Did You Get the Vibe?

Did You Get the Vibe?

KELLY JAMES-ENGER

KENSINGTON PUBLISHING CORP.
http://www.kensingtonbooks.com

For Erik, who still gives me the vibe

STRAPLESS BOOKS are published by

Kensington Publishing Corp.
850 Third Avenue
New York, NY 10022

All Kensington titles, imprints and distributed lines are available at special quantity discounts for bulk purchases for sales promotion, premiums, fund-raising, educational or institutional use.

Special book excerpts or customized printings can also be created to fit specific needs. For details, write or phone the office of the Kensington Special Sales Department. Phone: 1-800-221-2647.

ISBN 0-7582-0558-9

First Kensington Trade Paperback Printing: November 2003
10 9 8 7 6 5 4 3 2 1

Printed in the United States of America

Acknowledgments

I'm a big believer in thank-yous, so without further ado—thanks to my editor, John Scognamiglio, who acquired this book, and my agent, Laurie Harper, for making it possible. Special thanks also to my parents (even though my mom claims "every writer's first novel is largely autobiographical," I *swear* it's fiction, really) and the rest of my family, especially Andy (no, you don't get a cut of the royalties), Stephie (my fellow Solid Gold dancer!), and Mark. Thanks to Abby Gnagey for insightful tarot readings, awesome cards and letters, and unfailing support, and to Cindy Gendry for singing songs that made me laugh, suffering the same neuroses that I do, and as a result, always knowing where I'm coming from (even if you do refuse to buy my secondhand clothes).

I've been lucky to have fellow writing friends who have encouraged and inspired me throughout my writing career, especially while I worked on this novel. Special thanks to Polly Campbell, Sharon Cindrich, Sam Greengard, Leslie Levine, Margaret Littman, Nicole Burnham Onsi, Kris Rattini, and Jeff Stone. Thanks also to Lin Bresnahan, Deanne Jones, Burt Siegel, Ph.D., and Dorothy Vickers-Shelley.

And finally, the biggest thanks to my partner in marriage and life, who is still the funniest, sexiest, and sweetest man I know. I couldn't be who I am today without him—thank you, Erik, for listening to me worry about Kate and Tracy for months, and for making my happiness possible.

Chapter 1

So, Have You Ever Googled Anyone?

Brokenhearted women are supposed to lose weight. So why was she getting so *fat?*

Kate frowned at her reflection in the full-length mirror that hung inside the door of her closet. She'd already given up on her hair. It was only early April, but the humidity of the Chicago spring made maintaining any reasonable hairstyle for any length of time impossible. It looked decent now, but a few minutes outside and it would flatten like soggy roadkill. She'd opted for minimal makeup—mascara, blush, a nice pink lipstick—dangly silver earrings, nude hose, and her favorite black Sam and Libby's.

Her head and feet were ready. The problem was with what to do with what stretched between the two. She'd already considered—and rejected—four different outfits, all of which were lying crumpled on the bed where she'd tossed them.

She had nothing to wear. She had suits and she had jeans, and very little in between. Her closet was filled with tasteful, conservative (read: boring) suits and traditional, long-sleeved blouses for work and an assortment of T-shirts, baggy sweaters, and khakis—most of which dated back to law school if not college—for weekend wear. She had clothes for work and clothes for hanging out, but not many outfits appropriate for a cocktail party, especially not in Lakeview.

The reason—the only reason—she was going was because Tracy had begged her. "Pleeeeease, Kate! I promise there'll be some hotties here. You'll have a good time," Tracy had said on the phone just thirty minutes ago, when Kate had called with a pathetic last-minute excuse. Then she lowered her voice. "Come on, you can't leave me here with Tom and all his lawyer friends."

"Thanks a lot! You're talking to one, remember?" Kate checked her face in the bathroom mirror. There was definitely the start of a new wrinkle between her eyebrows.

"You know what I mean. You just happen to be a lawyer. Those guys from the firm all fit the profile."

"Uh-huh? And what about the hotties? Do they fit the profile, too?"

Obviously Tracy had already forgotten about her bribe, but she recovered smoothly. "Oh, yeah, what's his name . . . Bob, I think. He's a new associate at Tom's firm. He's cute, he's nice, he's single . . ." When Kate didn't answer, Tracy changed tactics. "Look, you've got to get out of the house. Happening women do not stay at home on Saturday nights watching the Discovery channel, especially when they live in Lakeview, the hippest, most happening Chi-town neighborhood save Lincoln Park. They're out seeking adventure, new experiences, new thrills, new men . . ."

"Give me a break. So I like *Raging Planet.* That's what I need, you know. A guy who will stay home and watch natural disasters with me instead of this whole getting dressed and going out thing."

"Yeah, well, you have to go *out* first to find someone to stay *in* with, remember? There's no shortage of guys around, Kate! You just have to get out there."

"Remember, honey, we live in the same neighborhood. And haven't you noticed that a lot of these 'great guys' also happen to be gay?"

"But not all of them." Tracy was relentless.

Kate knew when she was beat. "All right, all right! I'll be over there in a while."

"OK, sweetie. I promise you'll have fun. Just show up."

That was the difference between Kate and her closest friend. Tracy always saw the bright side of things. She was an incurable optimist, doubtless because she'd grown up with a mother who had insisted on continually pointing out to her three daughters how blessed they were. If you had arms and legs, and could see, hear, talk and use your brain, Dotty Wisloski liked to say, you had no reason to complain about anything. Kate couldn't recall her own parents infusing her with anything other than a streak of practicality tinged with stoicism— if you had to sum up the Becker family philosophy, it would be "work hard, don't talk too much, and turn up the TV." Something along those lines.

Back to the appropriate outfit. Kate pulled on a straight black knit skirt and turned to check her profile in the mirror. Her premenstrual stomach bulged out like a huge swollen tick. Tucking in a shirt was out of the question, even with fat-smooshing control top panty hose, so she pulled out a vee-neck pink Liz Claiborne shirt and pulled it on, smoothing the stretchy fabric over her stomach and hips. Well, it wasn't terrible, but she could see the lace of her bra underneath the slick material. Shit.

She slipped out of the shirt, and changed into the only smooth bra she owned—which happened to be a WonderBra she'd bought in a hormone-induced haze at Victoria's Secret, not long after she met Andrew. She'd thought it might impress him, and it had—although it hadn't stayed on long. She smooshed her boobs into the bra, pulled the shirt back over her head, and checked her reflection.

Holy shit! Her breasts oozed out over the vee-neck of the shirt. They wobbled a little dangerously, and looked as if they might burst free at any moment. She hesitated and then shrugged. What the hell. At least no one would stare at her stomach.

Kate walked the six blocks to Tracy and Tom's apartment, cutting east on Wellington to Sheridan. Yesterday, it had been in the forties—now it was warm and muggy. She nodded at a gorgeous pair of guys. Living near so-called Boystown—a largely gay neighborhood—she'd already learned that if a guy was beautiful to look at, had a killer body, and was well dressed, chances were that he played for the other team. Which was great, after all . . . it just meant that there weren't as many players to choose from.

The doorman at Tracy's smiled at her—what was his name? Roger? Roy? "Going up for the party?" He was in his sixties, wearing a maroon jacket, white shirt, and blue and maroon striped tie.

"Yup. Tracy insists. There're supposed to be *men* there," she confided.

The doorman laughed. "Well, you're looking real pretty. I'm sure they'll all want to meet you."

She smiled back. "Thanks." Boy, with the geriatric set, I have no trouble. Why can't it be this easy with guys of my own generation?

"Have fun!" he called.

Kate could hear music, the sound of people talking, and occasional laughter as she walked down the hall from the elevator. She stood there for a moment and took a deep breath. Why did this feel so hard? Still, Tracy had insisted, and she knew how important these parties were to her best friend. At least she knew Andrew wouldn't be there—Tracy had never liked him anyway. She shut her eyes, exhaled, forced a smile that hopefully didn't appear forced, and rang the doorbell.

Tracy opened the door, an expectant smile that reached her eyes when she saw her friend. "Kate! You made it out of your cave!" she teased. Then her blue eyes opened wide when she caught sight of her outfit. "Whoa. So, what's up with the dramatic cleavage?"

"Shut up. It's supposed to distract you from my huge bloated stomach." Kate looked down at her chest in alarm. "Shit, is it that bad?"

"Are you kidding? You look great. I'm the one who looks like a cow." Tracy was wearing a sleeveless red shift that ended above the knee and strappy red sandals. Her blond hair hung sleekly from her head, swinging with every motion she made.

"You look fabulous. I love that dress," said Kate with a smile. She'd known Tracy long enough to know that her self-critical comment was her way of asking for reassurance. She glanced around Tracy and Tom's apartment. "So, who all is here?"

There were a half-dozen guys standing in the kitchen drinking Heinekens, several with slender, attractive women at their sides. All the men had fashionably short hair, several with that annoying hairstyle where the front bits stuck straight up as if they'd just stepped out of a hurricane wind. What were they thinking? Freddie Prinze Jr. could carry off a look like that. A chubby-cheeked, ruddy-complexioned, high-foreheaded guy in his thirties could not.

"Mostly lawyers from Tom's firm. A couple of my friends from the bank. Elizabeth was here a while ago, but she had another party to get to." Tracy rolled her eyes at Kate.

"Oh, I'm so sorry I missed her!" Kate shook her head. "I don't know why you're still friends with her. She has the depth of a kiddie pool."

"I know. But we've known each other so long, you know?"

Kate glanced around the apartment. It was a living homage to Pottery Barn from the mission tables to the overstuffed couches, intentionally battered-looking recliners and colorful throw rugs scattered about. Photos of Tom and Tracy from various trips and clusters of candles decorated the mantel above the fireplace, and black and white photographs of various Chicago landmarks hung on the walls. The apartment was on the twenty-seventh floor of the high-rise, and the sliding glass doors faced Lake Michigan. It was funky, comfortable, and very hip.

"God, I love this place. When are you going to help me with mine?" Kate sipped from the glass of pinot grigio Tracy had bought her without being asked.

Tracy smiled a huge smile. Technically the apartment was Tom's—he'd bought it with money he'd inherited from his grandmother after graduating from law school two years ago. By that time, he and Tracy had been dating for three years, and it had made sense for the two of them to live together. Tracy had worried about Tom committing to her if she was willing to live with him instead. "It's the whole why-buy-the-cow-when-you-get-the-milk-for-free thing," she had confided in Kate, who thought the idea was ridiculous.

"Um, first, you're not a cow. Second, you know he loves you. And you know he wants to marry you. What's wrong with living together?"

So Tracy had moved out of her tiny one-bedroom in Edgewater and moved to Lakeview, which meant she was closer to work, and best of all, closer to Kate. Even though they lived together, the truth was that she spent more time with her best friend than with Tom, but at least they slept in the same bed every night.

"Hey, these are cool." Kate was looking at a pair of wrought-iron candlesticks on the mantel. "Where'd you get them?"

"That Cost Plus World Market on Broadway. We should go there and look for furniture for you. Or let's hit IKEA. We can take Tom's car out to Schaumburg and furnish your whole place. But you have got to get rid of that couch, Kate, seriously."

"I can't. That couch and I have a serious bond. It's seen me through every bad relationship of the last six years. I can't just dump it for the Swedish furniture fad of the moment."

"Kate. It's way ugly. Think about it, please." Kate smiled as Tom sidled up to his girlfriend and slid an arm around her waist.

"Trace, what'd you do with those mini quiches?" He leaned over and kissed Kate on the cheek, trying—and failing—not to ogle the vee of her blouse. "Holy cow! Glad you and your, ah, two friends could make it tonight!"

Tracy laughed and elbowed him. "Quit staring at my friend's chest, honey."

Tom grinned, and rubbed his hand over his face. "Hey, this is *Kate*, Trace." He made a face as if the idea he would check out Kate was beyond his comprehension. "She's like my sister! I was just noticing in a completely nonsexual way that she looks very nice." He winked, kissed Tracy, and wandered back to the kitchen. Kate recognized another one of the lawyers he worked with—a petite brunette named Julia. He walked over to her and said something and she laughed.

"What is it with men and boobs? They're, like, mesmerized by them." Kate looked around the room. She was trying to slide into her I'm-having-a-great-time party mode but the effort of standing and making conversation—even with Tracy— was draining her. *I could be home, on the couch, watching avalanches or earthquakes or tsunamis, after all. And what if Andrew happened to call . . . ?* Enough of that. He wasn't sitting home alone, that was for sure. Still, her couch was calling her. "OK, I'm not seeing any hotties! Time to split."

Tracy wouldn't let her off the hook. "Come on, you've been here five minutes." She beckoned. "I want to introduce you to a couple of people from work."

Perhaps an hour had passed, and Kate was now talking to a guy who worked with Tracy at the Federal Reserve Bank. He was telling her about something he did with computers—who knew what?—and she was wondering if she should have another drink.

"That's the great thing about the Internet," said her companion, Mark? Mike? Matt? She had no idea. He was incredibly skinny, with thick Brillo-pad hair and a paisley patterned shirt. *J. Crew*, she thought. *And ugly*. "You can find out anything about anyone if you Google them."

"If you what?" It sounded vaguely kinky and possibly illegal.

"Google. It's a search engine on the Net. You type in the

person's name, and it pulls up all kinds of hits. Court records, newsgroup posts, if they sold stuff on eBay, stuff like that." Mark/Mike/Matt took another swig of his beer.

"But why would you want to?" Kate drained the last of her wine. Screw it. She *was* getting another drink, even if it was only to provide her an escape from this tech head.

"You get the inside track on whether someone's being honest with you or not. Say you get fixed up with someone or you meet someone new." Was it her imagination or was he leering at her? "This way you can check them out in advance, you know," he said, pushing his glasses higher up on his nose. "Know what you're getting into."

"Aha." She nodded. Forget another drink; she wanted to go home. Her mind was wandering, her feet hurt, and her Wonder-Bra was digging into her flesh. She couldn't leave without saying good-bye to Tracy, though, so she excused herself and went in search of her. By this time, the party had filled up and there were at least forty people crammed into the apartment. The noise level made it hard to hear. She spotted Tracy, laughing with several of her friends from the bank, and then she saw *him.*

He was leaning against the waist-high breakfast bar that divided the kitchen from the dining and living area. He was several inches taller than the two guys he was talking to, and he had broad shoulders and dark, slightly messy hair. He wore a faded-looking shirt the color of butter, and a pair of dark gray chinos that fit perfectly—snug, but not gigolo-tight.

Kate maneuvered over to Tracy, her eyes barely leaving this gorgeous specimen of manhood. "Who," she said in a whisper, poking her friend in the side, "is that?"

Tracy followed her glance and grinned. "Told you!"

"Quit gloating. Who is he? How do you know him? Where did he come from?" Not that she was jaded, but come on. This guy couldn't be a lawyer. He couldn't even be real. You didn't run into guys like that at your best friend's party. Standing among the other geeks only enhanced his appeal, even from across the room.

"Gary Vincennes. He's single, I'm pretty sure, and does bankruptcy work. Tom played basketball with him last winter," said Tracy. She gave him a long, appraising look. "You know, he is pretty gorgeous. He's nice, too."

"Gary Vincennes. Gary Vincennes. Gary, Gary, Gary," Kate said dumbly.

"Get a grip, girl." Tracy set her drink down. "Come along. You're about to be introduced." She swerved gracefully through the crowd, nodding and smiling, Kate in her tow, and walked up to the trio.

"Hi, Gary. Have you met my friend, Kate? We went to law school together, but she stuck it out. She practices here, too." She nudged Kate, who was trying to conduct a quick tongue check to make sure she didn't have any stray broccoli bits wedged in her teeth.

"Nice to meet you, Gary," she said, offering her hand, and smiling what she hoped was a friendly and not drooly smile. "Kate Becker."

"Nice to meet you, too. So where do you work?"

"Cassell, Stevens, in the Loop. We do some corporate stuff, some litigation, a lot of insurance work."

"How many attorneys?"

"About eighty. What about you?"

Gary worked for a much smaller firm, one that Kate hadn't heard of. They stood there talking about their respective jobs for a few moments while Kate racked her brain for something fascinating to say. Something intelligent, something witty, something insightful.

"So, have you ever Googled anyone?" is what came out of her mouth.

"Google?" He looked confused. Kate was trying to study his face more closely without looking like she was staring. What was it about him? At this distance, she could see little smile lines around his eyes and a few faint acne scars. His imperfections—she couldn't even think of them as that—only added to his appeal.

"You know, it's where you use a search engine to look someone up on the Internet," she explained. Her upper lip felt slightly sweaty and she knew without looking that her makeup had slid off her face hours ago for parts unknown. Gary still seemed nonplussed, so she tried to explain it to him, realizing that she was probably coming off like some kind of cyber stalker. She thought she'd better change conversational tactics before his confused expression changed to alarm. She managed to work in the fact that she was dealing with a Chapter 11 case and knew little about the bankruptcy procedures. Would he be willing to explain it to her sometime?

Sure, no problem, replied the incredible Gary, who seemed relieved that all the Google talking had come to an end. He reached in his wallet and handed her his business card. "Give me a call and I'll bring you up to speed." His attention was diverted by two other guys, who were standing near the apartment door and pointing at their watches and making "wind it up" motions with their hands.

"Hey, ah, Kate, right? I've got to go. We've heading to Rush Street. Nice meeting you."

He strode off, and Kate watched how his ass perfectly filled out those gray pants and then glanced down at his card. His office wasn't far from hers.

"So?" Tracy materialized at her side.

"So what?"

"So, did you get the Vibe?"

"I don't know. He's hot. But I couldn't get a read on him, Vibe-wise." Kate pursed her lips, considering. "Maybe gay."

"You and the Vibe." Tracy rolled her eyes.

"Hey, it's never failed me before. You should be able to tell if someone wants you and you want him within five minutes of meeting. If the Vibe's not there, why bother?"

"Um, because you could be missing out on a really great guy simply because he didn't overwhelm you with sexual magnetism in the first five minutes." Tracy took a sip of her drink—water, Kate noticed. Tracy liked to drink a glass or two of wine, but Kate had never seen her friend drunk.

Kate considered. "Well, Vibe or not, he does seem nice and fairly normal. Except they're going to Rush Street. Probably wants to hit one of those thong contests or something."

"Oooh, ick." Rush Street was the catchphrase for a handful of bars like Mother's that invariably attracted college students, tourists, and suburbanites, and catered to the young end of the twenty-something crowd. To draw in the drinkers, several had forgone the wet T-shirt contests and Ladies' Nights in favor of thong contests where women stripped down to the tiniest G-strings imaginable, paraded in front of the cheering crowds, and competed for cash prizes.

"Yeah, can you imagine? There's not enough money in the world for me to flaunt my butt in public. I still do the back-away whenever I go to bed with someone new."

"What do you mean?"

Kate demonstrated. "You know, when you back out of the bedroom, so he won't see your bare ass. Like this." She started walking away from Kate without turning away from her. "So, can I get you a cup of coffee or anything? Anything else?"

Tracy started laughing. "You don't, really."

"Sure. Let me tell you, Tracy, you don't know how it is. Every time you're with someone new, you have to worry about whether they'll think your boobs are too small or your stomach is too squooshy or you have too much cellulite. You're lucky. You don't have to worry about that anymore. You've got Tom."

"That doesn't mean I don't worry about how I look." Tracy glanced down, smoothing the front of her dress.

"Please. You're beautiful, Tracy, and Tom loves you. I wish I could find a guy I could be that comfortable with." Kate took another swallow of wine. "I felt like that with Andrew, you know? Well, at least when we were having sex. Afterward, I felt like a big moose," she admitted. She sighed.

Tracy shook her head. "Remember, you said no Andrew talk. I'm supposed to remind you."

"You're right. Forget I said it. Let's talk about the Amazing Gary instead."

Chapter 2

Different Means Better

Tracy rolled over in bed. Tom was still asleep on his side, his breathing slow and steady. She curled her body around him, feeling his warmth, and kissed him between his shoulder blades, smelling his familiar scent, musky with a lingering odor of Drakkar. He still wore the same cologne he had since college.

"Ummmm." Tom, still half asleep, shifted a little, and she put her arm around his waist to pull him closer against her.

"You feel so good." She stroked his stomach and then slid her hand lower, to the front of his briefs. She wasn't surprised that she could already feel his erection starting to grow.

"What is it with you?" she teased, kissing his ear. "I've barely touched you."

"The wind blows." It was their joke—he could get erections at the drop of a hat—or at the drop of her underwear, as Tom liked to say. He rolled toward her and lay on his back, slipping his arm under her shoulders. He yawned. "I'm going to have to go in for a while today, though."

"Again?" She pulled her hand away. "Tom, you worked almost all day yesterday, and I had to do all the party stuff myself. Can't you take *one* weekend day off?"

He reached for her hand. "Come on. I told you I've got to help get that case ready for trial." He played with her hair with his right hand, using his left to place hers back on his cock. "You're not going to leave me like this, are you?"

Tracy was still annoyed, but she softened. She loved sex with Tom. He was the biggest guy she'd dated—at 6'3", he had six inches and at least seventy pounds on her. Before she'd met him, she'd always felt large and awkward, even unfeminine around men. It didn't help that she always fell for the smallish Rob Lowe types who were often barely her size. Is there any greater horror than looking at your thighs—and those of your boyfriend's—and realizing yours dwarf his? But with Tom, she felt protected, small, almost delicate—and incredibly desirable.

The first few times they'd slept together, though, Tracy had been half afraid he would hurt her from his sheer size. She'd admitted she felt a little smothered when he was on top, and he'd teased her about it. "What, do you think I'm going to pass out on you and crush you to death?" he said one of their first mornings together.

"No, it's not that. I love how big you are. You're so solid and strong and I like being able to grab you as hard as I want. It's just, well, different, being with someone so big."

"Different means better, right?" He'd grinned and pulled her completely on top of him. Even now, five years later, she couldn't believe how lucky she was. With Tom, what you saw was what you got. Like any guy, he tended to compartmentalize his life. He had his job, he had his friends, and he had her. Sure, he might not always anticipate what she wanted—and she sometimes did wish that he not push himself so hard all the time—but that was what she'd been attracted to, too. She'd liked his single-mindedness when she met him—the other guys she'd fallen for tended to be tortured artist types who waited tables while they wrote their great American novel or screenplay or short stories.

By the time she got to law school, she was growing a little tired of dating "flakes," as Kate would call them. She didn't mind when a guy didn't have much money. Sometimes she even preferred it. She just couldn't stand laziness. Too many of the guys she met were used to having everything handed to them and had no real plans for their future. And law students? Ugh. Most did "fit the profile"—anal, uptight, overly concerned about their careers, typical golf-playing, Mercedes-driving, money-making wanna-bes.

Tom, though, was different. He was open, easygoing, comfortable to be around. He was smart, but he wasn't a natural student. He'd worked for every grade in law school, graduating near the top of his class. She'd graduated two years before him, and they'd only seen each other once a month so he could focus on his studies.

It was that same focus he now applied to his career. He intended to make partner at his firm within six years. He was up for consideration for senior associate later this year, and had spent at least part of every weekend in the office since she could remember. "Face time," he explained. "Partners have got to see you there whether you're working or not."

After they made love, Tracy lay with her head on his chest. With him, without any distractions, she felt completely safe and comfortable and warm. She ran her fingers through the thick hair on his chest. "I love you."

He bent and kissed the top of her head. "Love you, too, babe." But she felt the slight movement of his shoulder as he twisted his left arm to check his watch. She sighed, annoyed. All the good feelings slipped away in a rush.

"Just wanted to know what time it was." They'd had this argument before. She hated it that he even *slept* with his watch on. "Trace, give me a break, all right? I promise I'll make it up to you."

He had slid out of bed and was walking naked to the bathroom. Tom could stand to lose a few pounds—he had the barest suggestion of love handles around his waist—but his ass was still muscular and his thighs bulged.

"I know." She sighed. "It'd better be good!" She got out of bed and pulled on his old Michigan sweatshirt, picking her underwear out of the sheets. "Do you want some eggs?"

"That'd be great, babe!" Tracy made him breakfast, feeling sweet and domestic, and poured a bowl of Total for herself. She couldn't stand hot food first thing in the morning. Tom gobbled his breakfast, slurped down a huge glass of orange juice, and stopped to kiss her.

"Hey, I'm sorry. This place is still kind of trashed. You want help?" But he was already slinging his briefcase over his shoulder. He used to carry a J.Crew shoulder bag, but about a year ago, had started with the briefcase bit. Part of looking the part, she supposed. Partners—or the associates who want to be partners—must not carry canvas bags, even monogrammed ones.

"No, that's all right. We did most of it last night anyway." After she cleaned up the party remnants, she curled up on the couch with the Sunday *Trib*. She felt vaguely bored, out of sorts. She reached for the cordless and dialed the second number on speed dial. Tom's office was the first.

"Hello?" Kate sounded cheerful, expectant.

"Hey. What are you up to?"

"Thinking about . . . the Amazing Gary," Kate answered. She sounded almost like her old self this morning. "Was it the alcohol or was he as hot as I recall?"

"The latter. Nothing like Scary Steve."

"Shut up!" Kate squealed. "You never let me live that down. You know, you probably shouldn't be so smug. I recall the PT days after all."

"Yes, I remember the parade of losers well." PT meant "pre-Tom." It was their code for the first two years of law school, when both had been single, and looking, and hooking up with various guys who had little in common with them except for the inappropriateness of any kind of long-term relationship with them. Kate had even gone out with the twenty-year-old pizza delivery guy. Now that Tracy was "married"—in every sense of the word except the legal—she channeled her single energy into helping Kate find someone, too.

Not that Kate *had* to have a guy, she corrected herself. Tracy didn't believe you had to have a man to be happy, but she also knew that was easy to say when you had one. After all, she no longer worried about what she'd do on Saturday nights or whether she'd ever meet someone she really loved. She loved Tom, and she knew he loved her. They had a great apartment together, they had fun friends, and they both liked their work. They'd talked about getting married—after he made senior associate, of course—and she'd already fantasized about having a baby with him. So why did she feel so alone?

"What are you doing today?" Kate's voice in her ear drew her back to the present.

"Nothing. Tom just went in." She drew a circle on the countertop with her finger.

"On Sunday? Man, they really make them work for that six-figure salary, huh?"

"Yeah, you could say that." Tracy's voice sounded bitter, and her friend picked up on it.

"Hey, what's the matter? You sound kind of bummed."

"Yeah, I guess." She didn't want to explain about Tom, though. At least she had someone who loved her, and she'd been attracted to the fact he worked so hard. It seemed petty and childish to complain about it now, after all, and she hated to whine. Then she mentally calculated and spoke. "It's probably PMS."

"Evil, nasty PMS or be-alone-and-feel-sorry-for-yourself PMS?"

"I don't know. I guess I haven't decided yet."

"Well, you want to hook up at Borders or something? Or we could go downtown. I realized last night I've got to get some decent date clothes." Kate chewed something. "Everything in my closet smacks of college grunge."

"Yeah, that sounds good," said Tracy, standing up and carrying her cereal bowl to the sink. "Give me a half hour to get ready."

"No problem. I've got to take a shower anyway. Why don't you pick me up, and then we'll get the el."

"OK, see you then." Tracy hung up the phone, relieved to have something to do. Lately Tom had been spending so much time at work, she'd started to dread coming home. She'd stop by the gym after work, but still there were empty hours to fill, and all that time made her feel anxious. She'd been bringing work home with her to have something to do, and had watched more episodes of *True Hollywood Story* on E! than she'd care to admit.

Tracy wished she were easier with people. She didn't make friends quickly—she couldn't relax and just connect with people the way Kate could. Sure, she could make small talk and she loved entertaining, but it seemed like she rarely talked about anything important with anyone other than Kate, and sometimes, Tom.

At least she and Tom had had a chance to connect this morning, no matter how briefly. Lately, though, sex with Tom sometimes left her wanting more. Sure, she could have an orgasm if she really focused on it, but she missed the old excitement she used to feel. Of course, they had been together for five years. *Maybe this is what happens when you're married,* she thought glumly. *What a great thought. I guess I am PMS.*

Chapter 3

I'm a Lawyer—Now What?

Kate frowned at the message on her desk. It was written on one of those ubiquitous pink "while you were out" message pads. "See Me ASAP," with the scribbled initials of Richard Lawless, one of the partners at the firm. He was arguably the best lawyer there as well as the most universally hated by the associates. In the four years she had worked at Cassell, Stevens, Kate had been assigned to only a few of Lawless's cases. Every one of them had been a nightmare.

There was no question that Lawless was a talented attorney. He was also short, fat, and tended to spit in your face when he got worked up over something, which was frequently. He also thrived on humiliating the other lawyers in the firm. It was trial by fire—you hadn't really gotten your feet wet until he'd torn you a new one, preferably at a meeting in front of your peers. He seemed to think that was a great motivator, and he was right. She and other associates would spend hours toiling on his files just to make sure they hadn't left any matter, no matter how seemingly insignificant, unaddressed.

Lawless was on the phone when she walked into his office, gesturing angrily from behind his expensive cherry desk. He scowled at a chair, which Kate perched on. She hated slick leather furniture—you could feel the cold, even through your clothes, and the chairs always felt like you might slide right off them. And she certainly wasn't about to make herself comfortable there.

As he continued his tirade, something about producing corporate documents, she scanned his office. Heavy, expensive-looking cherry furniture, olive and burgundy wallpaper in a particularly noxious checkered print, and a half-dozen English hunting scenes hung on the walls. She didn't know what it was with the lawyers here—they all seemed to be Anglophiles.

Abruptly he hung up. "What's going on with the Jacobsen case?"

Good morning to you, too, she thought. Aloud she answered, "We're still in written discovery. We've provided them with our docs and I'm doing the production request on site on Thursday."

"Have the deps been scheduled?"

"Working on it." Shit. Kate had no idea if Tiffany had started scheduling the witness depositions, but she could guarantee it would be the first thing on her list. Hopefully he wouldn't check before she could get to it.

"This is a bullshit case. Total bullshit. I've promised the client we should get out on summary judgment so make sure you get copies of everything that supports our position. The more change orders you can find that didn't get architectural approval and the like, the better. And give me a memo covering everything from written discovery by Monday."

In other words, your weekend is screwed, thought Kate. "Sure. No problem."

She hurried out of his office. First stop, Tiffany's desk. Her twenty-four-year-old secretary was sitting with her transcription headphones on, typing furiously and chewing her gum. Her long red nails clicked effortlessly over the keys, and her head bobbed slightly as she worked. Rhonda, the secretary who sat next to her—the support staff were grouped in pairs throughout the office—apparently hadn't arrived yet.

"Tiffany. Tiffany!" she said her name again, more loudly, and waved her hand in front of her face.

"Huh? Oh, Kate! How's it going?" Tiffany grinned. She wore blue mascara, heavy foundation, and her brown hair was outgrowing what looked like a bad home perm. She was wearing a cream-colored sweater with batwing sleeves. Her clothes were always a season or two behind the latest trend. Not that Kate was any fashion plate—without the help of T.J. Maxx and Filene's Basement, she'd be wearing the same military-looking double-breasted suits that had been in when she'd been in law school.

Kate started to ask about the depositions and then caught herself. "Not bad. How are you?" She had promised herself when she started practicing that she would treat the so-called underlings of the firm with respect. After clerking for two years, she'd been disgusted by the cavalier attitude that so many lawyers—even junior associates—displayed toward the secretaries, paralegals, and tech support staff at the firm. That was, unless they were male (the lawyers) and the staffers were female, pretty, single, and young. Then you had a whole different thing going on.

"I'm good. Oh, listen to this! Margo and Janice and I went out last night and we ran into Brian! He was trying to get over on me all night. I let him think there was a chance and then I totally dissed him." Tiffany grinned again and cracked her gum. "He was pissed! But that snake deserves it."

"Oh, yeah?" Kate paused for a moment. Much as she would love to hear more about the dissing of Brian, the thought of Lawless on the rampage overcame her commitment to treating her fellow coworkers as equals. "Tiffany, where are we with the deps in Jacobsen? Are you scheduling them yet?"

"No. I'm sorry! Did you ask me to?" Tiffany gestured to the neatly handwritten "to-do" list sitting on the corner of the desk. She was religious about writing down and dating every request, calling it her CYA list.

"No, I don't think I did," Kate admitted. "Call the other sides and see if you can set something up ASAP, will you? Lawless is breathing down my neck."

"Sure thing." Tiffany smiled at her. "Don't let him get to you. He pulls that shit with everyone, you know." She gave Kate a cheery wave as Kate walked back toward her office.

If only she could have that unflappable attitude. But Lawless *did* get to her. Kate sighed as she waded through the stack of mail on her desk. And it wasn't only him—he was just the most obvious symptom of the problem, the problem being that she was a lawyer. A string of seemingly insignificant decisions had put her here. In college, she'd majored in English, which didn't exactly provide you with a wealth of career options. Not that she'd thought about her Career—or even her Future—in school. She worked, went to class, went out with her friends, fell in love and back out of it, had mostly so-so sex, some great sex, some downright icky sex, and entertained two crushes on guys from afar. The thought that she was in school to prepare for the real world had simply never occurred to her. She took the LSAT on a whim, scored well, applied to law school (also on a whim), was accepted, and then spent the next three years trying to cram her head full of knowledge to regurgitate it during finals. After another two months of the same frantic cramming, she took the bar, and passed—and she was an attorney.

Law school seemed like so long ago. She remembered little about it than that overwhelming sensation of being the wrong person in the wrong place at the wrong time, and the incredible sense of dread during finals week. She'd carried a bottle of Mylanta with her and chugged it during exams. All her fellow students seemed so sure about what they were doing. Their fathers had been lawyers or they'd always dreamed of being lawyers or at forty-five, with their kids out of school, it was time to realize a long-standing dream. No one there had simply fallen into the profession the way Kate had—or at least no one would admit it. The closest she got was Ricky Garcia, who admitted that he'd applied because of Arnie Becker's character on *L.A. Law*, which by that time was in reruns. He'd confided that if he did divorce law, he'd have no shortage of women. While she'd been incredulous at his admission, she also knew that it made as much sense as her being there did.

Thank God for Tracy. They'd met the second day of class and for the next three years, suffered through contracts, torts, property, and constitutional law together. That alone had made it bearable. All you really need to get you through the worst of times is one person who thinks the same way that you do—or close enough that you laugh at the same things. And that was Tracy.

But Tracy was even less motivated than Kate had been. For her, law school was just an alternative to grad school. She'd wanted to get her master's in history, but her stepdad had refused to pay for it and Tracy hadn't wanted to take out loans to go. That made the choice law school or her MBA, and Tracy had opted for law. She'd studied diligently but then had flunked the bar the first time she took it—and the second as well. She hadn't seemed that concerned. "I didn't think I wanted to practice, anyway," she'd told Kate over drinks after the results from the second exam came in. "This just confirms what I already knew."

By that time, Tracy had nabbed her job in human resources at the bank, and she seemed quite content. She did take the bar one last time—and passed—but she really didn't care that she wasn't practicing. By that time, she and Tom had been dating for two years, and it was clear that he'd look for a job in Chicago when he graduated. Her life sometimes seemed very neat and orderly to Kate, but she knew her friend thrived on routine.

Tracy had probably had the right idea anyway. Even with two years of clerking at the firm, Kate had had little idea of what her life as a new lawyer would be like. During the first few months, she shadowed older lawyers at the firm, attending motion hearings and depositions and client interviews. Once her bar results came in and she was sworn in, she was expected to apply the skills she had learned in school and to bill a minimum of fifty hours a week, preferably more.

Those first few months of actual practice—arguing in court, her voice stammering, her hands sweaty, and her heart pounding with fear—now seemed like a distant memory. You racked up appearances in front of judges until you no longer felt like you'd puke when you had to argue a motion. After twenty depositions or so, you ran through the initial questions—name, age, address, occupation, marital status, social security number—without even stopping to look at your notes. You strolled into court without a glance at the other attorneys there, stepped through the gate that marshaled the lawyers from the ordinary folks, and immediately felt like you belonged.

But there was something missing. She'd gone into law for the intellectual stimulation (at least that's what she'd told herself), but being an associate at a big firm wasn't that different from any other grunt job. You were essentially a warm body for the partners—sent to appear in court on routine motions, conduct depositions in less important cases, and most important of all, wade through the written discovery conducted by both sides in civil lawsuits. It wasn't rewarding or stimulating or even interesting, but at least she could say, "I'm a lawyer."

Kate sighed again and checked her watch. It was just after noon, and she could hear some of the secretaries scuttling off for lunch. She'd probably just make some microwave popcorn and eat at her desk. Again.

"Katie-girl! Whazzzup?" Danny O'Malley stuck his head in her office. "You wanna grab some chow?"

"I can't. I've got too much to do and Lawless is on me. You know how it goes."

He glanced down the hall and stepped in her office, shutting the door. "You'd better watch it with him. I heard his wife just slapped him with divorce papers." His ruddy face lit up. "She had him served here at the office!"

"No way." Kate hadn't heard any such thing, and Tiffany would have been sure to tell her. "When?"

"Try this morning. Try ten minutes ago. He's on a tear and chewing everyone's ass."

Talk about good timing. "Shit, I must have just missed it. His wife really served him *here?*" That was a low blow, even for Lawless. His soon-to-be-ex must have really wanted to demean him. She couldn't help grinning at the thought.

"Yup. Serves the cocksucker right, though." Danny grabbed his crotch in the inimitable way that all males seem to master by the age of fourteen. "He can bite me."

"How old are you again?"

Danny smirked. "I gotta get going. We're going out for Thai, but I'll catch you later. Sure you don't want to come?"

"No, thanks. I'll see you later."

Danny was one of the few people at the firm she felt any kind of connection with. He'd grown up on the south side of Chicago, and his dad, uncle, and two older brothers were all city cops. Danny had thought about "the job," but had ended up in law school instead. He intended to be a prosecutor (with his pedigree, there was no real chance he'd be a defense lawyer) but after two years in the state attorney's office, the firm had made him an offer he said he couldn't refuse. The partners had liked his connections and his balls-to-the-wall attitude.

"You work your ass off, but they pay for it," he had told Kate before. "And it's not all politics like working for the city."

But then, Danny thrived on conflict. The messier and the nastier a case got, the happier he was. Kate didn't enjoy the back-and-forth the way he did, but she loved his no-shit attitude. You knew where you stood with him—he wasn't one of these plastic guys like most of the ones she worked with who mouthed all the right words but didn't mean any of them. And people wondered why she never dated lawyers.

It was Danny who had introduced her to Andrew, and also Danny who had studiously avoided mentioning his name since their breakup. Or, to be exact, since he dumped her for a woman taller, thinner, prettier, and most likely, smarter, than herself. Come on, she had been dating Andrew. How smart could she be?

She might be friends with Danny, but short of needing an organ donor, nothing could make her abandon her pride and ask him if Andrew had asked about her. Besides, if he hadn't, she'd be crushed. Better to picture him pining away for her, beating his head against a wall in frustration and berating himself for dumping her. In Kate's fantasy, his new girlfriend had dumped *him* (see, it's karmic revenge), and he'd realized his terrible mistake in hurting Kate. Or he was sitting at home in that ratty brown plaid recliner, the lights off, listening to Pink Floyd and experiencing existential depression of a degree he'd never known before. Or better yet, munching mindlessly through a giant bag of Doritos, watching *Where are they now?* on VH-1, and getting fat. Nice and chubby. She didn't really hope that he wound up on the losing end of an encounter with a fully loaded eighteen-wheeler Peterbilt semi truck while out on one of his interminable bike rides—nothing that drastic. But if he was suffering a little—or preferably a lot—she could live with that. She could certainly live with that.

Not that she shouldn't have seen it coming. Andrew was simply too beautiful for her. It was a fact that people hooked up with people who were at their own level of attractiveness. If you were a liver-spotted, humpbacked, octogenarian millionaire a thousand times over, you might hook up with Anna Nicole Smith. But in the real world, the beautiful people paired off together, the homelier folks always seemed to find each other, and all those in between—like Kate herself—played in the middling range.

Her instinct had warned her from the outset. Andrew had green eyes fringed by dark curly lashes, a striking bone structure, and perfectly straight, white teeth. Even his skin, which was tanned from the long hours he spent outside running and biking—not to mention those open-water swims all summer long—was smooth and perfect. She doubted he'd ever had a blackhead or even a pimple. His body was all smooth, tanned muscle except for a round, tight white ass that was always amazingly warm to the touch. His natural temperature seemed just a few degrees higher than anyone else's, and he couldn't stand to sleep under the sheets.

She'd known on some level that she just couldn't measure up to his nearly impossible beauty, but she'd fallen for him, despite it all. OK, maybe she hadn't been in love, but she'd been in lust and that was sometimes worse. Lust addled your brain and made you think it might be love, and even if you admitted that it wasn't love, you hoped that over time, lust would grow and adapt and transform magically into love.

But what she really missed wasn't the sex, or even Andrew himself, but that sense of potential she'd had at the outset. That's what made relationships so hard. Somehow, some part of your heart—a tiny little piece secreted away, crafted from the most resilient, hopeful, indestructible fibers of your being— that microscopic piece gave you hope every time you met a man who made you stop and think, "Hey. What about him?" Despite the fact that you'd been burned before and had your heart broken more than once and even loved men who didn't love you back—is there any greater humiliation—that secret little piece gave you a speck of faith, of courage, of hope that *this* time would be different. Even if you dared not admit it to yourself, it was there—every time you felt that little twinge the first time he made you laugh, really laugh, or that barely detectable lump in your throat you felt after he rolled on his side and you stroked the long, smooth line of his back, or when you'd spent two hours getting ready to meet him for drinks and had squeezed into your black leather miniskirt and dark cherry-red sweater and you were probably wearing too much red lipstick and felt quite not so much sexy as whorish, to be frank, and he took one look at you and an unreadable expression crossed his face and then he grinned and said "oh, babe, you look smokin!"—that little kernel of hope was there. Screw what you knew. Screw what you'd learned the hard way. You hoped that this would be it.

She was twenty-eight and she'd been in love—as a grownup anyway, she wouldn't count the crushes and fleeting relationships and the short-term flings—three times. No, four. Was that a lot? It didn't seem like it. She ticked them off on her fingers. Ben, Victor, Randy. And Mike Cooper, the first of the three Mikes, but the only Mike she'd loved. How she had wound up with so many Mikes—three in a row certainly seemed excessive—was a mystery to her. By the time the third came along, she'd nearly accepted her destiny as a permanent Mike-lover. When she met him at a party and he introduced himself to her, she'd groaned aloud.

"What?" This Mike, Mike number three, was probably nearly forty, wearing an expensive suit. He wasn't tall, but he bore something of a resemblance to a tired-looking Tom Cruise. At least if you didn't look that closely.

"Oh, you're a Mike. I seem to have a weakness for Mikes of late." She had flirted with him, emboldened by tequila—it was a Cinco de Mayo bash—and the pulse beat of the Vibe. When he'd leaned closer to her, she'd gotten that distinct little twang, and when she felt it, it was hard to resist, especially during a sexual dry spell. Within four hours of meeting him, she and Mike number three were in bed together, and he was proving himself the superior of his predecessors with apparent ease. She'd known from the outset that she was only a transition relationship for him—when a guy starts complaining about his ex-wife within ten minutes of meeting you, it's usually a clear sign you won't be invited home for the family Christmas bash.

But when it came right down to it, wasn't *every* relationship a transition relationship? At the outset, you were in a particular place in your life. At the end of it, you were in another. A transition had occurred on some level, like it or not. You weren't the same person you were before—after all, you never walk in the same stream twice. And if you loved the person, it only made matters worse. Love affected the way you looked at things, the way you felt about the person, how much you expected from him. Love someone and you opened yourself up to the resulting Pandora's box of ugly emotions—jealousy, anger, frustration, disappointment, insecurity. At least if you just stuck with sex, you didn't get as entangled, but that could be dangerous, too—see exhibit A, Andrew.

Kate couldn't understand how some men and women actually *stayed friends* when they ended a relationship. She had severed ties with each former lover as neatly as hacking off the end of a carrot, but lately she found herself wondering about some of them. Where was Ben now? Had he found someone he loved as much as her? Was Victor the same selfish, sexy, overly confident guy he had been at twenty-four or had he changed as he'd gotten older?

It was strange. She'd always been able to move on after a relationship in the past. There might be a grieving period that lasted for weeks—OK, months in Ben's case—but she'd gotten over each of them in turn. Why now did she keep wondering about them?

"Kate." Tiffany's voice on her intercom jolted her back to reality. "I've got those deps scheduled. I set them up for a week from Thursday."

"Thanks, Tiff." Kate reached for her calendar to write the dates in. Most of the other lawyers in the firm swore by Palm-Pilots, but she'd sworn off of them after a month of punching in data with that tiny little stylus. Something about a pencil and paper seemed much friendlier. She wrote down the date, noting that it would mark the one-month anniversary of her breakup with Andrew.

Chapter 4

Viva Las Vegas

Tracy slung her briefcase over her shoulder and adjusted her grip on her carry-on bag. Outside the airport, she could see the harsh unrelenting glare of the Las Vegas sun. Squinting, she followed the signs to the taxi stand, and climbed in the back of an amazingly clean cab. She was sweating already, but the desert air felt good after the overly air-conditioned airport terminal.

"MGM Grand, please." Sitting back in the cab, she looked out at the city's "skyline." The pyramid of the Luxor marked one end of the Strip, and a cluster of high-rises—Treasure Island, the Mirage, and the Bellagio, among others—jutted out from the desert floor on the other. The sky seemed vast and empty compared to Chicago, and she felt a little lost.

She was here for what was called an educational conference but in reality was an excuse for human resource professionals from throughout the country to gather in Vegas to drink, gamble, make passes at each other, and generally have a good time at their employers' expense. She'd been to Vegas before, and she wasn't much of a gambler, but Betsy had insisted.

"It will be fun! Go out there and enjoy yourself," her boss had said, reaching for a Tootsie Roll out of the bowl on her desk. "You work too much. Besides, I think we could improve the way we handle some of these internal complaints. And I need to be here for that meeting with the EEOC."

Tracy had agreed, but had dreaded the trip. At least it was only for three days—the conference ran tomorrow and Friday, and then she'd be free. She hated to admit it because it made her sound so boring, but she didn't like to travel. She didn't like the feeling of not knowing where she was, or the unpredictability of vacation. Even in college, when everyone else had looked forward to spring break, she'd worried about what they would do, and what time they'd eat dinner, and whether she'd brought the right clothes. Kate sometimes teased her about being anal. "Loosen up, Tracy! You don't have to control every single thing every single minute, you know."

At least she'd managed to sidestep Betsy's urgings to spend the weekend; instead, she'd catch a flight out late on Friday evening and be home that night. Fast forward some forty-eight–plus hours and she'd be back in Chicago where she belonged. The thought comforted her.

The first day of the conference wasn't as bad as she'd expected. She listened to the speakers and took detailed notes on the handouts that were passed out. By the end of the afternoon, many attendees had already snuck out, no doubt lured by free drinks and all-you-can-eat buffets, but she finished the last session. It was close to five and she thought she might grab a glass of wine, call Tom from her room, and then get some dinner. Room service sounded good.

Of course, getting a drink meant sitting in the casino—part of the Vegas conspiracy. She sat down at a low table next to the bar and ordered a glass of merlot from the waitress, who wore a tight red and gold uniform, and a name tag that identified her as Steffi from Portland, Oregon. She paid the waitress and took a sip of her drink, looking around her.

She wasn't sure if it was Vegas in general or the MGM Grand in particular, but most of the gamblers at the slot machines fell into one of two basic groups—overweight, badly dressed, middle-aged drinkers or skinny, badly dressed, middle-aged smokers. Women wearing too-tight stretch pants sat perched on bar stools, dumping in coin after coin, sipping drinks with cherries in them, and sucking on long skinny cigarettes. Men whose bellies hung over their belts gathered in groups to sit at the blackjack tables, rattling the ice in their drinks as they scratched on the table, motioning for another card. The slot machines *ding-ding-dinging* chimed incessantly, punctuated by occasional whoops and shouts of the winners. The losers were quieter.

Tracy slid her shoes off under the table and stretched her legs. She'd finish her wine, head upstairs, take a long shower, and see what was on the tube. She nodded at a woman she recognized from the conference walking by. Her fellow attendee still wore her red-bordered name tag that identified her as "Mary."

"Aren't you going to try your luck?" Mary smiled at her, fluffing her permed bangs and nodding at the casino floor.

"Maybe later. I think I just want to unwind a bit first." Tracy gestured to her drink.

"OK. Make sure you have some fun tonight! Tomorrow will be another long day!" Mary bounced off, rattling her pail of quarters as she did so.

Maybe she should have told Mary about the name tag. Tracy had peeled hers off as soon as she left the conference room, hating the idea of strangers knowing who she was. And what was everyone's insistence on having fun out here anyway? Sitting lumpily at a noisy slot machine hardly counted as fun. Fun was . . . well, spending time with Tom. Planning a party and having people tell her how great it was. Hanging out with Kate, who could always make her laugh. She stopped, unable to think of anything else.

" 'Management Strategies for the New Millennium,' right?" She heard a voice and looked up. He stood there with a glass of beer circled in his left hand, a canvas briefcase slung over his shoulder.

"Uh-huh." She didn't remember him, though. He was about

her height, maybe an inch taller, light brown eyes, black hair that fell over a slight widow's peak on his forehead. It made him look boyish, contrasting with the lines around his mouth. She offered her hand. "I'm sorry. I'm Tracy Wisloski. From Chicago."

"Tracy from Chicago." His hand felt hard. "I'm William Brown. But my mom's name is Kowalski."

"Oh, a fellow Pole, huh?" She smiled.

"Lithuanian, actually, but close enough. Actually, my family history pretty much includes every European country, it seems." He gestured at the chair next to her. "Mind if I sit down? Or are you getting ready to leave?"

She had been planning to go back to her room, but she surprised herself. "Have a seat. I'm just watching the show."

"People watching never gets old." He signaled to the waitress, glanced at her glass, and ordered another round of drinks, a Stoli on the rocks for himself. "Not a big gambler?"

She shook her head. "Not really. I've been out here once before, but even then it didn't do much for me. A group of us came out after law school before we started studying for the bar."

"You're a lawyer?"

"Technically, yes. I don't practice, though." She gave him the short version of the story, downplaying the part where she failed the bar the first two times she had taken it. Even though she'd found her job at the bank by then and knew she didn't want to practice, she couldn't let it go. She had signed up for the bar an unthinkable third time, spent another two months studying for it again, and passed—finally.

"Tom kept bugging me to try it again," she said. "He said a law degree wasn't worth much without a license to back it up."

"Your boyfriend?"

"Uh-huh." She sipped at her second glass of wine. "Oh, here." She reached into her wallet. "This is for the drink."

William waved his hand. "On me. So, your boyfriend's a lawyer, too?"

"How'd you guess?"

"Your comment about the law license."

"Oh." Suddenly Tracy felt utterly brain dead. She couldn't think of anything at all to say. Why was small talk so hard for her?

William was watching some of the people in the casino. "Don't you sometimes wonder about the gene pool?" He nodded his head at a couple that couldn't be more than twenty. Both wore tank tops, and sported multicolored tattoos up and down their arms. "Would you ever get one?"

"A tattoo?" She laughed and shook her head. "I don't even think I could get my ears pierced again. That whole needle/pain thing doesn't do anything for me."

"I guess I have yet to see one that I find attractive. Although navel rings can be pretty hot."

"Uh . . . I guess." Tracy wasn't about to say that the idea of a navel ring just brought up all kinds of visions of infections and injuries resulting from snagging it on your clothes when you were changing in a hurry. She wouldn't want to be drawing attention to her stomach anyway. She hated it when Tom touched her there.

"How about him?" He touched her arm, nodding at a man wearing tight, dark blue Wrangler jeans, a plaid shirt, string tie, cowboy boots, and a huge hat. "Does the cowboy look do anything for you?"

"Maybe he's just trying to do right by his state, 'Look at me—I'm from Texas.' " She tried to affect a Southern drawl. "Ah'm just here to try my luck at the gambling tables and maybe lasso a pretty little filly while I'm at it."

"Lasso a filly?" William laughed. "That's got to be the worst accent I've ever heard."

"Thanks a lot!" Tracy leaned back in her chair, letting the mellow feeling of the wine run through her body. It felt good to laugh. For the first time since she left Chicago, she didn't feel lonely.

It turned out William was a Midwesterner too—he'd grown

up in the Twin Cities and still lived in St. Paul. "The winters are a nightmare, but the summers are great," William said, reaching into the bowl of pretzels the waitress had brought. He ate the pretzels one at a time, she noticed, in neat careful bites. Tom would have grabbed a handful and shoved them in his mouth. "A lot of places have summer hours, too," William was saying. "My family's all there, too. I've got three older sisters. All married, all with kids. I get to be the 'fun uncle.' "

"Really." Tracy smiled. As they talked, Tracy became aware that she needed to use the bathroom—needed it desperately in fact—but ignored it.

After their third drink, she couldn't wait any longer. "I'm sorry. I'm going to die if I don't use the bathroom."

"Me, too!" He laughed. "I couldn't admit it first, though—don't want to appear unmanly," he said in a self-deprecating tone. "Why don't we both use the bathroom and get some dinner afterward? I heard there's a great Southwestern place somewhere in the casino." He looked around. "Although I have absolutely no idea where it is."

"I don't know." She stood, feeling a little wobbly. "I should probably get back to my room." She was embarrassed to admit that she'd been planning on ordering room service—it made her sound like a big geek.

"Don't make me eat alone. A good meal is always better with good company. Besides, we can continue our sociological study of 'people who come to Vegas and why they dress the way they do.' "

She felt the smile spread across her entire face and suddenly felt completely happy. "All right, you got me. With an offer like that, how can I refuse?"

In the huge, brightly lit bathroom, she checked her reflection in the mirror as she washed her hands. She fussed with her hair and reapplied her lipstick, then exposed her teeth to check for stray bits of food, a bad habit she'd picked up from Kate. She felt strangely light inside. It was probably the wine.

After a few wrong turns, they did manage to find the

restaurant William had mentioned, tucked away along one of the main hallways of the casino. They waited a few minutes for their table, and then were seated in a booth along the wall. The décor was done in terra-cotta, dusty blue, and shades of brick and tan. Georgia O'Keeffe prints hung on the wall. Lots of painted pots, cattle skulls, and cacti as décor. But it was dim inside, and quiet, miles away from the incessant noise of the slots.

"I love this place." She looked around. "Who'd believe you'd find it *here?*"

"One of the women I work with told me about it. She was out here with her husband several months ago, and I knew I wanted to check it out." He smiled at her. "I'm just glad I don't have to eat alone."

"Me, too. This is great."

William suggested they order a bottle of wine—a California chardonnay—and they munched on the assortment of rolls and muffins the waiter left on the table.

Later, Tracy couldn't remember how it had happened. Somewhere between the appetizers of tortilla soup and the coffee they both ordered at the end of their meal, she felt something shift inside her. Something was happening.

When she excused herself to use the bathroom, she briefly wished Kate were there. Kate was always talking about the Vibe. "Oh, he wants me," she'd say with confidence after the two of them had met a new man. "I definitely got the Vibe."

"You're insane." Tracy would shake her head, but she couldn't help herself. "How do you *know?*"

"You just do. You feel it. It's like a current running between the two of you. You might not acknowledge it. He might not acknowledge it. It doesn't matter. It's there."

"What does it feel like?"

"Come on, Trace! You know what I'm talking about. That feeling where you're hyper-aware of everything you're doing, hyper-aware of everything he's doing. You smell him better. You notice every detail. You feel stupid and then in the next second, you feel sexy, and smart, and hot. Half the time you can't even think of anything to say, but if it's really strong, it doesn't even matter. You *know* what I'm talking about."

"Oh, that." She had nodded knowingly, but she still didn't get it. Sure, she got turned on with Tom—they knew each other's wants in bed so well by now, their sex together was almost always mutually satisfying—but she wasn't sure if she'd ever felt the *Vibe* with him. Or with anyone—not that her sexual past had been that exciting anyway. She'd only slept with two guys before Tom. She was so inexperienced she hadn't even been able to have an orgasm with either of them, and she was pretty sure that eliminated any possibility of Vibeage.

But before it hadn't seemed to matter. She'd never say it to Kate, but sometimes she thought Kate was too picky. She wanted some perfect guy, not realizing that sometimes you had to settle. That was part of being a grown-up. She'd known once she fell in love with Tom that she'd never have to look for someone again. And she trusted him. He wouldn't take off like her dad had done. It just felt right with him. But now . . . now, she was wondering if this was what Kate was talking about. She felt incandescent with energy, bright, witty, insightful, alive. Even her face looked different—more animated, more color.

When she came back to the table, William stood up, the way he had when she'd left. "Please." She motioned for him to sit, but it secretly thrilled her. She couldn't remember Tom ever doing that. Come to think of it, she couldn't remember any man ever doing that for her. And she couldn't remember when she'd felt so damn good.

"I have to tell you. This has been so much fun," she began. "I was really dreading this trip, and look what happened! I'm having a fantastic time."

He smiled, and she noticed again the dimple in his left cheek. "I am, too. You're a fascinating woman."

"I am?"

"Of course. You're funny, you're obviously intelligent, you're gorgeous . . ." he stopped. "Shall I go on?"

Tracy looked at him and managed to speak. "Stop. You're embarrassing me." She looked down at the table, but she couldn't hide the smile. "It's weird, William." She loved saying his name. "I feel so totally comfortable with you. It's like I've known you forever. Does that make sense?"

"Of course it does. Sometimes you meet someone and you immediately connect. It doesn't happen often, but sometimes fate intervenes."

"Oh, this is fate, then?"

"Possibly. I think everything happens for a reason. And I think—" he started and then broke off. "Forget it." He looked at his watch. "We should probably get going—we've got an early morning tomorrow."

"What?" She leaned forward. "What were you going to say?"

He pursed his lips for a moment. "I was going to tell you that I'm incredibly attracted to you. I don't know what it is— your eyes, your mouth, the way you play with that piece of hair when you're thinking—but it's driving me crazy. *That's* what I was going to tell you."

She sat perfectly still. Her heart was thudding so hard she felt slightly breathless. She couldn't even form an appropriate response. But her mouth opened and the words spilled out.

"I know," she admitted. "I guess I'm attracted to you, too. I can't tell you how much I've enjoyed talking with you. And I guess I've been flirting a little."

"You guess?" He rubbed his lips and smiled. "I thought so. But did you hear me complaining?"

She smiled, looked at him and then down at the table. She took a sip of water and forced herself to think logically. "But I don't know what we can do about it. I mean, we're both in relationships. I couldn't do that to Tom." Just saying his name was like an ice-cold splash of guilt, a twist in her stomach. Nothing like a hard dose of reality to jolt you back to earth. She sighed and closed her eyes for a moment. "I really can't."

"Relax, Tracy. Nothing has to happen. But sometimes it's nice to feel this way, isn't it?"

She recrossed her legs. "Nice? Oh, I'd say it's more than nice." She exhaled. "It's pretty much . . . I don't know. Mind-bending."

He raised his eyebrows. "Mind-bending, huh?"

She exhaled again, trying to explain herself. "I don't know. Maybe that's not the right word. It's just that this has never happened to me before." She played with her butter knife and then looked up at him and met his eyes. "Ever."

He looked skeptical. "I find that hard to believe, Tracy. I'm sure plenty of men find you attractive."

"Maybe," she admitted slowly. "But I've never felt what I'm feeling now." She shook her head and tried to laugh. "Which means my life is pretty dull, huh?"

"I don't think that. I think maybe you're just too private to notice. You seem like someone who doesn't open up very easily, someone who doesn't share very much of herself with people," said William. "And it's when you do open up to someone that you're likely to feel something beyond 'oh, I wouldn't mind going to bed with that person.' You feel passion for the person instead. That's the difference between being just physically attracted, which is easy, and being attracted to everything. Which is what I am to you." He paused and lowered his voice. "And I'd like to take you up to my room, and take your clothes off, and just look at you. Then I'd like to make love to you very slowly. That's what I'd like."

"Well." She shifted in her seat. Her face felt hot and her panties were—*admit it, Tracy*—they were damp. "Well. William, I can't do that," she finally blurted. "I'm feeling guilty already, just for having this conversation." She shook her head and held up her hand. "I know. Don't say it. I'm pathetic."

"You're not pathetic, and there's no reason for you to feel guilty. I don't want you to feel bad about anything. We've had a wonderful night and I've really enjoyed getting to know you better," he said. "If we don't go to bed together, that's fine. It's nice to think about it, though, isn't it?" He looked at her eyes, and at her mouth, and smiled.

She bit her lip and tried to act nonchalant. "Um, yes. You could say that."

When they left the restaurant, they walked to the elevator lobby in silence, pressing the buttons for seventeen—her floor—and nineteen—his. The doors slid open.

"Good night, William." She was glad he hadn't suggested coming to her room for a nightcap. She didn't know if she could have turned him down.

Chapter 5

Making the Call

"So what do you think?" Kate stretched out on her striped blue couch, moving two pillows to make herself more comfortable. "Should I do it?"

"Yes! How many more times do I have to tell you?" Tracy sounded slightly annoyed. Not that Kate could blame her—she'd been obsessing over the subject for the past week.

"But what if he's totally not interested? I couldn't get a good read on him. There wasn't a clear Vibe. At least I don't think so," she said. "But I can't help it. He's so incredibly hot."

"How could you tell if there was a Vibe anyway? You talked to him for what, five minutes? How do you even know him well enough to be interested?"

Kate pulled the cordless phone away from her ear for a moment and frowned at it. "OK . . . I guess you've got a point. Hey, Tracy, is something wrong? You sound kind of upset."

Her friend's voice sounded distracted. "I'm sorry. I'm just tired."

"What's wrong? Is it work?"

Tracy sighed. "No, it's not work."

"Tom, then?"

"No. It has nothing to do with Tom. I'm just feeling bitchy." She sighed again. "I'm probably PMS or something."

"Geez, already? Say no more." Kate shifted position and tucked her feet underneath her body. "I promise, this is the last time I'll ask. I *should* call him, right?"

"Call him. Tomorrow. And then call me and let me know how it goes. OK?"

"OK. I'm going to call him right at ten," said Kate. "I'll approach it just like a business call. Then I won't be so nervous."

But her strategy didn't work. By nine-thirty the next morning, her stomach was in knots. By the time ten rolled around, her mouth had gone completely dry. She chugged down an entire bottle of water, took several deep breaths, forced herself to smile, and picked up the phone, punching in his office number.

"Gary Vincennes, please. It's Kate Becker calling."

The receptionist connected her. "Gary Vincennes."

"Hi, Gary!" she nearly shouted, then forced her voice down to a more normal decibel level. "This is Kate. Kate Becker. We met at Tom and Tracy's a couple of weekends ago? I was asking about bankruptcy law?" *I had the enormous pink breasts*, she thought of saying, but thought better of it.

There was a pause before he responded. "Oh, Kate. Sure, I remember. What's up?"

"Well, I was wondering if you'd like to go to lunch sometime. My treat. In exchange, I get to pick your bankruptcy brain." Her heart was racing and she could feel sweat beading on her upper lip. Thank God this wasn't a face-to-face encounter.

"Lunch? That'd be fine. I've got a busy couple of weeks coming up, though," said Gary. "Let me look at my calendar."

"Oh, that's all right," she interrupted him. "If you're too busy, that's fine—I totally understand." He was obviously trying to refuse, in the nicest of possible ways.

"No, hang on. How about a week from today? You want to meet at the Potbelly's on State?"

Standing in line for a sandwich was not quite the romantic tête-à-tête she'd hoped for, but hey, it was something. "Next

Wednesday sounds great. I'll just meet you there at noon, all right?"

"See you then."

"OK, bye." She hung up the phone and raised her arms in triumph. She had done it! She'd called the Amazing Gary and made a date! Well, maybe not a date, exactly, but certainly a pseudo-date. At this point, she'd settle for what she could get.

Chapter 6

Making It "Official"

Tracy poked at her chicken and then put her fork down. It had sounded good, but she'd eaten three pieces of bread before it arrived. She'd better not finish her dinner.

"Aren't you hungry?" Tom glanced over at her, halfway through a massive plate of spaghetti. They were eating at Luigi's, an Italian place a few blocks from their apartment. Around them, fellow up-and-coming young urban professionals sat at pristine white-tableclothed tables, drinking glasses of white wine and imported beers. Most of the men ate with relish while the women picked at their plates.

"No, not really. I guess I'm just tired." She took another sip of chardonnay and flexed her fingers in her lap.

Tom had finished his dinner and beckoned at hers. "Well, if you're not going to eat it, you mind if I finish it? I'm still hungry."

"Sure." She pushed the plate over at him and watched as he cut the remaining chicken breast into three pieces and forked them into his mouth.

"That's good." He finished and motioned to the waitress, ordering decaf for both of them. "You know, you've hardly said a word all dinner. What's up?"

"You've got something in your teeth, honey." She put her fingernail between her own teeth to show him where.

"Crap." He poked around in his mouth, first with his tongue and then with his index finger. Tracy watched him resignedly. Suddenly she felt extremely depressed.

"You didn't answer me. Is something wrong?" He leaned over and picked up her right hand from the table, gently massaging her knuckles. "I know I've been preoccupied. Just a few more months, I swear. Then I'll know about the senior associate gig and we can make our plans."

"Plans?" She looked at him.

He looked surprised. "Our plans, Trace. We'll make it official and set a wedding date," he said, draining the remainder of his beer. "I know you've waited, and you've been great. I just needed to feel set at the firm before I could take on the next step. You know, getting 'officially,' " he lifted his fingers to make little quote marks with them—God, she hated that—"engaged."

She didn't know what to say. A month ago, two months ago, she would have been thrilled. Hadn't she been thinking about this forever? She'd already planned most of the wedding in her head. Kate would be the maid of honor, she'd have her two sisters and Tom's sisters as bridesmaids. They'd have the reception at the Drake if her mom and stepdad could swing it, somewhere a little cheaper if they couldn't. They'd honeymoon in St. Thomas and then she could get pregnant—after all, they'd both agreed to start their family before they were thirty. This had all been decided years ago.

So why did it sound unappealing all of a sudden? *You're tired,* she reminded herself. *And preoccupied.* Aloud, she said, "I'm sorry, hon. I'm spacing out." She forced a smile. "That sounds wonderful."

"Well, you deserve it. I want our wedding day to be exactly the way you want it. As far as I'm concerned, you've got carte blanche—whatever will make you happy will make me happy." He leaned across the table and kissed her. "In fact, you should start thinking about our engagement party. I know how you are with your parties."

"Yes, I know." She smiled back at him. When he slid his arm around her as they left the restaurant, she automatically pressed her body against his larger one. He felt the same as he always did. Solid, dependable, safe.

Tom didn't say anything on the way home, which was uncharacteristic of him. When they walked through their apartment door, he stopped and looked at her carefully. "Go sit down on the couch for a minute, will you?"

She complied, slipping off her shoes as she did so. She should probably take an Advil for her head. It was starting to pound.

Tom came walking out of their bedroom, his expression unreadable. He swallowed. "I wasn't going to do this yet, but since we were talking about it . . ." He pulled out a brown velvet jewelry box from behind his back and got down on one knee. He gulped again. "Tracy, I love you. Will you marry me?"

She must have said yes, because he grabbed her and kissed her briefly, then hugged her body against him. "Jesus, I was scared shitless!" he said in her ear, laughing, then kissed her neck. "The reality of doing it feels different, doesn't it?"

She nodded, and looked at the ring he had slid on her finger. It was an enormous solitaire in a platinum setting flanked by two rectangular baguettes. "You remembered the ring." She'd shown him the kind of diamond ring she liked, what, four years ago? And now, here it was.

"Of course I did. I may not always be the best listener, but I pay attention when it's important." He lifted her hand and turned it from side to side so the stone could catch the light. "You like it?"

"I love it." She kissed him on the mouth, and surprised herself by starting to cry. "Thank you for asking me."

He stroked her face, and gently wiped at her eyes. "Thank you for saying yes. I promise I'll make you happy."

"You do make me happy already, Tom." He stood up and pulled her to her feet, leading her to their bedroom. He made love to her for a long time, using his mouth on her until she begged him to get inside her. She couldn't stand him focusing his attention on her like that. It made her feel too vulnerable, too exposed.

"I love you, babe," he said afterward, squeezing her shoulder. "We'll be great married, just wait." She opened her mouth to speak, but his slow steady breaths told her he was already asleep.

Chapter 7

Kate Makes Her Move

Kate wiped her sweaty forehead. Ten minutes on the elliptical trainer and she was dying. She could hear her harsh breath in her ears, and her calves and hamstrings were starting to burn.

"This—is—kicking—my—butt," she managed to puff to Tracy, who was on the machine next to her. They'd started at the same time, but Tracy hardly seemed out of breath. "How long—do we—have—to—do this?"

"Twenty minutes to warm up. Then we'll hit the circuit." They were at Tracy and Tom's gym, the Bally's on Webster. This was where the toned stayed toned and the fit got even fitter. Kate felt intimidated by all the perfect bodies around, and would've never come here on her own. But what she was calling the "terrifying skirt experience" had prompted her to take desperate measures.

The TSE had happened just one week ago. She was dressing on a Monday morning, sorting through the seven suits she owned to pick one to wear. Most were black or gray—appropriate garb for a firm as conservative as hers—but she had one red one and one that was sage green. The red was her favorite, but she only wore it on days when she felt like being noticed. It had been a while since she felt that confident—definitely before the Andrew breakup—but she reached for it. She and

Gary were meeting for lunch again today (their third lunch, but who was counting) and she knew it looked good with her dark eyes and hair.

Except. When she pulled the skirt up over her hips, she noticed it seemed rather—tight. She had to suck in her stomach to zip it, and found that she now resembled a stuffed sausage. The red material was stretched dangerously tight across her stomach and butt, and when she turned to check her reflection, she noticed in horror that the vent had been pulled nearly horizontal.

If it was tight at the waist, that was one thing—she could always keep her jacket on. But this—this was obscene. Not to mention impractical. To walk in it, she had to take tiny mincing steps.

"Shit!" She unzipped the skirt, let her stomach out with a *whoosh*, and picked one of her standbys—a plain black suit she had bought at Field's three years ago. It had been slightly baggy when she bought it, but now it fit rather snugly. It wasn't horribly, sluttishly tight like her red one, but it certainly wasn't loose, either.

She grabbed her stomach in frustration. That was it. She could no longer pretend she hadn't been putting on weight, and no wonder. Some women, when they got stressed or depressed or anxious, quit eating. Tracy was like that. But Kate was the other kind. She ate more when she was feeling bad. The food was a welcome distraction.

Come to think of it, she'd been eating a few too many pizzas lately, justifying it by the fact she'd been putting in long hours at work. And her M&M consumption had definitely increased. She turned and looked at her profile in the mirror. Yup—her stomach was blossoming. She could pass for four months pregnant, big time.

It must be a sign—it was a Monday *and* the tenth of the month. Like nearly every woman she knew—except Tracy— Kate dieted sporadically. Nearly every diet was brought on by an occasion—New Year's resolutions, the approach of summer short (and horror of horrors, swimsuit) weather, the beginning of fall. Regardless, though, all diets must start on a Monday—it was the only day of the week that would do. It was even better if it was also the first of the month, or at least a day divisible by five. It just seemed to make things so much neater.

So she had embarked on another diet. She had been afraid to check her weight that morning, but she forced herself to dig the scale out from under her bed. "Oh, my, *God!*"

One-fifty-two—an all-time high. No wonder Gary hadn't taken their lunch dates to the next level. At least he'd reciprocated by asking her to lunch, and then a week later, she had called him again. But she was still unsure of potential vibeage.

It was now day four of Kate's "get serious, get skinny" all-out diet plan. She'd enlisted Tracy to help as soon as she'd gotten to the office that morning. "Major fat pig calling here," she'd said. "Need help, and fast."

"What? Oh, come on, Kate. You look fine."

When Kate related the TSE, Tracy laughed. "I'm sure it wasn't that bad."

"Come on, Tracy, you're my best friend." Kate took a swig from her water bottle sitting on her desk. Minimum of sixty-four ounces a day from now on. That should keep her from feeling hungry. "Can you tell I've gained weight?"

Tracy paused. "Do you want me to answer like your friend, or like your best friend?"

Kate sighed and covered her eyes. "Best friend."

"OK, well, I guess a little, now that you mention it. But I'm only saying so because you asked."

"What? Oh, my *God!* Why didn't you say anything?"

"You're too hard on yourself. I just figured you were getting over Andrew. You know you'll lose it when you feel better."

"Hey, hon, guess what? It's been more than a month and I'm getting fatter by the day! Soon I'll have to shop in Lane Bryant. I saw this stuff—the Hollywood Miracle Diet?—and I think I'm going to try it. Supposedly you can lose eight pounds in three days."

Tracy laughed. "Don't go psycho on me. I'll whip up a plan for you if you want, but you have to promise not to get pissed at me. If you're serious, I'll help you."

"I am extremely serious. This little piggy needs your help. Bad."

So Tracy had sketched out a diet plan for her, and Kate enlisted her as her nutrition consultant and personal coach. Kate had always envied Tracy's body. She was taller than Kate, but slimmer too—she'd worn a size six since Kate had known her. Tracy was one of those women who stayed thin without really trying, but she did seem to know an inordinate amount about food and fitness. She wasn't annoying about it the way some women were—always moaning and bitching about their thighs and picking at salads for lunch and flagellating themselves if they had a Hershey's—but she always seemed careful about what she ate. If they had a pizza together, she'd only have two slices, on rare occasions three, while Kate could easily polish off a twelve-inch alone. Of course that was the problem—look at her now!

Tracy's program included minuscule portions of All Bran with fruit and skim milk for breakfast, lunches of broth-based soups and salads, and dinners of lean chicken, vegetables, and more salads. "And you should eat a minimum of five fruits and vegetables a day," she told Kate. "It will help fill you up."

The other part of the plan was exercise. "Do I have to?" groaned Kate.

"Unless you want to be skinny and flabby simultaneously," her friend answered. "You can start by walking at least thirty minutes a day, and I want you to come to the gym with me at least three times a week. I'll show you how to use the equipment. You'll like it after a while, I promise."

"Doubtful. Very doubtful."

"Hey, just think of the—what did you call it—the TSE? And do you really want Gary caressing your fat rolls when the two of you go to bed together?"

"Oh, God. You're right. I can't even imagine getting naked

with him. Keep reminding me of all this, will you, please? Even if I turn into super bitch?"

Tracy had agreed, and now she was here, sweating alongside her friend. At least they had hits of the eighties pumping out from the stereo system; listening to *Too Shy* and *The Safety Dance* helped boost her motivation, at least somewhat. If they started playing *Let's Get Physical*, though, she was outta there.

Three weeks later, she met Tracy for breakfast at the Golden Nugget on Sunday. She resolutely ignored the menu although she looked longingly at the short stack of pancakes the waiter carried past her, and ordered a bowl of fruit, dry toast, and coffee. Tracy had a toasted bagel, and spread a paper-thin layer of cream cheese on it.

"Hey! I'm proud of you! You didn't even look at the menu," said Tracy.

"Yeah, it's becoming automatic." Kate drained her water glass. "And guess what? I've already lost six pounds. The other day, I even saw an actual muscle in my arm."

"Woohoo!" said Tracy, Homer Simpson-style, and they both laughed.

"I'm feeling a lot better. Another fourteen pounds and I'll be a svelte, gorgeous babe. Gary won't be able to resist me."

"So what's the latest?"

Kate shook her head in frustration. "Tracy, I have no idea. We've gone out to lunch three times, and met for drinks once," she said. "But he hasn't even tried to kiss me!"

"I can't believe that." Tracy considered for a moment. "He *must* be gay," she said with finality.

"Oh, thank you!" She beamed at her friend. "No, I don't think so. He's talked about old girlfriends before. Maybe he's just not very sexual."

"And he's a man? Not very likely."

"Well, his time is up. Gay or not, I'm having him over for dinner tonight and I'm making my move."

"What are you making?"

"That spicy baked chicken and broccoli casserole and bread.

I figure I'll seduce him with food, get a couple of beers into him, and then pounce."

"What's the plan?"

"I don't know. I'm thinking a casual hand on the knee, maybe a meaningful glance, and then I lick my lips . . . what? Is there anything wrong with that?"

"I don't know. It just seems so contrived."

"Maybe, but I can't take much more of this," said Kate. "If I've got my signals crossed, I'd like to know now."

But things didn't turn out quite the way she'd planned. Gary arrived on time and even brought a bouquet of flowers with him. (So they were slightly wilted and still had the 7-Eleven price tag on them—*It's the thought that counts*, she reminded herself.) He had a Heineken and they talked about work mostly. Somehow they got to talking about urban legends—like the one about the Mikey kid from the Life cereal commercials, who had supposedly blown up his stomach by eating too many packages of Pop Rocks and Coke.

"There's a great Web site on those," said Kate. "Snopes.com, I think. Hang on, I'll show it to you." She motioned to the computer on her desk in the corner, and pulled up an extra chair.

"See?" she said, bringing up the Web site. "They've got hundreds of them here."

Gary leaned forward with interest, reading the screen closely, and she sat watching him. She could smell his cologne—was it Obsession? how ironic—and her knee was less than an inch from his leg. Even through his jeans, she could see the outline of his quadriceps muscles.

Moving slowly, she reached out and put her hand on his back, between his shoulder blades. As she did so, she could swear she saw him hunch forward away from her touch. It was as if his very flesh was trying to crawl away from her. After a long moment, she extricated her hand verrrrry slowly and returned it to her lap.

Neither said anything about it, and after another half hour of surfing, Gary pointedly looked at his watch. "Thanks for dinner, Kate—it was great," he said. "I should be hitting the road, though."

"Gary, wait a minute." They were standing near the doorway of her apartment. She balanced her weight on her left leg, a habit she did when she was nervous. "I can't believe I'm asking you this." She looked down and then swallowed hard. "What's going on here, anyway? Are you interested in me or are we just friends or what?"

He looked slightly constipated for a moment. "Interested?"

"Oh, come on, don't make it worse than it already is. You know what I mean. You've asked me to lunch, we've gone out for drinks, and now dinner here, and I guess I've kind of been waiting for you to—well, you know, make a move."

Gary looked around her apartment for help, but none was coming. He pursed his lips several times, looked at Kate's face and then away, and then finally spoke.

"How honest do you want me to be?"

Shit, this was sounding familiar. "As honest as you want to be." Then it occurred to her. "Oh, *God*, you're gay, aren't you!" She truly *was* an idiot.

"What? No. No!" He crossed his arms over his chest. "I think you're a great girl. You're smart and fun to talk to and I like the way you don't put up with any crap." He paused. "You remind me of my sister, actually."

Uh-oh. This wasn't sounding promising. "But . . ." she prompted.

"Kate, I know I'm picky. I've always dated the same type of girl before—you know, blond, in great shape, early twenties."

"Oh, this is because I'm too fat! Look, I've lost six pounds already!" She made a muscle for him. "See how strong I'm getting?" She poked at her biceps hopefully. "Check it out!"

He interrupted her. "It's not that. Kate, you're just not my type. I like you but I'm not interested in you, well, sexually." He reached for her hand and squeezed it—the first time he had initiated any physical contact other than a handshake, she realized. "I'm really sorry. I should have said something before now, but I kept hoping something would kick in. You're just the kind of girl I'd like to be with . . ."

"Except you don't *want* to be with me," she finished for him. There was no possible way she could feel more humiliated than she already did.

"I don't want to piss you off," he said reasonably. "I think I'm a pretty nice guy and I'm telling you the truth."

"Yeah, yeah, yeah." She opened the door for him. "Look, I'll be fine with this soon, I'm sure. Right now, though, could you leave and put an end to my total, complete embarrassment and shame."

"I'm going. I'll talk to you later, OK?"

"OK. See you!" she nearly shouted, and closed the door behind him. She checked the freezer—there was a half pint of Ben & Jerry's Chunky Monkey still in the door. It was a start.

Chapter 8

It's Called Lust

"**T**race?" Tom shouted. "Your mom's on the phone!"

Tracy rolled her eyes. Since their engagement, her mother had done an abrupt about-face. No longer did she complain about Tom and Tracy living together; now she was pestering her almost daily with wedding details, the latest on who they simply *must* invite, recommendations of vendors for the flowers, for the cake, for stationery, and insisting that Tracy find a dress *immediately*. "You don't want to wait too long," had become her favorite refrain.

"Hi, Mom." Tracy slid onto one of the bar stools in the kitchen and fiddled with the ratty end of a dish towel. "How are you?"

"I just got off the phone with Phyllis Epstein—you know, Kiki and Brad got married last summer and they had this beautiful ice sculpture. It was just exquisite—had likenesses of the bride and groom and even these adorable little cherubs," her mom's voice trilled in her ear. "And it was done by a caterer right there in Chicago!"

Tracy sighed. "Do we really need an ice sculpture, Mom? Isn't it just going to melt?"

"Of course you don't need one, dear. But every little detail makes a difference. And it'd be a wonderful centerpiece."

"You're right, you're right. We'll check it out, all right?" She waved her arm frantically at Tom, who was watching *Sports Center.* He caught her glance.

"Yo! Tracy! Come here a sec, will you?" he bellowed.

"Mom, Tom's calling me. I've got to go. Is there anything else?"

"Oh, all right. I'll speak to you later, then. Bye-bye."

"Bye, Mom." She pushed the button to break the connection and smiled at Tom in thanks. "She's driving me insane."

"What is it now? Horse-drawn carriages for us and all of our guests?" He lay sprawled on their leather couch, his head propped on his arm. He had come home from work at seven, the earliest in weeks, but had been lying on the couch most of the evening.

"Don't give her any ideas, please." Tracy went and slid under his legs at the end of the couch, gently squeezing the soles of his feet.

"Oh, yeah, baby. Work it," he teased. He arched his back and wiggled his toes in her lap. "More, please!"

She sat absently massaging his feet while he caught up on the latest baseball scores. Tom didn't seem bothered by the swirl of wedding plans, but then again, he was pretty much leaving everything up to her. It was her responsibility, as usual. Grasping the toes of one foot in her right hand, she moved them forward and back with more force than she meant to.

"Hey! That's getting painful, babe."

"Sorry." Why was she feeling so totally bitchy? It was probably trying to make all these wedding decisions on top of everything going on at work, where she'd been busier than she had been in months. The bank had had a slew of discrimination claims filed with the EEOC, and she was responsible for investigating all of them and filing the preliminary responses to the claims.

One of the attractive aspects of her job at the bank was that she usually worked reasonable hours—starting after eight and leaving around six. They weren't true banker's hours, to be sure, but they were much preferable to the typical fifty- and sixty-hour weeks most of the lawyers like Tom and Kate worked. She had been spoiled—most nights she had time to stop off at the gym on the way home, and if she was lucky, Tom got home about the same time she did. But lately she was always rushing from work or making phone calls at lunch or scheduling appointments or dress hunting on weekends. So far she'd spent four Saturdays looking for a dress—and had tried on at least forty—but hadn't found one that she liked.

Kate had been great about it although Tracy could tell she was stifling her impatience. By the third Saturday in a row, though, she let out an exasperated sigh when Tracy complained that the mermaid gown she had on made her look fat.

"Fat? Tracy, you're a stick. You have a perfectly flat stomach and barely any ass." Kate shook her head and took a big swallow of water. Lately she'd been carrying a bottle with her everywhere, and then she spent half the time when they were shopping looking for bathrooms. "You couldn't look fat if you tried. Not even in that hoop skirt nightmare you tried on."

Tracy turned in the three-way mirror to check her reflection from all angles. "I don't know," she said miserably. "I just don't like the way it looks."

Kate looked up from the chair where she was sitting with her head in her hands. "Hey, I'm sorry. I'm hungry and cranky. I didn't mean to snap at you."

"It's not you." She turned so Kate could unzip the dress for her, and slipped the shoulders off. "I don't know what it is." She lowered her voice. "I always thought dress shopping would be so much fun! But I hate it. I don't think I'll find anything I like."

Just then the impeccably groomed saleswoman strolled in, wearing a Pepto Bismol–pink suit and pearls. "How are we doooooing?" she sang. "Oh, I'm sure that mermaid looks incredible on your figure. Is that *the one?*"

Kate stood up and pulled back the curtain to the dressing area for Tracy. "It looks beautiful, but I think we're done for the day," she said with an apologetic expression. "The blushing bride needs a break."

"Oh, certainly, certainly. Here's my card if you need anything in the future." She whisked away on her elegant pink pumps.

Tracy stuck her head out the curtain. "Thanks."

"Hey, what are maids of honor for? Let's get some lunch and have some wine and talk, OK? Forget the wedding for a while."

They found a litte pizza place a few blocks away, and Kate ordered a glass of chardonnay for herself, a glass of merlot for Tracy, and salads for both of them. "If you don't feel better, we'll treat ourselves to some Garrett's popcorn, OK?"

Tracy didn't answer, and Kate waited until their server set down their glasses of wine. "Come on, I'm offering to blow my diet for you!" She took a sip of her wine. "OK, Trace, what's the matter? You don't seem very happy lately."

"Is it that obvious?" Tracy smoothed her hair, tucking it behind her ears. "I suppose it's just wedding jitters or something."

"That won't work with me. You've wanted to marry Tom since you met him, remember? You said that even before you slept with him. Although I don't know how you could decide that before you had sex with him."

"I remember." Tracy sat there glumly for a moment, playing with the stem of her glass. "I know that. But lately everything he does annoys me. The way he leaves dishes in the sink, the way he works late all the time and doesn't even feel guilty about it, the way he leaves hair bits from his razor all over the bathroom, the way he'll always make time for his buddies but never wants to go out just with me, the way he wears those horrible Dockers every casual Friday . . ."

"This is serious, huh?" Kate interrupted her, grinning. "Are you telling me that none of these things bothered you before?"

"Maybe a little. But now it's like they're extremely important, and if I have to live the rest of my life putting up with them, I don't know if I can." Tracy teared up and sniffled. "I know I'm crazy. I love Tom and I know I wanted to marry him. But now . . ." She took another swig of her wine. "I can't believe I'm saying this. But I guess I don't know if I'm sure this is the right thing."

Kate sat back in the booth, her mouth open. "Wow. Tracy, I don't know what to say. Does he know you feel this way?"

"Of course not! I keep thinking it's temporary, but it's not going away." She rearranged the silverware in front of her, lining up the bottoms of the knife, fork, and spoon so that they were perfectly aligned. "There's something else, too. I—I—I met someone."

Kate choked on her wine. "What? Hang on." She signaled at the waitress to bring two more glasses of wine. "I think we're going to need this. You met someone? Who? Where? Who is he?"

"In Vegas, when I went to that conference."

"And?"

"And—I'm embarrassed to admit this, even to you. You know how you always talk about the Vibe? Well, I don't think I've ever felt it before. I've just never been that sexually attracted to anyone."

"What about Tom?"

"No, even him. I liked him, I thought he was good-looking and sexy, and he's good in bed, but this is something different. This is like a chemical, all-over body thing. Whenever I think about him, my heart starts pounding." She forced a laugh. "Like right now, I feel sick and dizzy and nauseous for no reason. I can't concentrate on work, I don't care about the wedding, and when I look at Tom, all I can think is that he's not William."

"Wow." Kate sat there for a moment. "You don't have to tell me if you don't want to, you know, but did anything . . . happen?"

"No. We had drinks and then we had dinner and we talked. He told me how attracted he was to me," she lowered her voice, "and that he wanted to make love to me. I've never had a guy tell me that."

"Not even Tom?"

"Not beyond the 'hey, why don't we go home and play hide the salami' or something," Tracy answered and then saw her friend's face. "He's not that bad. He's just not that romantic, I guess. And I've known that all along. Jeez, I'm pathetic."

"You're not pathetic!" said Kate with feeling. "You're just . . . I don't know, Trace. You've got a lot going on right now, you know? And it's totally normal to be attracted to men other than the one you're with! That's part of being a grown-up."

"No. It's not!" said Tracy. "If you love your husband or wife enough, it doesn't happen. Look at my dad. He wouldn't have left my mom if he really loved her. The very fact that I was attracted means there's something wrong between me and Tom." Tracy blushed. "And I *liked* it. I loved it. I loved every minute of it. I talked about things with him I've never talked about with anyone, except maybe you."

Kate watched her friend carefully. "Like what?"

"Like sex."

"You talked about sex? With a guy? I can hardly get you to talk about sex to me."

Tracy grinned for a moment. "I know. And I brought it up! We went out for dinner again the second night of the conference, and I couldn't help myself." She pushed aside her empty glass and took a sip of the new one. "Kate, he is so incredibly sexy. He has these eyes . . ." her voice trailed off.

"He has eyes. OK, that's good . . ."

"He has these eyes that look dark brown but when you look really closely into them, you see that they have different colored flecks of brown and green and gold in them and his upper teeth are perfect but his lower teeth are kind of jumbled and he has a long scar down the inside of his left arm from where this dog attacked him when he was seven . . ."

"Geez, you've got it bad. And nothing happened?" Kate sounded skeptical. Very skeptical.

"No. After our second dinner, he walked me back to my room. I had to pack and get to the airport, but I waited until the last possible minute. I just didn't want to leave him," said Tracy. "I was a total dork. I tried to shake his hand. And he stood there and said 'I'm not leaving you without a hug' and then he hugged me." She swallowed. "Kate, my heart was beating so hard I couldn't believe it. We just stood there holding each other for like two minutes. I could feel how small he felt compared to Tom—that's what was so weird, I kept thinking 'it's not Tom, it's not Tom'—and I could smell him and I couldn't help myself." She looked down. "I kissed his neck, and then he kissed me."

"And?"

She swallowed. "And we kissed for a minute and," she lowered her voice and leaned toward Kate, "I was, you know, soaking. Just from the kiss."

"Oh, my God!" Kate picked up the dessert menu placard from the table and fanned herself with it. "I think I'm getting wet just from listening."

"Shut up." Tracy colored a little. "It was perfect. We kissed and he didn't try to do anything else, but I could *feel* him, and how hard he was, and I wanted him so bad. All I could think was 'Tom doesn't need to know, this has nothing to do with Tom,' you know, that was going through my head even as we were kissing. And then he pulled away from me and kind of groaned and said, 'you have no idea how much I want to make love to every inch of your body.'"

Kate stared at her, openmouthed. "I cannot believe you haven't told me this! You're killing me."

Tracy giggled. "And then I said, 'well, I think I have some idea,' and I just kind of traced my hand against him, you know?"

"You did that?"

"I know. I was addled by hormones. I didn't know what I was doing. And he groaned and grabbed my hand and squeezed it really hard and said, 'If you do that again, I won't be able to help myself.'"

"So, the big question is—did you do it again?"

"No." Tracy's face fell. "Then it all blew up. I thought of Tom and how I would never be able to explain this to him, and what about AIDS and I had no birth control with me, and I had on ugly underwear and I hadn't shaved my legs, and I had to catch that stupid plane and I just couldn't. So we kind of separated and he left and then I had to race to the airport and I almost missed my flight, and I couldn't stop thinking about him. And then as I soon as I saw Tom, I felt so guilty I couldn't stand it."

"Wow." Kate stared at her and then took a bite of salad. "I actually forgot about being hungry for seven minutes! Tracy, that is one of the sexiest things I have ever heard. I'm jealous!"

"But I feel terrible about it. I feel so guilty all the time."

"Why? You didn't do anything. You kissed a guy and brushed his dick with your fingers through several layers of clothing. I don't think that constitutes a mortal sin."

"I don't feel guilty about that. I'm glad I did it! I feel guilty about wanting him so much. How can I love Tom and feel this way about someone else?"

"Hey, it's called lust. It happens to everyone, Tracy. You don't need to beat yourself up about it."

Tracy opened her mouth to add the rest, and then shut it.

Chapter 9

Kate's Birthday, Milwaukee-Style

Since the Amazing Gary fiasco, Kate had been remarkably celibate. Not only had she not had sex, she hadn't thought about having sex—at least not that often. She had even managed to make it through several weeks without torturing herself about what Andrew might be doing. The only drawback was that she'd developed a new bad habit instead.

She was surfing the net out of boredom one night and decided to check out the Google.com site that geek at Tracy's party had told her about. First she typed in her own name, and came up with nothing. She typed in Andrew's and found it on several sites, most of which listed the results of local triathalons. That figured. This was supposed to be how you found out the dirt on someone? It didn't seem likely.

She thought a minute and then typed in "Michael Cooper"—her first Mike—but she got thousands of hits. After wading through a few pages, she gave up. Too bad—she wouldn't mind knowing what he was doing now. Clearly it helped to stalk people with unusual or distinctive names. Then in a flash, she tried typing in Victor Musnisic. With a name like that, he'd be easy to find—and he was.

Victor now appeared to be a C.P.A. at a firm in Los Angeles. She also found several listings of his on eBay.com; apparently he collected old Beatles paraphernalia. Interesting, but again not the treasure trove of information she'd been led to expect. Then she thought of Ben, and typed in Ben Yaeger. Just typing in his name left her feeling slightly sick. When she saw his home page—complete with photos of him, his wife, and three little boys—she was immediately depressed.

Might as well go for broke. She looked up Randy. After using Randall Hendrickson, she got lucky—he'd written three books and was teaching in Seattle. The two other Mikes—Pierce and Rogers—led to dead ends. Like Michael Cooper, they pulled up thousands of hits. Why hadn't she realized there were so many Mikes out there? Oh, yeah, she'd dated three of them. That should probably have been her first clue.

Kate got up and got an apple. She'd prefer a bag of M&Ms, but lately it'd been easier to stick to her diet. Still, she felt vaguely depressed. OK, maybe she'd never really gotten over Ben. Maybe she wouldn't. But it wasn't like she still loved any of these guys. In fact, Victor had been an asshole, come to think of it, and Randy had cheated on her at least once that she knew of, and probably more. And so had Mike Cooper. What was her damage, anyway?

But she was going to be twenty-nine in less than two weeks. That left her one good year before she turned thirty. It was all downhill from there, and her life just seemed pretty lame of late. Work, dieting, exercising, and televised natural disasters. How could it get any worse? Tracy had tried to cheer her up, but it hadn't worked.

"Why don't we have a party?" Tracy had asked. "We can do it at our place, and you can invite whoever you want."

"I'm not having a party. Besides, other than you and Tom and maybe Teresa, I wouldn't know who to invite. I could invite Danny and some of the guys from work, but that's all I know anymore. And I don't want to hang out with lawyers for my birthday." She sighed.

"Quit moping," said Tracy. "OK, then. I'll plan something for your birthday—you just have to agree to go along with it."

Which is how Kate found herself the victim of a stealth road trip to Milwaukee a few weeks later.

"Milwaukee?" She'd only been there twice, both times to Summerfest. Lots of beer, lots of loud music, and lots of people wearing tank tops who should have thought better of it.

"Don't be such a snob. It's a fun town and we'll celebrate by ourselves." She and Tracy searched for two hours for the bar known as The Safe House, which was hidden away in a downtown basement. By the time they got there, Kate was ready to go home. But in the crush of tourists at The Safe House, Kate had even exchanged significant glances, then smiles, and finally spit with a tall, blond Norwegian-looking guy. She was only a few countries off. It turned out he was a German—Hans—and on holiday with a group of his buddies, who seemed intent on drinking as much Yagermeister as possible and ogling the "hot American girls." When Tracy had explained to him that it was Kate's birthday—and the tradition of the birthday kiss—he had obliged with a smile. She'd drunk just enough to thoroughly enjoy the kiss and even considered sneaking out into the alley to make out with him. How old was she, anyway? Then his increasingly rowdy friends had dragged him out of the bar while she looked on in regret.

"OK, you're right. I needed this," she said over bites of a panzarotta, which resembled a pizza, folded in half. Screw the diet—it was her birthday. "God, this is good."

"I know. Tom and I came up here a few times when we started going out, and he introduced me to them." Tracy had actually finished her entire meal, Kate noticed—that was rare for her.

Kate took a swallow of beer. It was almost two in the morning, but she didn't even feel tired. The night reminded her of college, when she'd go out with her roommates, drink beer until closing time, and then eat burritos at two in the morning. You flirted with guys, maybe made out with one at a party—whatever happened to party mashing, anyway?—and maybe even met someone you really, really liked. She looked at Tracy.

"So, how are you doing?" asked Kate. "You know, about the William thing."

"Better, I guess." Tracy bit her lip. "Actually, I wasn't going to tell you this. We've been E-mailing each other."

"You have? How long?" Another thought occurred to her. Blame the lawyer in her. "Who initiated it?"

"He did, actually." Tracy refolded her paper napkin. "He just sent me a little note about a new federal employment case, and mentioned how much he'd enjoyed meeting me, and he hoped I was doing well, that kind of thing."

"And did you tell him you're engaged now?" God, Kate hated the way that had sounded, priggish and judgmental, but she couldn't help it.

"Of course." Tracy looked away from her. "We're just friends. Colleagues. I don't think there's anything wrong with E-mailing each other."

"I'm sorry, Trace. You're right. I didn't mean to sound like your mother or something."

"You couldn't sound like her if you tried. Weren't you the one who said what, that groping a guy through his pants was no big deal?"

"I still think that." Kate finished her beer. The waistline of her pants was digging into her, but she didn't care. "But because it was a one-time thing, with a guy you're never going to see again."

"Well, of course." Tracy answered quickly, changing the subject. "But I guess I'm still not sure about everything else. Maybe I'm just not ready to be married. But then I think of how long we've been together and how we have the apartment and all the furniture and how hard we've worked and I can't see walking away from all that. I mean, it's been five years."

"Tracy, if you're not sure, I don't know if you should marry him. Maybe Tom isn't the right person for you."

"I thought you liked him!"

"I do. You know I do. I love him. Tom's great. But it's the rest of your life, you know?" Kate took another bite, chewed and swallowed. "And, well, you haven't seemed like yourself lately. Even if you and Tom broke up, it wouldn't be the end of the world. You'd find someone else, you know."

"How? How do you know that?" Tracy shook her head. "I'm not you, Kate. You're so independent. You say you want a guy, but you don't really need one. Before I met Tom, I always worried about what people would think of me and whether I was dressed wrong or would say something stupid or make a fool out of myself. With him, I feel . . . I just feel secure. I feel safe, you know?"

Kate didn't know what to say. Something didn't feel right, but she couldn't figure out what it was. "Security doesn't seem like a good reason to get married, Tracy."

"Are you kidding?" Tracy practically snorted. "Why else do people get married? Because they want to know that that person will be there for them, no matter what. That's what marriage is all about. Commitment. Trust. Growing old together. Sharing your lives. Sticking together when you'd prefer to leave."

Kate tried to lighten the mood. "I think you're reading too many of those bridal magazines, you know? Look, I'm not criticizing you. You just don't seem all that happy lately."

Tracy smiled. "I am. I'm happy. I'm just busy with all the wedding stuff. I'm sure that's the problem." She reached across the table and squeezed Kate's arm. "This is your birthday, remember? So let's talk about what we're going to do tomorrow."

Chapter 10

Little Hearts

Tracy surveyed the damage. The kitchen counter was littered with an empty pizza box, a half-eaten bag of Cheetos, and the melting remains of a half gallon of chocolate ice cream. She felt bloated, nauseous, and disgusted with herself.

She'd been doing so well! Sticking to healthy foods, always careful to watch her portions, exercising every night after work. What was wrong with her? Why couldn't she just be *good?*

Tracy sat on a kitchen stool, her head in her hands. How long had it been since she had succumbed to her out-of-control hunger? Three weeks? Four? She'd let herself believe she was over it. But then she got sucked in again. Why couldn't she just eat like a normal person?

She'd felt the binge coming on all week. She had too much to do at work, too many wedding details to take care of, and obsessing over William didn't help. A normal woman would just chalk up what had happened as no big deal. That's what Kate would do. But no, not her. She let all this stuff build and build until she couldn't help herself. She stopped at the 7-Eleven on the way home, hurriedly grabbing a bag of Cheetos, a bag of M&MS, and ice cream, ordering a pizza from her cell as she walked home. For a few minutes, while she ate, she thought of nothing but the food. Her mind was completely blank.

But now it was over, and she had to get rid of all those calories. She walked in the bathroom and pulled her hair back in a
ponytail. In one practiced move, she put her right hand into
her mouth and jabbed with two fingers until she gagged. It
took several tries before she was able to vomit up everything
she'd eaten. Half-digested chunks of pizza and fluorescent orange bits of Cheetos and runny brown liquid floated in the toilet. She sat on the floor, sweaty-faced and sickened for several
minutes. Finally, she flushed the toilet three times and then
heaved herself into the shower.

She stood under the water for at least fifteen minutes, letting the spray beat her until her skin turned red. Then she
climbed out, scrubbed her teeth with her toothbrush and a
generous amount of Crest, flossed, and then rinsed with Act to
disguise any leftover smell. She had changed into what she
called her "comfy clothes"—the bottoms from an ancient pair
of J.Crew pajamas and an XXL faded green sweatshirt—and
was curled up watching *Survivor* by the time Tom got home.

"Hey, babe." He set his briefcase down by the door and
walked over to kiss her forehead. "How was your day."

"OK. Yours?" She got up, swaying slightly. She'd felt dizzy
ever since she'd thrown up. But she followed him into the
kitchen, where he opened the refrigerator.

"I'm starved. You want to get take-out? Chinese? I'll get it
if you want."

"All right. Some sweet-and-sour soup and some chicken
fried rice, I guess."

"Is that it?"

"Yeah, I'm not that hungry." She said that a lot, but tonight
she meant it. Her throat felt raw anyway.

"All right." He called in their order and then took a quick
shower, emerging in jeans and a T-shirt. "Be right back."

Tracy ate most of her soup but had only a few bites of rice.
Tom picked up the cartons to put them in the fridge and
looked into hers in surprise. "Trace, come on. You've got to
eat something. Are you sick?"

His concern made her tear up, but she shook her head. "I'm just tired, honey."

Tom came back from the kitchen and sat down next to her, pulling her to him. He started massaging her neck and shoulders, and she let herself relax against the feel of his large, warm hands. "Mmmmm. That feels good."

"Um-hm." She felt his fingers squeezing her shoulders and then reaching down to cup her breasts. Immediately she stiffened and squirmed away from him.

"I don't feel like it."

"Come on." He bent and kissed the side of her neck. "You know it will make you feel better."

She sighed and closed her eyes. They hadn't had sex for seventeen days—it was a new record for them. Tom didn't realize she always marked the dates on a calendar with little hearts—one heart for each sex act. At first it had been a diary of sorts, a way of tracking their relationship and remembering certain nights or weekends. Even when little hearts bloomed all over the pages of her day planner, she'd been able to look at them and remember each time. But over the years, the hearts had grown farther and farther apart, looking more and more lonely. And lately—well, lately there were only two or three a month.

She wished she could tell him no, but it *had* been two weeks. She allowed herself to be convinced, allowed Tom to kiss her and stroke her breasts the way he knew she liked. He even went down on her, but she couldn't have an orgasm. She could tell he was only doing it to make her come—then he'd get inside her and thrust until he came. She hated that. Didn't guys know that the only way you could really enjoy oral sex was when you felt like they were loving every second of it—not counting the minutes until they could stop?

She tugged on his hair gently. "Come up here. Why don't you let me get on top," she murmured. Even after all this time, it was hard for her to say what she wanted. But she knew she'd come more easily if she could ride him, if she could control the pace. The only way she finally got there was by shutting her eyes and imagining that it was William kissing her mouth, William sucking her nipples, William's fingers digging into her hips as she rode him. Finally, she came, and Tom flipped her over in a practiced move and pumped her for another thirty seconds before his orgasm.

"Mmmm. Love you." Tom pulled her closer to him, kissing her hair. She knew he'd be asleep within thirty seconds. As she heard his breathing deepen, she bit her lip. She carefully extricated herself from his hold, slipped her clothes back on, and padded out to the refrigerator to finish her dinner.

Chapter 11

Kate the Animal

Kate pulled up her favorite jeans—Old Navy low-slung hip-sters—and looked at her ass in the mirror appraisingly. Certainly not a supermodel's, but it wasn't bad. She'd lost nearly twenty pounds in the last ten weeks, and could wear a size eight for the first time in . . . OK, for the first time since high school. A few small pockets of cellulite clung to her thighs, but all in all, her diet and exercise plan had been a success.

When she had started—prompted by the TSE—Kate had focused only on reaching her goal weight of 133 pounds. She was sick of being fat and worrying about the way she looked, and she was willing to do anything—including sweat and breathe hard for reasons that had nothing to do with sexual activity—to get there.

What she *hadn't* considered was how good she would feel once she got going. When Tracy had first dragged her to the gym, every workout had been torture. Now she had her own membership—Lehmann Sports Club, which was closer to her apartment and cheaper than Tom and Tracy's—and she'd started running. She could jog for thirty minutes at a stretch now, and had even developed actual visible muscles in her thighs and arms. When she got out of the shower, she some-times flexed her biceps just to admire them.

She'd started running three mornings a week, before she went to work. Now that summer was here, the days had turned steamy, but at six in the morning, the air was still relatively cool. She'd usually run down Wellington toward Lincoln Park, and make several loops or run along the lake for a mile or so before heading back home. After six weeks of this routine, she started recognizing and nodding at some of the other runners she saw. She'd even run into Gary one morning near North Pond.

"Kate!" Gary was wearing black shorts in the extreme baggy style that hetero guys in their twenties and thirties favor, and a stretched-out snot green T-shirt. It didn't change the fact that he was, even sweaty and red-faced, incredibly hot. "I didn't know you ran!" He changed direction and loped over to her.

Kate tried to keep from sounding out of breath. "Yeah," she panted. "I started a couple of months ago."

Was it her imagination or did he look her up and down? "You look good. Really good. You've dropped some weight, haven't you?"

Ha! He noticed. "Some," she said noncommittally.

"Well, you can tell." He fell in beside her, jogging easily while she tried to keep her breath from rasping. "Have you ever thought about doing the marathon?"

"A marathon? What, are you kidding? That's like twenty miles, isn't it?"

"Twenty-six point two. It's a great race, though. They get twenty-five, twenty-six thousand runners out in the streets and you have a million spectators cheering your on. It's a blast. You gotta do it at least once."

"I don't think so. I can barely do three miles."

"All you need is a decent base. Once you work up to fifteen, twenty miles a week, you can start doing long runs. CARA— you know, the Chicago Area Runners Association—has groups that meet on Saturday and Sunday mornings, and you gradu-ally build up your long runs. Plus you're with a group, so it goes a lot quicker." They came to a stoplight and let a couple of early morning commuters clear the intersection. "Think about it. I'll even coach you if you want."

"Oh, you will?" she said, glancing over at him.

"Sure. I meant what I said. I like you. It's just not a sexual thing with me." They jogged in silence for a few moments while Kate marveled at how lightly he ran for someone his size. His footsteps made little noise while hers sounded like a small elephant. "Actually it'd be good," he admitted. "You know, I don't think I've ever had a woman friend before."

"Oh, now I'm an experiment for you?" She rolled her eyes, but she couldn't help smiling. He was kind of a doofus under those gorgeous looks. Probably better off as friend material, anyway. They ran along for a while, chatting about work, and then veered back south, and Kate snuck a look at her watch. She'd been running for almost forty minutes, a new record for her! "Hey! I think I've done about four miles!"

"See? The time goes a lot faster when you've got someone to talk to." He glanced at his watch, too. "I've got to hit it. Hey, do you play volleyball?"

"That depends on your definition of play. I'm OK, but not great or anything."

"No problem. We need another female on our coed team tomorrow night down at North Avenue Beach. You interested?"

"What if I suck? Are you guys super competitive?"

"Not at all. Well, a little. But you can't be worse than the sub we had last week. Why don't you meet us at seven at the volleyball courts and we'll play a couple of games."

She considered. What the hell. "All right. I'll see you there."

"Great!" He gave her a friendly pat and sped off, while Kate turned back to her apartment. She dashed to work with her hair still wet, but it was worth it. She'd run four miles! She was an animal.

Chapter 12

Soaking Wet Panties

Tracy stared at her day planner without really seeing it. Less than four months to go—Saturday, November 16 was circled in red. Why had it sounded like such a good idea to get married in November, anyway? She'd finally given in and hired a wedding consultant who had taken over the responsibilities of selecting every possible detail from how many sprays of baby's breath would be included in the bridesmaids' bouquets to the choice of paper, lettering, and wording of the wedding invitations they'd send. Tracy had gratefully surrendered the job to Maxine Geraldi, a no-nonsense woman who appeared to never lose her temper. She was expensive but her mom was paying for it. Besides, her mom had spoken with her as many times as Tracy herself. She figured diverting the phone calls to Maxine was worth nearly anything.

"She's a gem, an absolute gem," her mother enthused while going over the final guest list and potential seating arrangements for the five hundred millionth time. Her mother was fretting over how they would seat all of their relatives without anyone's feelings getting hurt. Apparently in the Wisloski family, being seated close to the bride and groom was a question of pride. During the interminable dinner, she and Tom would be surrounded by a swarm of relatives she barely knew—while her closest friends would be relegated to the outside tables. She groaned inwardly.

"Mom, we don't have to worry about this yet," said Tracy. "We won't mail the invitations for two more months at least. And even then, who knows who will come?"

"Well, it doesn't hurt to be prepared. And anyway, everyone from your family will be there. How could they miss the big day of my youngest daughter?"

Gag. "Yes, Mother dearest."

"Stop calling me that!" But her mom wasn't really annoyed. "I'm probably driving you crazy, aren't I?" Tracy said nothing, just sat at her desk, twisting the phone cord. Her mother continued. "I just want everything to be perfect for you, honey, that's all. It's the most important day of your life."

And besides, it's a reflection on you, too, thought Tracy but didn't say it. She made an excuse to get off the phone—lately her mom had been calling her at work as well—and hung up. Not twenty seconds later, it rang again.

"Mom, enough. I'm not discussing this until the RSVPs come in."

"Fair enough." The voice was deep, much deeper than her mother's. "But this isn't your mom."

"William?" Her heart immediately thumped wildly.

"Hello, Tracy. What are you doing at the office so late?"

She glanced at the little gold clock on her desk—that Tom had given her when she was offered this job. "It's barely after six," she said. "Not quite a late night."

"True. But around here, everyone clears out by five and straggles in after nine during the summer. We have to soak up all the sunshine when we can."

"Oh, that's right, the land of a thousand lakes, right?"

"It's ten thousand," he teased. "But you're close enough."

Hearing his voice in her ear seemed much more intimate than the E-mails they'd been exchanging. She'd thought about calling him a hundred times, but didn't want to be the first one to act. Besides, maybe their relationship was supposed to be limited to E-mail. It seemed safer that way, more like a fantasy. Like the way she remembered the dinners they'd shared, how intent he had been on her, how his attention had never wavered. She cleared her throat. "So, what's new?"

"What's new?" he repeated. "What's new is that I'm coming to Chicago next week for work. If you're free, I thought maybe we could go to dinner or something. You could keep me company in the Windy City."

Hmmm. Dinner "or something." "Next week?" she squeaked. "Hold on, let me grab my calendar. What night were you thinking?"

"How's Thursday?"

She looked. Tom was supposed to be out of town for a trial all next week, but it might cancel. What would she tell him? What kind of excuse could she make? Aloud, she said, coolly as she could manage, "Thursday's doable. You want me to pick the restaurant?"

"Why don't you. It's been a while since I've been there. I'm staying at the Palmer House, downtown. Do you know it?"

"Oh, yeah, it's right in the Loop, not far from my office. There are some good restaurants near there. We won't have any trouble finding a good place."

"I'm going to be hung up most of the day, but I'll probably come back to the hotel before dinner. Why don't we meet downstairs, in Trader Vic's then," said William. "Or is that too much a tourist thing?"

"No, that's fine. Besides, it seems to draw a lot more people during the winter anyway." She paused. "Um, it will be great to see you again, William. I'm looking forward to it."

She could hear the smile in his voice. "I'm looking forward to seeing you, too."

That's why she found herself unable to function for the next week. She was distracted at work, misplaced her keys no fewer than four times, and twice walked past her building's door on the way home from the gym. Her eating habits had been bad, too. Normally, she could keep her eating in check. So she slipped once, maybe twice a week. But now it was becoming an almost nightly occurrence.

Thinking about William made her feel both sick and anxious. She replayed their evenings together in her head over and over, feeling that excitement again. Then she'd remind herself she was supposed to be in *love* with Tom. What kind of person was she, having thoughts like this? And look at how her thighs bulged when she sat down. They were definitely bigger. She had to get things under control. She wanted to look perfect for the wedding. She couldn't stand the idea of everyone staring at her, being the center of attention. The anxiety made her want to eat. At least Tom had been working late, as usual, which made it easier to hide the empty ice-cream containers and chip bags.

Why did he want to see her? The safe thing, the smart thing, the rational thing, would be to simply call him and cancel. She didn't even have to call his office; she could just leave a message at the hotel. Or send an E-mail. Or just not show up. He'd get the message.

But that would be incredibly rude, and Tracy was nothing if not polite. It was probably all in her head, anyway. Sure, they'd flirted—seriously flirted—but that didn't mean anything. They'd had a chatty E-mail relationship. Sure, it was fun looking forward to his messages in her inbox and they had talked about a lot of pretty personal stuff, but he had a serious girlfriend and she was getting married, for God's sake.

So why did it take her two hours and seven different outfits to get dressed that morning? She had finally decided on a beige Ann Taylor pantsuit she had bought at something like seventy percent off. And a creamy soft pink shell underneath. And white silk panties and matching bra from Victoria's Secret. *Admit it*, she thought. *You want to look good. You want him to want you. You want that same feeling you had before.* But she didn't want to lead him on, either. What she wanted was for her outfit to speak for her. Her clothes should say, "I'm glad we met and I find you incredibly attractive, but I love my fiancé and am not going to sleep with you." This was as close as she thought she could get.

She purposely arrived at the hotel a few minutes early to duck into the bathroom at Trader Vic's. Her cheeks were pink, her eyes looked bright, and her hair actually looked good. It was sleek and smooth against her head due to a rare low-humidity summer day.

As she walked down the hall from the bathroom, she saw him walking toward her. He seemed to almost roll as he moved, his stride was that easy. Tom walked with a slight swagger; William moved more stealthily. She liked watching him.

"Tracy from Chicago!" He smiled, and she outstretched her hand to shake his. He surprised her by kissing her cheek.

"Hello." Her voice seemed strangled. In that moment, she could smell his cologne and instantly felt a wave of desire sweep over her. It was almost nauseating.

"Ah, did you . . . did you have a good flight?"

"It was fine. You look gorgeous," said William, who looked quite gorgeous himself. He was wearing flat-front gray pants, a black short-sleeved sweater of a light, expensive weave, and a gray and black checked sport coat. He wore simple black loafers and a silver watch, no other jewelry. His hair looked shorter than it had before, but he still had that piece that hung over his forehead.

"What?" He noticed her appraisal and looked down at his chest. "Did I forget to zip or something?"

She laughed. "No, you just look—you look great." She smiled. "I thought maybe I had imagined how good-looking you are," she teased.

"Well, I thought I remembered how you look, but you're even more incredible than I remember." He was looking directly into her eyes, but she watched as he let his gaze travel down her body and back up. She stood there, unable to say anything. William broke the tension, gesturing toward the bar. "May I buy you a drink? I hear they have drinks called things like 'rotten bastard,' although I'm leaning toward a margarita."

"Um, sure." They sat at the bar, and she ordered a banana daiquiri, gesturing at the décor, which was done to look like a Tahitian outdoor bar. "When in Rome."

William took a sip of his margarita. "Oh, that's excellent." He offered her the glass. "Want a taste?"

"OK. I'm not a huge tequila fan, though." He handed her the glass and she briefly felt the warmth of his fingers. She nearly dropped the glass, but he managed to catch it in time.

"Hey, are you OK?"

"Yes." She nodded. "No." She shook her head. "I don't know. I'm so nervous. I can't believe it."

He lifted his chin. "Why are you nervous, Tracy?"

She loved hearing him say her name. She bit her lip, playing with the straw of her drink. "Because I don't know why I'm here. Because I think this is nuts. It's much easier having you be three hundred miles away."

"Maybe." He watched her carefully. "But I knew you'd meet me."

She shook her head. "Really? Am I that predictable?"

He reached over and touched her arm. "Don't get angry. I just knew that you had the same feelings I do. You can't deny that."

She sipped at her drink. "Look, can we change the subject?" She forced a smile. "I'm not sure I know what to say right now."

He opened his hands in a *sure, why not* gesture, and then caught the bartender's attention. By the time they started their third round of drinks—she'd switched to wine after the cloying sweetness of a couple of daiquiris—Tracy felt a lot better.

"Can I ask you something?"

"Anything." He was sitting facing her, his legs apart. She had turned her body toward him so that they formed their own little corner. She loved feeling him so close to her. She'd forgotten her earlier worries about anyone seeing her with him. They were just two friends, business colleagues actually, having a drink. And besides, no one she knew would hang out in

Trader Vic's. The bar wasn't crowded and it felt very good to be with him, not thinking about Tom or the wedding or her job or her body or anything.

She smiled a huge smile, and he smiled back. "What?" he asked. His voice was gentle, teasing.

"Nothing. I'm just really enjoying this." She stretched a little, pulling her shoulder blades together. God, she felt so relaxed. "Oh, I was going to ask you." She giggled. "OK. William, why are you here? I mean, why did you want to see me?"

A smile twitched at his lips. "Why wouldn't I want to see you?"

"Don't play with me. You know what I mean. Ever since you called, I haven't been able to stop thinking about you."

"Really?" He finished his drink and motioned for another round. "That's interesting. Ever since I met you in Vegas, I haven't been able to stop thinking about you."

"You haven't?"

"No. Tracy, I meant what I told you before. I think sometimes you meet someone where there's instant chemistry." The bartender set their drinks in front of them and William paid with a twenty. "Most of the time when you get to know the person better, that chemistry fades. You notice their faults or find out that they're not intelligent or time goes by and the attraction peters out. This isn't like that." He paused. "And E-mailing you has been great. I feel like we've gotten to know each other, you know what I mean? I can really talk to you, tell you things I can't tell anyone else, not even Cythnia." He smiled. "I've thought about you a lot, actually." He lowered his voice and leaned close to her. "And I've fantasized about you, too. A lot."

She drew in her breath and pulled away from him, looking past him at the huge—what was it, a clam?—hanging on the wall. There was a long, long pause. "I've thought about you, too," she said finally. "A lot. I can't help it. But my fantasies are way too convoluted! Tom has to have broken up with me and found someone else, or died, and Cynthia has broken up with you and found someone else or else she's died, and you and I are both doing OK and recovering from those horrible things and then we meet again and we have this incredible relationship and we make love and have wild passionate sex and it's fantastic and incredible and we can't believe how good it is . . . and it's simply right and good and supposed to be and there's no guilt," she finished.

"Wow. That's a pretty complicated scenario just to get to have sex with me."

"Are you kidding? I spend more time working out how we've both become single than I do thinking about the sex." She shook her head. "I know, I'm crazy."

"No. I'd say conflicted. But don't you wonder about what you'd be missing out on?"

"Of course I do. I wonder about it all the time. But it doesn't seem fair," said Tracy. "If Tom found out, he'd be devastated."

"Why would he have to find out?" He was sitting close to her, and she could feel the pressure of his leg against her left knee.

She closed her eyes and took another sip of her drink. "I don't know that I can afford to think that way, William," Tracy said. "Even if he didn't find out, I'd know that I'd done it."

"You know what I think? I think you and I both know this is going to happen. We're going to go to bed together. Maybe not tonight. But I know this is going to happen even if you want to pretend it won't."

"Thanks a lot," said Tracy. He wasn't giving her any credit. "You're giving me a lot of credit. What, do you think you're just going to overwhelm me with your sexual energy and I won't be able to resist?"

"No. And I don't want to overwhelm you or badger you or even talk you into it. I want you to want me as much as I do you, and for you to just lean over and say," he leaned very close to her, " 'I want to fuck you.' "

A thrill went up her spine. While she'd certainly said the f-word before—when she'd been really, really angry—she'd never used it for its true meaning. And Tom had never used it that way—he used euphemisms like "get busy" or "banging" or even "knocking boots." The idea of someone saying that he wanted to fuck seemed totally crude. So why was she suddenly so short of breath? And why were her panties, well, soaking? She didn't say anything, just looked in the mirror above the bar, and played with the stem of her wineglass.

"I've offended you." William's voice was quiet.

She shut her eyes for a moment and then turned to face him. "No. You've"—she took a breath—"totally turned me on."

Chapter 13

Sheer Horniness

Kate stretched out her arm, turned her wrist very slowly, and checked her watch without moving her head. God, it was already 5:38 P.M., and Lawless showed no signs of slowing down. As the head of the firm's litigation department, he was responsible for overseeing all the active cases. Once a month, all the litigation partners, associates, and paralegals met for the so-called file review which was in reality an excuse for Lawless to badger, harass, denigrate, and humiliate his fellow attorneys. The only ones who were safe were the two partners older than he—Lawless might make a snide comment, but he never let loose on them. Everyone else, however, was a possible target. Had you blown a discovery deadline? Lost an important motion? Failed to anticipate the appropriate next move in one of Lawless's cases? In other words, failed to have powers of ESP? Your shortcomings would be broadcast to the entire litigation department by meeting's end.

It was telling that he scheduled these meetings on the first Friday afternoon of the month. "Why not Monday morning or even another afternoon?" grumbled Kate to Danny. "He's got to know that this is the last time we want to be sitting here."

So far Lawless was on a streak. He'd implied that one of the junior partners was retarded, mocked another for his inability to win "a complete no-brainer" of a motion, and asked one of the younger associates if she might consider spending less time worrying about her hair and more time worrying about her billable hours. He sighed, rolled his beady little eyes, and proceeded down the agenda.

"Wright versus Carvello." He looked over at Michael Bough, who had just passed the bar a few months ago. "This is the appeal of that summary judgment motion over a coverage issue." He picked up a stapled sheaf of paper and waved it around. "I asked Mr. Bough to draft the brief for me to get a feel for his writing skills."

Lawless paused and Kate stole a look at the hapless Michael. She'd said hi to him but never really spoken to him—the last thing she needed was another Michael, particularly someone she worked with. He was a thin, slightly geeky guy with glasses, and he was looking very nervous.

Lawless removed his heavy glasses and rubbed his eyes. No one spoke. He replaced his glasses, picked up the brief again, and spoke. "The thing I want to know is—did you ever take a class in legal writing at the U of I, Bough?" He frowned at him. "Or are they no longer teaching that particular discipline?"

Michael shifted in his chair. "Of course I took legal writing," he said, obviously at a loss. "It's part of the curriculum there."

"Really? It is. And you have to pass it to graduate, correct?"

"Yes . . ."

"I see." With one swift move, Lawless tossed the brief so that it slid across the large oak table and landed in front of Michael. You had to admire his aim. "Because I would have never believed that from reading this, uh," he squinted as if trying to think of the right word, "brief."

"I'm sorry," said Michael, flustered. "Do you have a problem with it?"

"We don't have the *time* to cover all of the inadequacies of that brief, of which there are many," snapped Lawless. "It requires a complete reworking, not to mention an understanding of the most basic tenets of contract law. Get your shit together, and have an acceptable version on my desk by Wednesday." He continued down the list while the thirty-odd lawyers sitting around the table studiously avoided looking at Michael, who appeared as though he might cry.

After the meeting ended thirty-seven tense minutes later, Danny poked Kate's shoulder. "You wanna beer?"

"I want many beers." They were walking down the hallway, and she stopped in front of her office.

"Bunch of us are going to Harry's." Harry Carray's was a couple blocks away, a popular spot for the litigators at the firm after what Danny called the "Friday night reamings." "Want to walk with me or meet us there?"

She glanced at her watch. "I'll meet you there. I've got a couple of quick things to finish up first." She read through her phone messages—nothing that couldn't wait until Monday, and she'd be back in the morning anyway. She slung her briefcase over her shoulder, not bothering to turn off her office light. No one did. If you could imply that you might still be working in the library or had just stepped out for a quick cup of coffee or a bathroom run, why not?

Michael was, not surprisingly, sitting in his office with a shell-shocked look.

"Knock, knock."

"Oh, hi." He flipped his chair forward and tried to smile at her. "How are you, Kate?"

"I'm fine, now that the monthly ass-kicking is over. How are you?"

He pursed his lips and looked embarrassed. "Somewhere between humiliated and pissed off, I guess," said Michael. "I'd heard about those meetings . . ."

"But that can't compare to actually surviving one, can it?" she said with a smile.

"The thing is, I thought I did a good job on that brief. I

spent four weeks researching and writing it," said Michael. "I don't know what the 'inadequacies' are, so how am I going to rewrite it?"

"Hey, don't take it personally. Lawless has his own way of doing things. He likes to use certain phrases, cite certain cases, and he hates certain words like 'indicate.' That always pisses him off."

Michael started flipping through the pages in front of him. "Shit. Here's one, and here's another. That's just great." He seemed frustrated, tired, defeated, beaten down by life—which is exactly how Kate had felt her first year of practice. Throw in being constantly on the verge of tears and having the desire to down stiff drinks by ten every morning and you about had it.

"Michael, I've written lots of stuff for Lawless and I know what he likes. I'm sure the brief is fine law-wise, but if you want, I'll read through it for you and give you some ideas of how to make it more what he wants. OK?"

"Really? I'd appreciate it. I don't even know where to start."

"Don't worry about it. We were all first years once, you know." She thought of telling him that it would undoubtedly get worse before it got better, but he looked too fragile to handle the news.

Michael seemed unsure. "I don't know. Are you sure you'll have time?"

"Hey, what can I say? I have no life anyway. Let me take it home and I'll read it tonight or first thing in the morning. Will you be in tomorrow morning?"

"Are you kidding? On a Saturday?"

"I know. It's sad, isn't it? Stop by my office late morning and we'll go over it."

After saying good night to Michael, she walked up west on Water Street toward Harry Carray's. It was muggy and humid, and she could smell the fishy, dank smell of the Chicago River off her left shoulder. When she got there, Danny and several other lawyers were rapidly downing pitchers. Danny filled up her glass.

"He was brutal today, huh?"

"I know. I told Michael I'd take a look at the brief for him." Kate took a long swallow of her Miller Lite. She didn't go out with the other lawyers very often, but when she did, she drank what they did. Anything to fit in.

"Oh, Katey, you're such a softie." He grinned at her. "Why didn't I have a nice associate like you looking out for me when I started?"

"Maybe you didn't deserve one." She drained her glass, and glanced around the early Friday evening crowd. It was already starting to switch over from small clusters of coworkers to couples out for drinks and dinner. She heard a distinctive male voice behind her, deep but not quite baritone, and her stomach twisted, telling her who it was before her brain did. She should have known—after all, his office was just a few blocks away on North LaSalle.

She turned to see him greeting Danny. "Hi, Andrew." Her voice sounded steady. Good.

"Kate! I didn't even see you." *Or you wouldn't have come over,* she thought to herself. "How you doing?"

"I'm fine. I'm good. I'm great."

He raised his eyebrows. "Getting better all the time, I guess."

God, why couldn't she just hate him? He was still so appealing. That wavy blond hair, that tan, those impossibly green eyes, the sexy jutting lower lip. "I suppose."

Andrew drew back from her and looked at her appraisingly. "You look different. What, have you lost weight?"

Like it was his business now? "Maybe," she answered vaguely. "I've started running."

"You?" Andrew took a sip of his Coke. He rarely drank alcohol—it interfered with his training regime. "The couch potato queen?"

"I've become quite athletic, actually," she said proudly. "I'm running twenty miles a week now."

"That's great!" he said enthusiastically. He glanced at Danny for a moment, who was deep in conversation with one of the other lawyers from the firm. "You know, I've been meaning to call you. I've been thinking about you a lot lately."

Uh-huh. "You have."

"I have. Danny told me you'd been looking really good."

"He did?" Trust Danny, thought Kate. If she had *put on* an extra twenty pounds after they had broken up, she was sure Danny would have reported that fact to Andrew with glee. When it came down to it, guys were worse gossips than women.

"He's my bud. Hey, you know we guys can talk about relationships. We have needs too, you know."

"What, have you started watching *Oprah* in your spare time? This doesn't sound like the Andrew I know."

He shrugged. "Think what you want. I'm just glad to see you."

As always with Andrew, she found it impossible to stay angry with him. Sure, he had dumped her unceremoniously for an incredibly fit triathlete with a body fat ratio of nine percent, yet strangely round, perfectly shaped breasts. Can you say *surgery?* And when it came down to it, he wasn't the sharpest tool in the belt and had never even heard of Sylvia Plath. Maybe he was immature and incapable of truly committing to someone and he left shit stripes on his underwear. But he had that grin, and those eyes, and it had been, what four months, hadn't it?

They wound up back at her apartment—his was always a disaster and smelled vaguely like mildew from all the sweaty workout gear strewn everywhere—just after eleven. She'd had several more beers over the next couple of hours, but she couldn't blame it on that. As they talked, Andrew leaned up against the bar, eventually sliding his arm around her shoulders. She let it stay there.

After Danny and the other guys from work eventually trickled out of the bar, she turned to Andrew with an expectant look.

"What?" He turned his palms up, all innocent.

"You know." She shook her head. "Are we going?"

He picked up her briefcase. "Your place, Katydid." They left the bar and he slung his arm around her neck.

"Why am I doing this?" she said aloud. "You broke my heart, you know."

"Oh, come on. We'll go home, and I'll give you a massage if you want. And then we'll make the beast with two backs and have a good time and you'll wonder what ever possessed you to break up with me."

She twisted away from him. "*You* broke up with me, remember? For the Amazon?"

"I did?" He looked perplexed. "Are you sure?"

"Am I sure? Andrew, what can I say? Can't you keep track of your relationships?"

"Not really."

As they crossed the street, heading for the el station, she felt slightly buzzed—enough to not care that she might regret this tomorrow. And yet she was going to sleep with him anyway, out of nothing more than sheer horniness.

"And yet I'm going to sleep with you anyway, out of nothing more than sheer horniness," she said aloud.

Andrew grinned. "That works for me!"

Chapter 14

Being a Grown-up

"**D**id you hear me? Tracy?"

"Huh?" She looked up at Betsy, who seemed amused. "I'm sorry. What is it?"

"I need those new EEOC charge files. I know you're going to prepare the responses, but I have to look them over to finish one of these quarterly reports."

"Oh, right." Tracy reached into her current box and pulled out six blue folders. "Here they are. Two sex, three race, one age."

"Thanks." Betsy glanced at the files. "So, how are the plans coming along?"

"Plans?"

"Your plans. Your wedding plans? I figured you were probably daydreaming about your honeymoon."

"Oh, sure, yes, of course." Tracy forced a smile. "Actually, it all seems under control—the wedding consultant has been great. She's even keeping my mom happy."

"Yeah, weddings are all about pleasing your parents, aren't they?" Betsy, who had been married for twenty-one years and still rushed out of the office on Friday nights for her standing dinner date with her husband, smiled at her. "Don't worry,

Tracy. Even if something goes wrong, you'll always remember the day as being perfect."

Tracy tried to force her features into an expression becoming of a soon-to-be bride. "I know. You're right!" she said, a shade too brightly.

Betsy strolled out of her office and Tracy dragged her attention back to the new sick-day policy she was supposed to be writing. But all she could think about was last night.

She and William were just finishing their drinks when the hostess walked over to seat them. She'd been relieved that they'd been interrupted—the conversation was getting out of control. She also realized if she didn't eat something, she was going to slide off her bar stool, but once they sat down, nothing sounded appetizing. Finally she ordered a bowl of soup.

"I'm just not hungry," she'd said to William. How many times had she said that before, but always because she was trying to keep her weight under control? This was the first time she could remember saying—and actually meaning—it.

He ordered a steak and baked potato—*the same thing Tom would have ordered*, she thought—and they managed to make their way through the meal. He didn't bring up anything sexual again, instead asking her about her job and even how the wedding plans were coming along. She had trouble even finishing a sentence. It must've been the alcohol, but she felt like her brain had simply vacated her head. She found herself grinning like an idiot at half the things he said, and laughed hysterically when he told her about his first serious girlfriend, who had turned out to be gay.

"I'm sorry," she said, wiping her mouth on a napkin. "That wasn't funny."

"No, it's funny now," said William. "I guess all the signs were there—she was athletic, she played softball, wore her hair short, and wasn't really interested in sex."

"You're stereotyping."

"I suppose. But she also had this best friend who she did everything with—and who hated me. Josie was always spending the night at her apartment, but I never figured it out until I walked in on them."

"You did?" She took a swig of water. She hadn't ordered anything else to drink, but she still felt light-headed. "What did you do?"

"I just stood there. Then her friend—Penny—said she'd kick my ass if I didn't clear out."

"You're kidding!"

"No. And she could have done it, too." He finished his dinner and pushed his plate slightly away from him. Half of Tracy's soup still sat in the bowl, but he didn't comment on it the way Tom would have.

"I can't believe that."

"Oh, you would if you had seen me then. I was nineteen, as tall as I am now, but much skinner. Maybe 135, 140."

"Really? What happened?"

"Late puberty and lots of weights. I put on about thirty pounds, and that summer when I went home, people didn't recognize me." He grinned at her. "That was when I really discovered sex." He laughed. "I spent the next two years making up for lost time. Then I met Monica."

She nodded. "The first woman you loved, right?"

"You remember. Yeah, she's the one who broke my heart— really broke my heart. Josie was nothing compared to her." He looked away. "Actually, you kind of remind me of her."

"Get out."

"No, you do. Something around the eyes and mouth," said William. "And you have that same innocence about you. Maybe that's what it is."

Tracy uncrossed and recrossed her legs under the table. Her face felt warm and her lips dry. "I'm not all that innocent, you know."

"I know. Or you wouldn't be with me here now."

She felt momentarily stung. "What does that mean?"

"You know there's something between us. We were talking about it in the bar. You haven't left, you haven't made excuses, you haven't even brought up your fiancé," said William, his eyes looking directly into hers. "Have you?"

She was flustered and finished her water in one big glug. "Yes, I have! You asked about the wedding and I told you about his tux."

"Mmm-hmmm. I asked, you didn't offer. And to tell you the truth, you don't seem very interested in your own wedding."

To her horror, she felt tears welling up in her eyes. "That's not fair. That is not fair," she said, her voice rising. Glancing around, she hissed, "You don't know what I'm thinking or feeling. You don't know anything about me except what I tell you—what I choose to tell you. This dinner is as innocent as I want it to be."

He lifted his eyebrows. "Did I hit a nerve?"

"You know, you're right." She looked at her watch. "I think you did. It doesn't matter, anyway. I've got to go. I have to be at work early." She reached down for her purse.

William just looked at her for a moment, then leaned over and touched her arm. She could feel the heat of his fingers through the sleeve of her blouse. "Wait. I'm sorry. I was being a jerk." He squeezed her forearm gently. "Don't leave."

She looked away and then back at him, and leaned toward him. "I know this isn't innocent," she said quietly. "You have no idea of how paranoid I feel right now. I keep waiting for someone I know or someone Tom knows or someone he works with to walk in and catch us. And they'll know."

He leaned back. "What will they know? We're two business colleagues having dinner."

"They'll know!" she insisted. "I can feel it between us and other people will feel it, too. I can hardly even make conversation with you. I feel like a grinning moron. And when you bumped my knee under the table, I about jumped out of my seat."

He moved his legs under the table so that both of his knees

were gently gripping hers. "I noticed." She took a deep breath and he watched her. "Shall I stop?"

She didn't answer. What was going on? She could hardly breathe. How could the pressure of someone's knee feel so incredibly good? It was a *knee*, after all! Imagine if he touched her with his hands. She shook her head without looking at him.

"Tracy." He lowered his voice. "I can hardly stand this. You know what I want. All evening I've been thinking about taking your clothes off and making love to you. I want to touch you all over and feel your skin next to mine." His voice grew hoarse. "I've been hard this whole evening. I was hardly able to walk to our table from the bar."

She looked at him. She could swear she felt the heat coming off his body. "It's not just me?"

"Are you kidding? You've had the starring role in my fantasies since we met in Vegas. An attraction like this doesn't just go away," said William. "You either act on it or you stay away from the person. It's too hard—if you'll excuse the expression—not to."

"William, I want to. You have no idea how much I want to," said Tracy. "But I can't. I can't!" she said miserably. "I hate this."

He reached over and took her hand. "Would you relax? I've never seen someone get so depressed about having sex," he teased. "Look, Tracy, no one is going to make you do something you don't want to do." She felt his fingers on her own and then immediately looked around the restaurant and shook her head.

"I know that. It's just that I haven't felt this way about anyone. Kate has this thing about the Vibe—this feeling you get when you're really attracted to someone. I always acted like I knew what she was talking about. But I don't think I ever really felt it until I met you."

"Isn't that good?"

"No! It's awful! Now all I can think is, what have I been missing? And why did I meet you now? What am I supposed to be getting out of this experience? And why is this happening before I'm married? Is that a good thing or a bad thing? And . . ." she faltered, looking at his face. He was smiling.

"Wow. All I'm thinking about is how much I want you. Do you always have to complicate things?"

Again, she felt a flash of resentment. "Maybe I'm complicated."

"I like that about you. Tracy, if I just wanted sex, I could get it from almost any woman. I know how to talk to women, how to listen, how to tell them what they want to hear. Most women are easy to read that way. But I don't want to just fuck someone. I want to be with someone who turns me on, not just sexually, but intellectually. Emotionally. For me, it's about more than looks. True physical attraction is when you're attracted to every aspect of the person."

She had a sudden flash of two nights before, when she'd snarfed down an entire loaf of bread, toasted, with butter and cinnamon, and then puked it all up. *I wonder if he'd be attracted to that aspect of me, too,* she thought. She'd hardly eaten anything that day—she was taking one of those fat burners in a bottle that made her feel dizzy and sick—but when she got home, she promised herself she'd have two pieces of toast to settle her stomach. Then it was four slices, then six, then eight. She'd stuffed the wrapper down into the bottom of the trash, then run out for another loaf. What if Tom wanted a sandwich later? He'd wonder where the bread had gone.

But aloud, she said, "I'm attracted to you, too. How many times do I have to tell you that? I couldn't even think while I was getting dressed," she admitted. "But I just can't do it. Besides, what about Cynthia?" she added, as a last resort. "How would she feel?"

"She'd never find out. And besides, our relationship isn't a traditional one. We have more of an open relationship than most people."

"What does that mean? That you can go to bed with whoever you want?"

"Not exactly. It just means that we give each other more freedom to explore outside the confines of our relationship."

"Explore other women."

"Sometimes. But that's not what this is about, Tracy. I feel something between us, and it's only grown over time. I know you feel it, too."

She nodded miserably, but said nothing.

"So if you don't act on this, aren't you always going to wonder what it would have been like?"

"Of course." The waiter came by with the check, and refilled her coffee. "But that's the price you pay for being a grown-up, isn't it?"

"So being a grown-up means that you can't act on your desires?"

"Pretty much."

"How sad to be a grown-up. Maybe I'm not one, then."

She smiled and shook her head. "I don't know what you are."

They stood up and left the restaurant, turning toward the escalator that led to the ground floor and the lobby of the hotel. "Would you like to come up to my room for a drink? I've got a great view of Lake Michigan," said William with a straight face.

She actually laughed, and so did he. "Is that like, 'come on up and see my etchings'?"

"It was worth a shot. I know, I know. You can't." He gently took her wrists and pulled her to him. "Come here. Just give me a hug."

She put her arms around him, all too aware of his smell, which catapulted her back to the MGM Grand. He put his arms around her waist and pulled her against him with just enough force so that she could feel he was indeed quite hard. She sucked in her breath.

"Not fair," she murmured against his neck.

William shifted so that his erection pressed harder against her stomach, and she moaned involuntarily. For a moment she forgot that they were standing near the entrance of the building, in front of huge glass windows a mere eight blocks from her office, and just two miles from her apartment, the one she shared with Tom, the man who loved her and who she would marry.

"I've got to go." She broke away from him before he tried to kiss her. She didn't think she had the mental fortitude to resist him if he did. "Thanks for dinner. It was great. But I've got to go."

She turned away but he caught her wrist. "Are you OK?" His face was concerned. *He cares about you,* one voice in her head was saying. *He just wants to get laid,* said the other.

"No. My good angel and my bad angel are in a war, and I don't know who's winning," she said, trying to smile.

"Look, I'm leaving first thing tomorrow after this meeting. I'll drop you an E-mail when I get home, OK?"

She nodded. "I'd like that." She took a deep breath. "I don't want you to think I'm a tease. I really like you, though. I want to stay in touch."

"So do I." They stood there, two feet apart, and he reached out and gently touched her face. "Take care of yourself, Tracy. I'll talk to you soon."

She had walked to the el stop and then home in a daze. She felt turned on, guilty, conflicted, anxious, and full of dread. And turned on. Very turned on.

When she got home, she took a long shower, imagining that it was William's hands on her body, soaping her breasts, and sliding between her legs. She even tried to bring herself to orgasm—something she'd never been able to do before—but it was a wasted effort. Obviously she just wasn't good at sex.

She hadn't done anything wrong, she reminded herself. They hadn't even kissed. No clothes had been removed. There was no reason for her to feel so guilty. But she did anyway.

Chapter 15

Sex Just for Sex's Sake

The volleyball came sailing back over the net, faster than she had expected. She jumped and managed to barely tip the ball off her fingertips, knocking it vertically into the air. "Got it!" yelled Gary, who was playing next to her at the net. He timed his leap perfectly, spiking the ball across the net. Two other players on the opposite team dove for the ball, but missed.

"That's game!" Gary high-fived her. "Nice set." They walked together off the court to the side where the other four guys were chugging Gatorade and water and wiping off with towels. The volleyball courts at North Avenue Beach were all filled, and dozens of spectators sat in shorts and tank tops watching the action. Behind the courts, the bike path was busy with runners, walkers, bladers, and bikers. It was close to 8 P.M., but it was a gorgeous July night—in the low eighties with little humidity, a rarity for Chicago this time of year.

"I see what you mean, Gar," said Tony, who was wearing a sweaty blue tank top and ratty black shorts. He was losing his hair, but he grinned at her with an appealingly crooked smile. "She's not bad at all."

"Thanks." She wiped her face with a towel. "Actually, I'm enjoying myself." And she had, once she got over the fear of humiliating herself in front of Gary and his buddies. She'd even had some decent serves, and only missed a couple of shots.

She was chugging a bottle of water when Andrew rode up on his racing bike. He was wearing the ultra-tight black bicycle shorts he favored for long rides and a tight, hot pink, windbreaking cycling jersey. His arms and legs were shiny with sweat, and his blond hair was plastered to his head when he slipped off his helmet. "Say, Katey!" He glided over to her. "Thought I'd find you here."

"Hi, Andrew." She couldn't help admiring his body. The fact that she had seen it in its naked glory just two nights ago didn't help. "How far did you go?"

"About thirty. It's an easy day for me." He pulled a bottle of water from his waist pack and drained it. "How's the volleyball?"

"It's good." She raised her voice. "You have to deal with a lot of ball hogs, but that's OK." Tony and Gary heard her and rolled their eyes. They were gathering their stuff.

"Kate, we're going to shower and head out for a beer. Wanna come?" Gary called.

She had been prepared for just this exigency—her gym bag included a fresh change of clothes, some makeup, and a toothbrush. "Sure. I need fifteen minutes to get cleaned up." She gestured at the building that served as a bathroom and locker room for the beachfront crowd.

Tony, Gary, and the other three walked off in the direction of the locker room. "You're not losing any time, are you?" said Andrew.

If she didn't know him better, she would have sworn he was jealous. "What? Gary? He and I are just friends." She'd leave out the part about Gary deflecting the pass she'd made at him.

"What about the other guys?" Andrew nodded with his chin. "Tony was checking you out hard."

"You know, I'm missing something here." She looked closely at his face. "Did we get back together the other night and I missed it? I thought that was sex just for sex's sake. Right?"

"Right." He looked down and adjusted the grip on his handlebars. "Anyway, I should get going. I was riding and thought I'd say hi."

"All right." She slung her bag over her shoulder. "I guess I'll see you later."

Still, she thought about their exchange as she showered and dressed in a pair of khaki shorts and pink short-sleeved top. She could see the muscles in her biceps, and if she flexed, even the teeniest hint of triceps muscles. Not quite Linda Hamilton level, but still, it was something. Her waist looked trim and even her legs looked good. She made a mental note to thank Tracy—again—for giving her the advice and motivation she had needed. She turned and checked her reflection in the mirror.

"Not bad," she said aloud. "Not bad at all." Even Andrew had noticed. Andrew. She couldn't help herself sometimes. Sex with him was always so easy. That's what made it so dangerous. If you're with someone who just simply seems to know how you like to be kissed—softly at first and then harder, with a certain amount of tongue play but not dueling ones—how you liked to have your breasts stroked—squeezed gently with special attention paid to the nipples, please—or that your favorite position is straddling him, reaching down to balance yourself on his chest—it's very difficult not to feel that the two of you share some bond, some link, some special unique connection. When they'd made love the first time, Andrew had made her come three times, a record for her. She'd looked at him with something like amazement.

"What?" He had turned toward her, his face flushed and his smooth, muscular chest still damp. "You look like you want to say something."

"How?" she started and then stopped. "That was incredible," she said with feeling. "You're amazing."

He slung his hands behind his head, and she could see the soft, light brown tufts of hair under his arms. "I know."

She took a playful swing at him and he caught her hand. "Don't injure anything important," he murmured, pressing his cock against her. He was already getting hard.

"What's with you?" She looked down at him in amazement. "We just finished."

"Can't be helped. He's got a mind of his own."

Sex with Andrew was so good that she often completely forgot herself while they were making love. With other guys she might be worrying about whether her thighs were spreading out massively against the bed or whether she would win the motion for dismissal in court the next morning or whether she would have time to stop and get groceries on her way home from the store the next night. With Andrew, it was all mouths and fingers and tongues and sweat and skin and assorted body parts being inserted into various orifices and a complete loss of time. She'd never even had to fantasize to have an orgasm with him. It always just happened.

"It's flow," she had said once to Tracy. "You know, that state where you're so caught up in what you're doing that you lose all track of time and space and the outside world?"

"While you're having sex?" Tracy had been doubtful. "You don't think anything at all? Not even if the lights are on?"

"Nope. It's like my brain shuts off completely," said Kate. "It's incredible. It's the only time I don't hear that constant mental chatter, you know?"

And the other night had been no exception. They walked into her apartment and Andrew helped himself to a large glass of water from her kitchen tap. He drank it thirstily while she excused herself to put in her diaphragm. They'd use a condom, too, but Kate believed in serious birth control and STD measures. Especially with Andrew—who knew where he'd been?

When she came out, Andrew was already lounging on her bed, stripped down to his underwear. He always wore those horrible tight white briefs, but at the moment she didn't care. "Let's see what we can do about that horniess problem you mentioned," he crooned. She cringed inwardly at his words, but her body knew no such high standards. At the feel of his hands on her bare arms and his mouth on hers, she had one fleeting thought—this was only sex and she mustn't get reattached. Then she was only her body and Andrew was kissing her, touching her, teasing her the way he knew she liked.

It was only forty minutes later when she got up to use the bathroom that she had the first twinge of self-consciousness. She hated walking around naked in front of a guy, and when someone was as physically beautiful as Andrew, it only made it worse. She wouldn't go as far as backing away from him all the way out of the room, but her steps toward the bathroom were quick. After she peed, she slipped her black robe from off the back of the bathroom door and put it on.

Andrew was still lying in bed, flipping through a *Marie Claire*. "Wait a minute," he gestured at her. "Slip that off." She rolled her eyes and slipped the robe down to her wrists while Andrew looked at her carefully.

"Katydid, you're becoming quite the little hard body! I noticed before but you can really see the difference without your clothes on. You hardly have any cellulite at all now," he finished.

"Oh, thanks a lot." She walked into the kitchen. "You know, that would have been a lot more flattering without the last sentence," she called.

He pulled on his underwear and jeans and padded out to the kitchen. "I'm just stating a fact. You look much better—you've really toned up—but your butt and thighs still need some work. I can help you with that if you want," he offered.

Kate spun around. "What makes you think I want your help? And you know what, maybe I *like* having a little cellulite, OK? So just shut up."

"Touchy, touchy." Andrew came up behind her and slid his hands up the sides of her thighs. "Relax, Kate. I was trying to give you a compliment." He slid one hand inside her robe and idly played with her breast while he used the other hand to open the fridge. "Got anything good in here?"

"God, you never change, do you. There's bread and turkey and fruit and I don't know what else in there. Help yourself." He was already fixing a sandwich as she crawled back in bed. "I guess I'll see you later."

"You don't want me to stay?" He sounded surprised.

"Not really. Why should you? Your work is done here." The truth was, she wanted him to stay. It'd be nice to sleep with someone again after four months, and they could maybe grab breakfast tomorrow morning . . . but the fact that she wanted him to stay made it impossible to ask.

"Have it your way." He slipped into his clothes and gave her a quick kiss on his way out, munching his sandwich. "I'll see you."

"Bye," she called. After a minute, she got out of bed to slide the dead bolt on the front door.

The next morning, Kate woke with that complete, every-cell-of-your-body-relaxed, life-isn't-so-bad-after-all sensation you only got after a night of really good sex after months of forced abstinence. She was just sore enough to have pleasant flashbacks all day when she shifted in her seat or stood up from her chair. Forget weightlifting—this kind of workout was killer on your inner thighs.

She was surprised to find that not only did she not miss Andrew's presence waking up that morning, she was a little relieved not to have to make small talk with him about his upcoming day. She had been painfully aware in the past that she had been more interested in the day-to-day minutiae of their mutual lives—what he planned to do that evening, how his job was going, whether he wanted to get dinner later in the week—than he was. She was always trying to get him to talk about what he wanted out of life and share her own feelings and frustrations, but Andrew was completely present only in bed. Out of it, he was usually mentally elsewhere.

Why should I want something I can't have? she reminded herself. A night with him had been just what she needed to remind her that she was, in fact, a sexual being, and yet she could live without sex for a few months with no long-lasting negative consequences (at least that she knew of, anyway). Maybe what she needed wasn't a boyfriend, but a fuck buddy.

Chapter 16

Why Are We Still Friends?

Tracy scanned the menu. The restaurant was a little too pricey for her—she'd probably just get a salad. Nine was Elizabeth's choice. She always had to be at the latest happening spot—she'd die before she set foot in a Giordano's for pizza. Tracy wasn't sure why she had agreed to have dinner with Elizabeth, but the call had caught her unprepared. She'd found herself agreeing to meet her tonight without considering the consequences.

She wasn't even sure why they were still friends. They'd known each other since high school, but since then had steadily grown apart. While Tracy had gone to law school, Elizabeth had opted for her MBA. Now she was working at Accenture, making more than $200,000 a year. She drove a Saab, owned a lakefront apartment on Lake Shore Drive, and spent more on her monthly cut and color than Tracy spent on her hair in a year. How did she know all this? Because Elizabeth made a point of telling her.

It wasn't that Elizabeth bragged, exactly—her "here's-some-more-fascinating-information-about-me" comments were seamlessly worked into conversation. Her invitations to dinner always seemed to coincide with her latest job promotion, bonus or the fantastic vacation she had just taken—and Tracy spent most of the time listening and congratulating and very little time talking. Tonight would likely be an exception. Tracy sat and nursed a glass of merlot while she waited for Elizabeth. She entertained a fantasy about leaving the restaurant before she arrived, but knew she wouldn't. At twenty after seven, Elizabeth breezed in. Her size-four body was squeezed perfectly into an expensively cut royal blue suit and a large diamond solitaire ring decorated her right hand.

"Why should I wait for a man to get me one when I can afford to do it myself?" she had laughed to Tracy during their last dinner.

"Mmm-hmm," Tracy had answered, thinking with a secret smile that after all, she had Tom. The one thing Elizabeth hadn't managed to do was to have a lasting relationship. So far her record was three months. Tracy figured that's all a guy could possibly take, regardless of Elizabeth's good looks and hard body. Tom couldn't stand her, and had been barely polite on the few occasions he'd met her. "She's a bitch, Tracy. I don't know why you still hang out with her."

But they'd been friends for years, and it seemed like a waste of all that time to cut the cord. At least that's what Tracy told herself every time Elizabeth called her.

"Hi-yee!" Elizabeth trilled, leaning over to kiss Tracy on both cheeks, European style. You'd never guess that she'd grown up in Peoria, just a few blocks from Tracy. "I'm sorry I'm late. I've just been so busy!"

Tracy smiled. "That's OK." She gestured at her wine. "I'm relaxing."

"Oh, that's so good of you," said Elizabeth, signaling the waiter. "You must be simply crazed trying to get everything just perfect for the big day!"

Tracy checked her mental wedding list. Was Elizabeth even on it? Of course. She'd made the first cut to three hundred people, many from Tom's firm.

Aloud, she said, "Everything seems to be under control. I

hired a wedding consultant and she's working pretty closely with my mom to take care of most of the details."

"Oh, who are you using? Bethanne Latourni?" asked Elizabeth.

"Uhh . . . no." Tracy knew without having to ask that Bethanne Latouri would be the crème de la crème of wedding consultants in the Chicago area. No doubt everyone who was anyone would be using Bethanne Latouri for their momentous occasion. But of course she, Tracy Wisloski, would have no such consultant. Tracy Wisloski would have some second-tier, cut-rate wedding consultant that someone like Elizabeth hadn't even heard of. *I'm getting paranoid,* thought Tracy. *And besides, who cares what she thinks.* "I'm sorry?"

Elizabeth was beaming. "Didn't you hear me? I've decided to have a baby!"

"What?" She was stupefied. Elizabeth wasn't even married. Or had she finally successfully nailed the last element in her all-too-perfect life? "When did you get married?"

Elizabeth waved her hand in the air. "Who needs to get married? I'm working with a fertility specialist, and I've already chosen a sperm donor. He's twenty-five, tall, dark, and handsome, and he has a master's in philosophy from Yale and a Ph.D. in biochemistry from Michigan."

"Philsophy and biochemistry? You're kidding."

"No." Elizabeth leaned forward and widened her blue eyes. "I wanted a well rounded father for my baby. And he plays classical guitar, he swims and plays squash, and he speaks French and German."

"I don't get it. How do you know all this?"

"They have whole bios and profiles on all the donors," said Elizabeth. "You can search the database on the computer at the office or even at home. I was torn between my donor and a marathoner who's a surgeon, but you know how arrogant doctors are. Besides, some of those runners have those unattractive stringy leg muscles." She made a face, took a sip of her water, and patted her flat stomach. "Now I'm just waiting for the egg to drop and we're in business."

Tracy was still trying to catch up. "The egg to drop? You mean when you ovulate?"

"Right. Then I stop by the center, they inseminate me and, with any luck, a new life begins." She reached over and grasped Tracy's hands. "My baby, Tracy, can you believe it?"

Tracy finished her wine. Forget about sipping it to make it last. She signaled for the waiter. "But how are you going to do this? Who's going to take care of the baby while you work? How will you pay for everything?"

"Oh, that's no problem. I'm already considering nannies, and my parents are so thrilled about becoming grandparents, the whole father thing is hardly even an issue." Elizabeth smiled contentedly. "That's one of the advantages of being an only child—they know where the grandkids have to come from."

"Oh." Tracy tried to picture Elizabeth with a screaming infant in her arms, the kid puking all over the shoulder of her Ann Taylor jacket. She couldn't do it. "Well, it sounds like you've thought everything out," was the only thing she could think of to say.

"I think so," responded Elizabeth, apparently unaware of Tracy's discomfort. "And anyway, I don't want to wait forever. I'm twenty-nine now and I want to have a baby while I'm young enough to enjoy it. Besides, they say every year older you are, the harder it is for your body to bounce back. And I am *not* having breasts that hang to my waist. Not that I couldn't get them done, but come on."

Tracy glanced at Elizabeth's perfect perky A cups. "Yes, I can see that you'd be concerned."

Again Elizabeth missed or chose to ignore the sarcasm. "And your risk of birth defects—Down's and all those other chromosomal abnormalities—starts to skyrocket in your thirties. Of course, my baby will be perfect, though." She smiled. "Good genes. The best money can buy! Not to mention my own, of course."

"Of course." Tracy picked at her salad. She wasn't sure why she'd lost her appetite.

"You and Tom will start trying right away, won't you?" asked Elizabeth, picking up her fork. She'd ordered a salad, too. "You've been together so long I can't imagine you'd want to wait any more."

"Uh, yes, I guess we'll try after the wedding." That was true. That was what they had always talked about, wasn't it? They'd get married and have a couple of kids. Tom was making enough that she could choose whether she'd continue to work or not.

Before, she had fantasized about what their lives would be like with a baby. She'd meet him downtown for lunch with the baby dressed in adorable Baby Gap outfits, and he'd kiss them both hello. She'd introduce their baby to music and take long walks along the lake to watch the seagulls swooping along the shoreline, and spend weekend afternoons at Lincoln Park Zoo. She could remember a time when that fantasy had the power to make her smile.

So why didn't she feel jealous of Elizabeth? She was getting something Tracy had wanted well before she did. But she didn't feel the slightest bit envious of Elizabeth—simply annoyed. Annoyed at Elizabeth for being such an egotistical, wealthy little twit and annoyed at herself for agreeing to dinner. She'd see her at the wedding, Tracy decided. Then she'd be done with her.

When she got home from dinner, Tom was lying on the couch, his hair still wet from a shower. She bent over and kissed him.

"Hey, babe. Where were you?"

"Dinner with Elizabeth, remember?"

"Oh, right. So what's she gloating about now?"

She slid down on the couch next to him. "You won't believe it. She's having a baby."

"No shit? I'm surprised. Who was drunk enough to knock her up?"

"She doesn't have to worry about that, you see." Tracy paused. "Because she's getting a sperm donor."

"Get out of here. What do they do, pop her with a turkey baster or something?"

She swiped at him. "I think it's a little more technical than that, honey."

"Wow. Well, I guess she's got the bucks to do it, that's for sure. Feel sorry for the kid, though."

"Yeah, I suppose."

The next night, Tracy was leaning forward in the shower, letting the water beat against the back of her neck. She felt dizzy, and weak, and disgusted with herself. She'd been doing so well this week—carefully counting her calories and staying under 1,200 each day. She'd worked out every night except last night—dinner with Elizabeth—and then tonight she'd totally lost control. She'd stopped at the 7-Eleven, knowing full well what she was going to do. She bought a bag of Cheetos, a half gallon of chocolate ice cream, a box of Matt's chocolate chip cookies, and a bottle of sickeningly sweet peach wine.

She came home and left the food out on the counter to let the ice cream soften, turned on the television, and changed out of her work clothes. Then she poured a glass of the wine and systematically worked her way through the Cheetos. She finished the bottle of wine—by this time she had a decent buzz on—and started on the cookies, eating the entire package. Then she dug into the ice cream, wrapping a towel around it so she could hold it on her lap. She was almost finished when the phone rang. She let the machine pick up—it was Tom, who was going to be even later than he'd thought. She listened to the message and sat there for a few minutes, feeling slightly sick but strangely calm. Then she sighed, heaved herself out of her chair, and walked into the bathroom to make herself vomit.

She'd been doing this so long it was a practiced move, but she always had the same thought. Please let this be the last time I do this. Let this be the last time. It took four tries before she could puke up everything from her stomach, and by then she was so sweaty she peeled off her clothes and climbed into the shower.

What's wrong with me? Why don't I have any self-control? She looked down at her body with hatred. Her stomach bulged, her breasts sagged already even though she was only twenty-nine. And she didn't even want to talk about her butt.

Going to the gym should help, but instead it made things worse. She spent most of the time covertly eyeing all the other women there and mentally dividing them into two categories— women who were thinner than her, and women who weren't. She knew enough about dieting to understand that unless she limited the amount she ate, she would never lose that last five pounds. Then she'd be perfect.

"You're crazy!" Tom would laugh. "You have a great body. I love your athletic legs."

But Tracy knew athletic meant fat. She'd never told any-one—not even Kate—that she used to weigh sixty pounds more than she did now. When she got into college, instead of gaining the freshman ten or even fifteen, she'd gained thirty. Then she put on another fifteen the following year and wore sweatpants and baggy T-shirts and sweaters regardless of the temperature. It didn't help that she was working at Joey's, a pizza place where she wound up practically eating her weight in pepperoni every night.

The turning point had come when she had overheard a couple of guys she worked with at a party. The only socializing she got was hanging out with the people she worked with, and she was delighted to be at a campus party. Fat girls didn't get invited to many things like that—and shy, fat girls, definitely not.

She had just been in the bathroom and was walking down the hall toward the balcony of the apartment. JJ and Brian were standing on it, smoking a joint and reviewing their fe-male employees.

"What about Annie? Wouldcha do her?" Brian's voice.

"Yeah. Her face isn't great but she's got a nice ass." That was JJ, whose voice was strained as he tried to hold in the pot smoke.

"Tasha?" Intake of breath by Brian.

"Fuck, no. Those nose rings are nasty."

"How about Tracy?"

"Tracy? I don't know, dude. There might be more meat there than I can handle."

"More cushion for the pushin', though, right, dude?" Laughter from both, and Tracy froze in the hallway. She left the party without speaking to anyone, and walked home in a state of shock.

Her roommate was gone when she got home—probably at her boyfriend's—and Tracy locked her dorm room door and stripped off all her clothes and looked at her naked body in the mirror for the first time in months. She was a fat, lumpy, bulgy mess. She started to cry, thinking about JJ and Brian, who she had always had a quiet little crush on. No wonder she didn't have a boyfriend. Who'd want to have sex with *this?* Standing there crying, she promised herself she'd show them. She'd lose the weight and once she got thin, she'd never get fat again.

And that was the turning point for her. She gobbled fitness magazines instead of pizza and educated herself about nutrition. She slashed her calories to one thousand a day, measured everything she ate, and started walking for half an hour each evening. After two weeks, she could already see a difference in the way her clothes fit. After eight, her sweatpants hung on her. And six months later, she was sixty pounds lighter, thinner than she had ever been since junior high.

Only it had come at a price. Every week or so, she wouldn't be able to control the constant hunger that nagged her. It seemed like she never got enough to eat—she only ate enough to quash the harshest hunger pangs, constantly afraid she'd start gaining weight. The first time, she'd broken down and eaten an entire bag of Fritos and washed it down with a Big Gulp Coke. She immediately calculated the caloric content of her binge—close to three thousand calories, almost three days' worth of food. She snuck into the bathroom, checked to make sure there weren't any other girls around, and jammed her fingers into her throat repeatedly until her gagging turned to vomiting.

It certainly wasn't as if she were the first one on her floor to do so—she'd heard them in here before, throwing up their late-night pizza binges and then strolling out to gargle with Scope and return to their dorm rooms like nothing had happened. Before, Tracy had been disgusted by those girls, all of whom had appeared effortlessly thin. Now, with almost ten years of bingeing and throwing up behind her, she understood. Nothing was as bad as being fat. Your throat might burn, your stomach might ache, your heart might pound until you thought you'd pass out, you might get puke in your hair. So what. It was all temporary. Any of that—all of that—was better than being fat. Given the choice, she'd stick with her fingers.

Chapter 17

The New and Improved Kate

There are two kinds of women in the world—the kind that guys look at and the kind that they don't. Or so Kate's new theory went. She had spent all of her life up until now as being a member of the latter group, only vaguely aware that the former even existed. Now suddenly she was a woman who men noticed and really looked at.

It wasn't just her new and improved body. She'd gotten her hair cut—even though it took a full thirty minutes to dry it perfectly straight and sleek—and she'd invested in a few new short, straight skirts as well. Hey—they were all a size six. How could she resist?

She was so used to wearing twelves she tried on an armload of skirts in the wrong size her first shopping trip for her new body. They hung on her, and the tens and eights were baggy around the waist. When she zipped into a six—and it fit—she whooped aloud.

I know it's petty to be so excited about something so trivial, she thought, *but screw it. I've worked hard for it and I'm going to enjoy it.* She even found the occasional whistles and nods on the street flattering. One morning a black guy across the street yelled at her as she was finishing up her run.

"You are one gorgeous lady!" he said with a smile, and it

made her glow all day. The drawback, the big drawback, was that several of the guys at work had appeared to notice her metamorphosis as well. Suddenly Jason Keesling—one of the senior associates—was finding every possible reason to stop in her office. She'd heard he'd recently gotten divorced (the rumor among the associates was that he'd been screwing his secretary, a fact not appreciated by his wife of twelve years), but she didn't like the new attention. Before, she had blended into the background, and that was how she liked it. Even Michael seemed tongue-tied around her. And then there was Andrew, who had rededicated himself to her with new passion. He called her several times a week and had even made her dinner at his apartment, something he'd never done when they were dating.

"Is that all you're going to eat?" he'd asked when she'd taken a small serving of each dish.

She gave him a look. "Hello? Wasn't it you who was commenting on all the areas of my body that needed improvement?"

"I'm sorry about that." He twirled his pasta around his fork. "I forget how touchy women are about their bodies. You look great. That's what I should have said."

She lifted her glass to him. "Now, that's better. The bottom line is that women only want to know that they look gorgeous, sexy, beautiful, or thin." She took a sip of iced tea. "Or hot. Hot is good."

He slipped his hand onto her knee, squeezing it gently before running up the inside of her thigh. "Yeah. Hot is definitely good."

She paused, her fork in midair. She was wearing a powder blue tank top and black denim shorts, and his fingers felt very hot against her skin. She could feel goose bumps rise up along her bare leg. "What are you doing?"

"Just touching this hot body." He slowly lowered himself to the floor, on his knees next to her chair. Grasping it with both hands, he eased it away from the table so that he was sitting inside her legs, and slid his right hand farther up her thigh.

"You look so hot. And gorgeous. And sexy. And what was it?"

"Thin. And beautiful."

"Thin." He kissed the inside of her left knee and she shivered. "And beautiful." He started tracing a slow wet kiss up the inside of her leg, and she tensed in her chair. The feeling was close to tickling but much more intense—almost too much to take.

"Andrew . . ." She set her fork down. Suddenly she wasn't hungry anymore.

"Shhh . . ." His fingers were carefully unbuttoning her shorts and slipping them off over her knees. She closed her eyes and lifted her hips slightly as he slid her panties off as well.

"I think that's what I want for dinner," he murmured, sliding his head slowly up her thighs, the soft hair tickling her skin. Then he decided he wanted seconds as well.

OK, so it had been an amazing night. And after they'd picked themselves up off the floor, Andrew had even reheated the pasta. But Kate had been completely grossed out when she discovered the amount of dirt and grit that was stuck to her sweaty back and ass.

"God, don't you ever sweep in here? I'm taking a shower!" she'd yelled at him, annoyed. But she was more annoyed at herself. Why didn't she have more control around him? She knew this relationship—if you wanted to call it that—wasn't going to go anywhere, after all.

"Come on, Andrew." Kate shoved his sleeping body with her foot. "I've got to get to work."

"Hgrhm." Andrew made a not-quite-awake noise and then snaked his arm out of the covers to grab her leg.

"Quit it!" She was really getting annoyed. He'd come over unannounced last night, ringing her buzzer after eleven. It had been a week since their memorable dinner, and she was surprised to see him again so soon. She'd been in bed reading, and had made the mistake of letting him in.

"Katydid! Just thought I'd see what you were up to." He slipped off his jacket and immediately opened her refrigerator door. "Anything to munch on?"

She had stood there in her long white cotton T-shirt, her arms crossed over her chest. "Andrew, you can't keep showing up here whenever you feel like it. We're not going out together anymore, remember?"

"Then what are we doing?" He drained a glass of water and stretched his arms above his head.

"Having occasional sex." She crossed her arms over her chest. "It's called being fuck buddies. And for your information, I'm not in the mood for an FB tonight."

"Come on, Katey." He reached for her. "Don't be like that. I just felt like seeing you."

"Are you drunk, or what?" He was acting even goofier than usual.

"Nope. Just wired." He squeezed the tops of her shoulders. "Feels like you are too. Your shoulders feel like they're strung with piano wire. You could probably use a massage."

"I could use some sleep," she said pointedly, but he was already squeezing her shoulders with just the right amount of pressure.

"Come on, lie down and take this off so I can touch your skin," he said softly. "I promise you'll feel better."

"Andrew . . ." But she did. She always did. Their one-nighter six weeks ago had extended to an entire series of one-nighters. She saw him more often now than when they were dating.

Not that the sex wasn't divine—it was. And she wasn't even that worried about falling for him again. In fact, she was discovering that he was starting to really irritate her. His continual talk about his training regime, his narcissistic obsession with his own body, and his insistence on constantly having the television on were all adding up to one big annoyance. He didn't give a shit about his job, so he rarely talked about work, but he was unstoppable when it came to sharing the latest split times he'd clocked during speed work. The only time he didn't annoy her was in bed, which is probably why they spent most of their time together screwing.

Afterward, Kate had fallen asleep almost immediately. True to his word, he had started by massaging her shoulders, kneading firmly with his hands, and then slowly worked his way down her body. He stroked and rubbed and caressed her lower back, her ass, and her hamstrings and calves, finally focusing on her feet. She'd moaned.

"I know just what you like, don't I?" said Andrew, and bent to suck on her toes. The sensation was cool and warm at once, and it was so intense she threw her head up.

"Oooooh, stop that." She tried to squirm away from him. It did feel incredibly good, though. Andrew moved his mouth over her toes, stroking one of his hands up her leg as he did so. In a flash her exhaustion was replaced with heat, and a few moments later he was tugging her panties down, slipping a condom on, and sliding into her. He always made these moves look easy—it had occurred to her that he'd had lots of practice. But at the moments those unwanted thoughts skittered across her mental radar, she didn't really care.

Months ago when they were dating, she would never have guessed there was such a thing as too much Andrew, but clearly there was. She'd seen him so rarely before that she hadn't realized they didn't have that much to talk about. What had they talked about before? Mostly Andrew and his training regime. Andrew's idols were professional triathletes and his only long-term goal was to get good enough that he could command corporate sponsorships—basically, be paid to train.

Kate had seen him compete, and he was definitely one of the fastest triathletes in the Chicago area. He often finished in the top ten in local races and often in the top three. But was he world-class? She didn't know, and she wasn't sure she wanted to be the one to burst his bubble if he wasn't.

But he had been good for Kate in terms of her new and improved body. He'd suggested some simple strength training moves with free weights to build her arms and legs, and she could actually see more muscle definition in her thighs and biceps. The triceps—those muscles that run along the sides and backs of your arms—well, those were more elusive. She occasionally caught a glimpse of them when she worked out, but usually they stayed hidden away.

At the gym earlier this week, another guy had approached her as she stood in front of the mirror doing kickbacks. He was in his early forties, with graying hair pulled back into a ponytail. He wore a black muscle T, baggy gray shorts, and black leather lifting gloves. He was nicely defined—not huge, but you could tell he spent some time "with the iron" as muscle heads might say.

He'd been watching her for few minutes between his own sets of biceps curls. "Can I make a suggestion?" he said politely.

"Uh, sure," Kate grunted. She was red-faced and sweaty, and pushed some of her hair away from her forehead.

"You're swinging the weight too fast—a lot of the motion is coming from momentum." He gestured for her to bend over with her back parallel to the floor and had her extend her arm. "Bend your arm slowly and really feel the pump when you extend it," he said, lightly touching her arm with his gloved fingers. "Then don't bring it back all the way—stop halfway like this and extend it again."

She did as he suggested. "Slow. Nice and slow."

"Whew!" Three reps and her arm was burning. "That's a lot harder."

He grinned. "That's the idea."

She tried a couple more reps so that she had the hang of what he had suggested. "Thanks a lot." She gestured at him. "You obviously know what you're doing."

"Technique is the critical part of lifting weights. Forget

how much you're lifting. The better your technique, the better your results."

She straightened and wiped her face with the back of her hand. "So basically the harder it is, the better?"

He seemed to miss her flirting. "You've got it." He wiped his hands on a white cotton towel and extended his hand. "I'm Ned, by the way."

"Kate. It's nice to meet you."

"You too, Kate. I think I've seen you in here a few times before, haven't I?"

"I'm still a newbie. I've been running and a friend suggested I start lifting weights, too."

"They've got the right idea. Lifting will do more to sculpt your body than any amount of cardio."

"How do you know so much about this anyway? Is this your favorite hobby?"

He looked down with a smile. "OK, you've got me. It's more than a hobby—I'm a personal trainer here."

"So I have to pay you for your advice now?"

"No, no, I was implying no such thing. Besides, you don't look like you need much help. You're in good shape." He said it matter-of-factly, without a hint of flirtatiousness. *Probably gay*, she thought. Good-looking, nice bod, friendly without coming on to her. Yup, gay.

"Thanks. I've been working on it."

Ned looked at his watch. "I've got a client coming in ten minutes—I'd better let you go. It was nice meeting you, Kate. I'll look for you here."

"You, too, Ned. Thanks for the tip! I'll have to see how it works." She waved at him and then turned to check her reflection in the mirror. She had zero makeup on but her skin was flushed and she didn't look half bad. Ned was right—she was in good shape. *Go, Kate!* she thought. Glancing around, she made sure no one was looking and then extended her left arm, trying to make her triceps muscle pop. A small bulge rippled under the surface.

"Hey!" she said aloud. "There it is!"

Ned suddenly stuck his head back into the weight room. "I saw that pose, you know!" he said with a laugh.

God, how embarrassing. "Shut up!" She laughed back. "I just wanted to see if it was paying off!"

Chapter 18

Quality Time

Tracy stared at the scale in disbelief, and then clenched her fists in frustration. She'd gained another two pounds.

Where was the weight coming from? She was practically starving herself. She'd been having coffee for breakfast, a salad and crackers for lunch, and a Lean Cuisine or a tiny portion of whatever she and Tom were eating for dinner. But the scale didn't lie and even her body looked different—heavier, more bloated. Rounder. Definitely rounder.

Tom stepped into the bathroom to grab his toothbrush, dressed but with his hair still wet from his shower. " 'Scuse, Trace." He squeezed toothpaste onto his toothbrush and began scrubbing his teeth vigorously.

"That's awfully hard on your gums, you know," she commented as she slid the scale back under the sink. "You should brush softer."

"Thanks, Mother," he mumbled.

"What does that mean?" She turned to look at him, her forehead furrowed. "Is that some kind of shot?"

He spit out the toothpaste, wiping his mouth on a hand towel. "For Christ's sake, Tracy. What is your problem? Lately all you've done is bitch at me for every frickin' thing. Is this wedding crap or what?" He ripped off a piece of floss angrily. " 'Cause I'm pretty sick of it."

It didn't help that the first thing that came to mind was to remind him to throw the nasty used floss into the wastebasket, not the general vicinity of same. She bit her lip. He was probably right—she had been sniping at him a lot. "I don't know, honey. I guess it's wedding stuff. I'm sorry." She reached up and touched his face. "Forgive me?"

"You don't want me having second thoughts, do you?"

He was teasing, but she misread his tone and responded back angrily. "What does that mean? You're having second thoughts?"

"Trace, lighten up. Please." Tom looked at his watch and quickly ran his fingers through his hair. "I've got to go. I'll probably be late tonight."

"That's fine!" she yelled. "Be as late as you want. Like I care!" Then she stopped. What was wrong with her? Lately everything Tom did drove her insane. The way he chewed his food, the way he swung his legs over the side of the couch while he was eating, the way he took over the breakfast bar with papers from his briefcase almost every night even though she'd asked him not to a million times.

But she knew what the problem was. It was guilt, plain and simple.

She'd E-mailed William the morning after he'd returned home, apologizing for running off after dinner that night and no doubt making an idiot of herself. He'd responded within fifteen minutes.

"Don't worry about it, Tracy," William had written. "It was great to see you and spend time with you. Like I said, I don't want you to do anything you don't want to do."

She'd replied to the E-mail, choosing her words carefully. "Maybe it's not that I didn't *want* to do it," she wrote. "Maybe it's that I was afraid of what would happen if I did."

He replied immediately. "Afraid of what? That your fiancé would find out?"

She typed carefully. "No. Afraid of my own reaction, I

guess. I was so attracted I didn't feel I could control myself. Maybe I was scared."

William: "Everyone needs to lose control sometimes. Maybe your body was trying to tell you something."

"That's what I'm worried about," she wrote. "My brain has always been in charge. What happens if my body gets the upper hand and I can't get the control back?" She hit send without stopping to consider what she was writing.

"That's not likely," William wrote. "It's much more likely that you'll discover you love the loss of control. We all need to do something good for our souls once in a while."

Tracy thought about what he said. What was she missing out on? It didn't seem fair, after all, to give up the one time she had felt the Vibe. Would she marry Tom without ever knowing what it was like to be with someone she wanted so incredibly much? The thought was bleak.

Yet she couldn't get her mind around the idea of being with William, either. How would the two of them meet with no one else finding out? What about condoms? What if it was terrible between them? Worse yet, what if it was great? She thought about him all the time.

When Tom suggested that they head up to Door County for a weekend, she had been excited at first. She couldn't remember the last time they'd taken a trip or had any quality time together. Though she might hate the phrase "quality time," she relished the concept. Quality time meant long leisurely breakfasts, reading the paper together in bed, strolling around the quaint little towns of Door County, idly stopping to pick up antiques or admire locally produced art.

She'd been bugging him for a weekend away for months. Now that it had arrived, all she could think about was how she didn't want to be here. She felt awkward around him, uncomfortable. She wanted to be home, lying on the couch. Sitting out on the minuscule balcony at Kate's place, talking and laughing. At work, preoccupied with whatever was on her desk. Anyplace but here.

And then there was the fight. Tom had taken along his pager—"just in case." A case that was set for Monday looked like it might settle, but the partner wanted him available in the event something new developed.

Of course he got paged. And when she discovered that not only had he worn his pager, he'd stashed his laptop—and the relevant documents from the file—in the trunk of his car, Tracy had flipped.

"Two days! That's all I wanted!" she said bitterly. "You can't even give me that." She knew her anger was out of proportion to what he'd done—he'd warned her about the case, after all— but she couldn't help herself. She heard how bitchy her voice sounded but she couldn't help it.

"Ten minutes, Tracy. Then I'll be done and we'll head out for dinner." Tom was already booting up, his attention elsewhere. "Why don't you check the menus at the B&B and find us a place to eat?"

"No problem. Whatever you need, you know I'm always willing to do it." She stomped from their cottage to the main building next door where they served breakfast every morning. The main room was empty, the fireplace set with logs for a fire later that evening.

She rifled through the stack of menus sitting in a wicker basket and realized she didn't care where they ate. Did it make a difference? They'd sit and she'd look for the lowest-calorie thing on the menu and he'd eat whatever he wanted like usual. Then he'd talk about his job and she'd listen and try to pay attention and ask insightful questions and then he'd remember to ask her about her job and then they'd talk about the wedding and then they'd come back here and have sex. He'd make her come, the way he always did, and then he'd come and then it'd be over and a minute later, Tom would be sound asleep. And she'd lie awake, wondering what William's hands, William's mouth, William's body would feel like.

But Tom's case had settled after all, and the dinner had been nice. She'd had three glasses of merlot, and had been feeling incredibly sexual. She'd teased Tom on the drive back. "Hey, why don't we just pull off the side of the road right here and make love?"

He'd looked at her in amazement. "Here? Are you kidding? How much wine did you have, anyway?"

"Enough." She scooted over toward him and unbuttoned her blouse. Maybe tonight wasn't a lost cause. Maybe they could recapture something they'd lost. "What do you say?"

He glanced at her breasts, considering, and then looked in the rearview mirror. "I don't know, Trace. This road's pretty dark. I'd hate to get rear-ended while we were getting busy."

"Come on . . ." Tracy picked up his hand, gently kissing his fingertips. "Let's do something crazy."

"Give me ten minutes and we'll be at the B&B and I'll take care of you then."

"Fine." She exhaled sharply. By the time they'd gotten back to the cabin, the quick sexual thrill she'd felt was gone. They made love exactly as she'd predicted, and she said little to him during the drive home. Monday morning, she was relieved to be back at work.

"Tracy, can you do me a favor and take care of these employee suggestions?" Betsy walked into her office, a stack of papers in her hand. "Just write them up along with any recommendations. And pull together the copy for the newsletter, would you?"

"Sure." Tracy motioned to her desk. "I'll start on it later today."

"Thanks. You're a lifesaver." Betsy glanced at her watch. "Tracy, if you don't have plans tonight, would you like to have a drink after work? Just something quick—maybe we could swing by Cactus. Are you up for it?"

"Um . . . sure. Yeah, that'd be great." They agreed to walk over at 5:30 and Tracy found herself wondering what the occasion was. She and Betsy got along, but they'd never socialized outside the office. While she liked working for a woman— Betsy wasn't unreasonably demanding and had recommended her for several raises in the past five years—she'd also thought it wasn't a good idea to get too chummy with her superior. Maybe she wanted to talk about work away from the office, Tracy thought. But on a Monday night? Weird.

But Betsy surprised her. They ordered a couple of glasses of wine and Betsy immediately started munching on pretzels from the little bowl. "These are here just to make you thirstier, you know," she said. "It's a bartender's trick." She gestured at the change the bartender had set in front of them. "Notice all the small bills? That makes him more likely to get a tip."

"Really?" Tracy took a sip of her wine. It was going straight to her head, which wasn't surprising—she'd only had a can of Slim-Fast and a salad all day. "How'd you know that?"

"Didn't you know I worked in a bar in my twenties? Finally decided to grow up and enter the corporate world," said Betsy, taking another sip of wine. "The hours are better, the money is better, and benefits! Bartenders don't usually get benefits. But I miss the people, and the conversations."

"It wasn't depressing?" A guy in a suit bumped into Tracy, and apologized. It was starting to get crowded, even for a Monday.

"What do you mean?"

"I don't know. I think seeing the same people come in night after night would be kind of sad."

"I never looked at it like that. People are lonely, that's all. And a lot of people would rather sit around in a bar and talk and be part of something than sit at home in front of the TV."

Tracy made a wry face. "I'm probably in the latter category."

"There's nothing wrong with that. You get a lot of interaction at work, so you probably don't need as much at home. Plus you have Tom. That makes a big difference, doesn't it?" Betsy brushed pretzel crumbs off her lap.

"Sure. Sure, it does. It's just that, well, with his job and everything, we don't see each other that much. He's pretty busy."

"Really? That must be hard on you, huh?"

"Oh, I don't know. I think I'm used to it."

"Well, I hate it when Roger travels. I can't sleep right unless he's next to me." Betsy stood up. "I'm sorry—I've got to use the restroom. I'll be right back."

Tracy wasn't lying—she had gotten used to Tom being gone. Lately she didn't even miss talking to him. They only talked about his job, anyway, or she dutifully filled him in on wedding details. She E-mailed William several times a day—he usually E-mailed her back with a funny or sexy response—and of course, there was Kate.

She wasn't that close to anyone else—forget Elizabeth—and all anyone ever asked her about were her stupid wedding plans anyway. Tracy reached over for a pretzel—she was starving. She crunched on several as she thought about what Betsy had said. By the time Betsy came back from the bathroom, the bowl was empty.

"It's all that water I'm drinking lately," apologized Betsy. "Every five minutes I have to take a bathroom break!"

Tracy smiled. Betsy was talking again, but she wasn't listening that closely. What had it been—two glasses of wine? She'd better pay attention—this might be important. "I'm sorry, what?"

"I asked whether you were planning to take any vacation time soon?"

"Um, no, I don't think so. We just went up to Door County, but like I said, Tom's really busy with work."

"Yes, you mentioned that. Tracy, one of the reasons I wanted to come out with you was because I like you as a friend and a coworker. But I have to tell you that lately your performance hasn't been up to par."

"What?" She was stunned and then panicked. "What do you mean? Am I in trouble?"

Betsy put her hand on her arm. "Calm down. I'm talking to you as your friend, not your boss. That's why I'm doing this here."

To Tracy's great horror, her eyes filled with tears. She took a deep breath and forced her eyes wide open so that they wouldn't spill. Betsy waited for her to collect herself.

"Are you OK?"

Tracy nodded.

"Listen, you're not in trouble. If you hadn't been such an exemplary employee, I probably wouldn't have even noticed. But it's been clear to me that the past month or so your mind hasn't been on your work. You're distracted and I've caught several mistakes—oversights, really—in your work that just aren't like you."

Tracy hung her head, her hands in her lap. "I'm really sorry."

"I'm not asking for an apology. I understand you have a lot going on with the wedding and all. Is that what it is?"

"Not really." Tracy brushed her hair off her face and took a deep breath. "Part of it is, I guess. I'm not sure—I've just been having a hard time concentrating."

"Maybe you *need* to take a vacation," suggested Betsy. "I know you've got the time built up—why not take advantage of it." She patted her arm. "I think you could use it."

"You're probably right." Tracy wiped at her eyes. "I'm sorry I'm reacting like this." She waved at the wineglass. "I'm a lightweight."

"Don't worry about it. I think it's better in a situation like this to bring it up outside the office. No need for this to affect your official employee standing. And I just want the old happy Tracy back."

Tracy forced a smile. So did she.

Chapter 19

No Job Is Worse Than a Bad Job

Kate adjusted her breasts in her sports bra, looking for the perfect amount of cleavage—not so much that it threatened to choke her but enough that you might, well, notice it. She smooshed her boobs closer together and checked her reflection. She was wearing a bright purple sports bra, matching shorts, and lifting gloves. Her hair was in a high ponytail and her makeup was minimal but perfect. She'd already learned that too much concealer wound up on her hand towel, so now she stuck to waterproof mascara, light powder, and cherry Chapstick for color. Did it matter? Probably not. Ned probably wouldn't even be in the gym today, after all. But still, she knew that was why she'd taken special trouble with her gear. She looked fit, almost perky, even. Gag. Time to hit the weights.

After warming up briefly on the exercise bike for five minutes, she strolled over to the free weight room, surreptitiously glancing around for Ned. Aha! He was there, spotting an overweight guy in his thirties while the latter struggled with a barbell.

She walked over to the smaller dumbbells and selected a pair of twenties, and lay down on another bench to begin her own set of bench presses. After resting, she finished another set. Her chest and arms were starting to burn, but she was aware of Ned's presence and pushed herself to finish all fifteen reps.

When she stood up to change weights, she felt his eyes on her. In the mirror, he smiled and raised his hand at her. She nodded and smiled back, concentrating on finishing her biceps curls. After about ten minutes, she saw him walk off with his client and was momentarily disappointed—until he appeared at her side.

"Having a good workout?" He looked even better this time, wearing slightly baggy sweats that still didn't conceal the fact that he had a tight, trim waist and an extremely nice ass.

"Pretty good." She paused. "I just don't get the same buzz from this as from running, though. Do people really get hooked on lifting?"

"Sure. It takes a while, though." Ned reached over and gently corrected her form. "Hold your arms closer to your body. There you go." He watched her and nodded. "When you start seeing results, you want to progress even further. That's what keeps most of us coming in day after day."

"But would you say you're addicted?"

"I don't know if addicted is the right word. Committed, maybe. I like the way I feel when I take care of my body. I don't have to tell you that, do I?"

Kate laughed. "You should have asked me that six months ago! If you told me I'd be running twenty miles a week and be a member at a gym, I would have laughed my head off."

"So what happened?"

"It's not anything specific. I just got tired of being fat," she admitted. *And being self-conscious about it*, she thought, but didn't add.

Ned shook his head. "Women are so hard on themselves. Guys have it easier. They don't have all that societal pressure to be thin and gorgeous and perfect." Ned stepped behind her to replace a few dumbbells. "Most straight guys just care about their chest and their guns. Of course gay guys are more body conscious," he admitted. "But women obsess about everything."

Hmm . . . so did that mean he was gay? It took Kate a minute to realize what he'd said. "Hey, that's not very nice! You're talking to a woman, you know."

"I don't mean it in a critical way. Women just have it harder." Ned nodded slightly at a gorgeous woman doing shoulder lateral raises. Kate could see her muscle definition from where she stood: lean, smooth muscles with no hint of excess fat. "See her?"

"Yeah," said Kate, a tiny bit jealous. "She's a knockout."

"She is." He spoke matter-of-factly. "But she's in here for at least two hours every day, sometimes three."

"What? What does she do the whole time?" Kate was stunned. "Does she have a job or what?"

"She's a secretary at some company downtown, I think," Ned said. "But that's not the point. There's no reason for her to spend so much time here. You can get a great workout and see results in less than an hour a day." He grinned. "Oops. Starting to do my PR thing again."

"So she's in here every day?" Kate felt sort of sorry for the woman. Sure, she was physically perfect as far as she could tell—but it seemed too high a price to pay. She looked back at the woman's tight washboard abs and then glanced down at her slightly rounded lower abdomen with a frown.

"Stop that. You look great."

"What?"

"I know exactly what you're thinking. You're comparing yourself to her and coming up short." Ned folded his arms across his chest, and she noticed how the veins in his forearms bulged slightly. Not scarily, the way extremely cut guys did— just sexily.

"How'd you know?" she admitted.

"Train women half the day and you know what they're thinking, believe me," said Ned. "I'm like Mel Gibson in that movie."

"Oh, *What Women Want*?" She'd seen the previews but skipped the flick. Not even Mel could make her sit through a Helen Hunt movie. "I didn't see that one."

"Not into movies?"

"No, I like them. I just prefer the less Hollywoodish stuff, I guess. I hate the predictable ones. Boy meets girl, boy loses girl, boy gets girl. You know, in a cop movie, the partner must die. That kind of stuff."

"Really? Me, too." Ned rubbed his hands together. "So, would you like to see something sometime?"

"With you?" Duh, Kate. "Sure, sure." She nodded like an idiot, reconsidering her "gay" assessment of him. "That'd be great."

"How about if I get your number from the desk and give you a call? I wouldn't ordinarily do that without checking—I wouldn't want you to think I was a stalker or anything."

Good thing he didn't know about her mad Googling. "No, give me a buzz. That sounds good."

Ned checked his watch. "I will. I've got a client, but I'll talk to you soon, Kate. Have a good workout!" he touched her lightly on the arm as he strode off. She watched his ass as he walked away. It was very nice, indeed. Way too nice for a guy in his forties.

She thought about him two nights later as she angled her wrist carefully so she could see her watch. She was becoming a master of slyly checking the time. God—only 9:30 P.M. She probably couldn't leave this early—everyone would notice and comment on it later, and somehow, somewhere it would wind up in her personnel file as "not interested enough in being a part of the firm."

Even though the party had only been rolling since 7:00 P.M.—timed to correspond with the end of the halfway point of their fiscal year—most of the lawyers there were feeling no pain. Kate had had a glass of chardonnay and filled her plate with fresh vegetables, carefully avoiding the cheese, egg rolls, and everything else that looked fried and/or fatty. Her plate was colorful, certainly, but it hadn't done anything to appease her appetite. She should have eaten beforehand, but she hadn't had the time.

She was having one of those experiences where you see yourself as if outside your body—almost as if you're watching a movie. She watched the other lawyers, ties loosened, joke and laugh and talk with each other. Did everyone have a drink in his hand or was it just her? She checked. Everyone, although admittedly a few were drinking Coke or water. There were at least two recovering alcoholics in the firm and ten times that many active ones.

Danny sidled up to her as she stood with her back against the wall. "Katey! Are you enjoying yourself?" His fair complexion was flushed and pink; he'd downed several Jack and Cokes while she was talking to him earlier and showed no signs of having slowed.

"It's going great." She nodded at Lawless, who appeared to be ranting about something to several other senior partners. "What's that all about?"

Danny leaned closer to her, and she involuntarily flinched at his breath. "It looks like we're having a shitty year. Losing Mutual Insurance really hurt the firm," he confided. "They're talking about canning a few people."

"You're kidding." She felt queasy. "Support staff, lawyers, or both?"

"They're starting with support staff but maybe lawyers, too."

"Shit." Kate turned and grabbed another glass of wine from the table. "Any idea who?"

He shook his head. "But if they're cutting back, you know they're going to look at the senior associates. High pay, no buy-in, you know."

"I do." She rubbed her lips together. "Danny, what should I do?"

"Take it easy. I'd just get your resume together and touch base with your network just in case. Doesn't hurt to be prepared."

"Uh-huh." *What network*, Kate thought. Other than Tracy and Tom, she didn't spend time with that many lawyers. Wasn't being surrounded by them all day at work enough? "In other words, cover my ass."

He lifted his glass. "You got it."

"Will you let me know if you hear anything? Anything, Danny, I mean it. I'm scared."

"Take it easy. I've got my ear to the ground and I'll let you know."

After Danny's revelation, Kate had felt compelled to stay at the party. She even made a point of starting conversations with as many of the partners as she could. Basic suck-up survival strategy. She made a mental note to spend more time in the office, and that meant most nights, too. She'd prove her dedication. She was already billing the hours but this was a serious wake-up call to go into overdrive.

Chapter 20

The Truth Dawns

"Tracy!" Tom knocked on the door again. "Are you all right in there?" He sounded genuinely worried.

"I'm fine!" She ran water in the sink and splashed it over her face, wiping it with a towel. "I'll be out in a minute."

When she opened the door, Tom was standing there naked. "Hey!" He reached to kiss her. "I was starting to get worried about you. You having a nasty case of the runs or what?"

"Uh-huh." She sidled past him. She was already running late for her appointment with the wedding coordinator. The ironic thing was that even with all the time she spent in the bathroom lately, this was different. She had been having terrible stomachaches lately. Even when she *could* eat, it went right through her.

While it was great for keeping her weight down—she'd stayed under 125 for the past week—it was making it impossible to concentrate. She'd been eating bland food but it hardly seemed to help.

She dressed quickly and grabbed her purse on the way out. She was in the lobby before she realized she'd forgotten her wedding notebook. She ran back to the elevator, dashed inside for the notebook, and dashed back out. She wound up only ten

minutes late, but was still out of breath from the sprint from
the el station to Maxine's office just off Michigan Avenue.

"I'm so, so sorry," Tracy was apologizing before she sat
down. "I got a late start and then I had to go back for the notebook . . ."

"Don't trouble yourself," waved Maxine, picking up Tracy's
file. "Shall we get down to work?"

"Sure." They spent the next forty minutes firming up details, most of which consisted of Tracy nodding, agreeing, and
signing off on Maxine's work. She had never seen a woman so
organized. When they finished, Tracy stopped off at a nearby
Starbucks and ordered peppermint tea and a low-fat cranberry
muffin. She was feeling a little better than she had this morning—probably just nerves.

It was nice to just sit and not think for a while. She watched
the people coming in and out—lots of them her own age, some
with small kids in tow, some obviously on their way to their of-
fices for what Kate called "face time."

A woman about thirty, slim, with fashionably cropped blond
hair, walked in holding a child maybe three years old on her
hip. She was wearing black Capri pants, a tight orange tank top,
and black slides. Her stomach was flat, her arms toned. She ordered a latte—decaf—chocolate milk and a muffin for her little
boy.

The two of them sat down on a purple couch next to her
and Tracy watched them. The little boy sat down on the couch
next to his mother and she handed him the chocolate milk
first. He took a couple of small sips and then nibbled at the
muffin, cuddling next to his mother. He had blond hair, like
her, straight and fine like cornsilk.

He saw Tracy looking at him and she smiled. He glanced up
and his mom and then shyly smiled back.

"He's a doll." Tracy spoke to his mom.

"Thank you." The boy's mother smiled, and smoothed his
hair back in a gesture of love, pride, and possession.

"Hi," said Tracy directly to the boy.

"Hi," he replied. Just then, a man in his late twenties—just over six feet, with a lean face and slightly receding hairline, walked in. He was carrying a newspaper and a bag from Field's. "Daddy!" The boy leaped up and dashed over to the man, hugging his legs.

"Hey, slugger," his dad teased him, stroking his head the way his wife had and then picking him up. "What, did you miss me? It's only been twenty minutes!"

His son wrapped his arms around his father's neck and squeezed him tightly. His dad smiled and looked over the top of his son's blond head at his wife, and their eyes met. Tracy's stomach suddenly twisted in a knot of—what? Jealousy. They were a family. You could tell by the way they looked at each other, and their little boy, that no one else in the world mattered to them. That guy would never hit on one of his secretaries. And his wife wouldn't flirt with her boss. They'd never even *dream* of cheating on each other. They loved each other, and people in love didn't do that.

Tracy wrapped her arounds around herself. She suddenly knew the truth. She couldn't marry Tom.

Chapter 21

Career Counseling

Kate added up the figures again, trying not to panic. It wasn't looking good. She had barely four thousand dollars in the bank and she owed about sixteen hundred on her credit cards. Sure, she had some money in her 401K at work, but that wasn't easily accessible. Other than that, her assets totaled her meager possessions in her apartment—her clothes, her computer, her furniture, and some gold jewelry that wouldn't bring much. Living in the city, she hadn't even bothered to buy a car—not that she could afford to park it anyway. What would she do if she got fired? She'd run through her savings in two, three months at the most.

Her non-lawyer friends just assumed she was rolling in money. Sure, she made just under sixty thousand a year, but factor in her rent and other apartment expenses, her student loans (she'd borrowed fifty thousand for law school), clothing, meals, cabs, the gym membership, occasional books and videos, and maybe even a once-in-a-great-while splurge on a trip somewhere or a really nice dinner out and you didn't have much left over. She'd thought she'd been doing the right thing by setting aside ten percent in her 401K—but now that wasn't going to do her much good if she couldn't get to the money.

God. What was she going to do? She knew she could ask

her parents for money if she absolutely needed to—it wasn't like they'd let her be cast out on the street, after all—but the potential humiliation of that encounter stopped her dead. She loved her parents, but they worked best as a family when they only shared the surface stuff. She'd put herself through college and law school, and would rather do almost anything than admit she needed their help.

She should be looking for another job. But the thought of working at a different law firm—any law firm, really—made her cringe. What were the chances another firm would be better than where she was now? *Slim*, she thought. Maybe she could consider a move like Tracy's—getting out of practicing law altogether—but she had no idea of what she would do otherwise.

She mentioned it to Ned briefly that night. He'd asked her out for a walk later that night. They met at the gym—he had a late client to train and she didn't mind the brief walk—and then they walked east on Diversey toward Lincoln Park.

Ned was wearing jeans and a faded T-shirt. It was unseasonably chilly for August and she was glad she'd brought a jacket along. Out of his workout clothes, he looked somewhat older but just as comfortable in his own skin.

"How goes your week?" They strolled along at an easy pace, to her relief—she'd been half worried that he'd turn the walk into a cardio workout.

"Not great, actually." She filled him in briefly on the rumors circulating at work. "I'm worried," she confessed. "I guess I'd gotten kind of complacent and now I realize I don't have any job security. I'm pretty nervous about it, to tell the truth."

Ned looked at her. "Have you started looking?"

"Not really. I've started working on my resume, but I guess I'm in denial." She smiled apologetically. "I know, it's incredibly stupid. I'm the ostrich who would rather put her head in the sand than deal with facing this head-on."

"Don't be so hard on yourself. It's got to be stressful," said Ned. "You probably need some time to figure out what you want to do before you take action. Are you considering other firms?"

"That's the thing," she admitted. "I don't even know that I want to keep practicing law. But I don't know what else I would do! I have no skills," she said with a half laugh. "All I know how to do is appear in court, argue motions, conduct written discovery, and take depositions. And oh, yeah—bill hours." She snorted. "I'm great at that. Not that it matters."

"What else can you see yourself doing?" They were rounding the northern part of Lincoln Park, near North Pond. A pair of roller-bladers whizzed by and he gently took her arm to give them room.

"I really don't know. Sometimes I feel like law has ruined me for anything else."

"I don't think that's true," answered Ned. "A career change might be just what you need. I should know."

"What do you mean?" She looked at him with interest, noticing how strong his jawline was. He had a jaw that some guys would kill for—she had read that plastic surgery was the latest thing for male yuppies, and that Michael Douglas's chin was the hottest commodity going. Ned seemed beyond considering that, though. "Did you change careers?"

"Sure. About half a dozen times now. Let's see. I've been a cop, a social worker, worked as a probation officer for a while. Oh, and I was a massage therapist, too. Finally I wound up a trainer."

"You were a cop? How'd you go from that to working in a gym?"

"It's not that different, when you think about it. You're helping people, hopefully. I liked the social work part of it, but it's disillusioning after a while." Ned motioned to a bench and sat down, stretching his legs. "Plus, I didn't like the hours— when you're low on the totem pole, you get the worst shifts, work holidays, the whole thing. I'd rather have control of my time."

She was fascinated. "How long were you on the job?"

"Just over five years. I started out in social work, then about the time I was thirty, thought I could do more as a cop and went to PTI—the police training institute," he explained. "I'd always been in good shape, but that was the motivation I needed to really get fit. A few more job changes later and here I am; I don't make as much money but I can set my own hours and I love the freedom."

"And you're happier?" She took her cherry Chapstick out of her pocket and ran it over her lips, offering it to him.

"Thanks." He used it and handed it back to her. "Are you kidding? Some of my clients can be challenging, but I get paid to stay in shape, and I help people improve the quality of their lives. It's rewarding work."

"Yeah, I can see that." She thought a minute. "I'd like to feel that way about a job."

"You can. You just haven't found the right one yet."

Chapter 22

Breaking the News

Tom stared at her. His mouth hung open and his forehead wrinkled. "What?" They were sitting on the multicolored couch with the huge pillows Tracy loved. "What did you say?"

Tracy twisted her hands together and took a deep breath. "I said," she started over, "I said that I think we should call off the wedding. Or at least postpone it."

"Call off the wedding." Tom still looked confused, and his cheeks were starting to flush the way they did when he was angry. "Do you want to give me some idea of what you're talking about? What's going on here?"

She gulped and blinked rapidly to keep from crying. "I don't know, Tom." She reached for his hands but he yanked them out of her grasp. "I've just been thinking about it lately and I don't think I'm ready. It just doesn't feel right, you know? I can't explain it."

"You're not ready?" His voice rose. "We've been going out for more than five years, Tracy. Living together for three. When do you think you're going to be ready?"

She hung her head. "I don't know."

"You don't know." He stood, shaking his head, and walked into the kitchen and then spun around. "What is this? Cold feet? Jitters? PMS? Help me out here, Trace."

"I don't know what it is," she said miserably as tears spilled over and began to roll down her face. She sniffled. "I just can't do it. Not right now."

He stood there, his hands flat on the kitchen counter. Neither spoke for a long minute. This is one of those moments you're always going to remember, Tracy thought. She noticed how Tom's hair was slightly messed up on the left side, and the bleach stain on his gray cotton T-shirt. And the kitchen floor really needed to be swept. She picked at one of the pillows. Fir green, eggplant, mustard yellow—what had she been thinking? This couch clashed with itself.

When Tom spoke, his voice was strained. "Tracy, what is going on?" She could tell he was trying to control his anger. "I thought this was what we both wanted. We love each other, don't we? Isn't this what people in love do?"

She leaped up and crossed over the stand by him, but he wouldn't let her touch him. "I *do* love you," she said, her voice breaking. "I'm just not sure that I want to marry you right now. And I want to be sure. I want it to be perfect."

"Would you mind telling me what the hell has happened?"

"I don't know." The truth—or at least part of the truth—danced around her mind, but she pushed the thought away. Tom wouldn't understand about William, even if nothing had really happened. She knew that once she told him about her attraction, she and Tom would be through. He wasn't the jealous type but he would know she'd lied to him—or at least omitted the truth. There would be no going back. "Tom, I am so, so sorry. But I can't marry you unless I'm sure. I don't want to be in the same situation my mom was." Geez, it was a cheap shot, but she was desperate.

His face softened. "Tracy, you know I'd never do that to you. I'd never leave you. Haven't you always been able to count on me for anything?"

She nodded, crying harder. He was right. He'd always been there for her—when she flunked the bar the first two times, when her family drove her crazy, when she had a bad day at work. Maybe he wasn't home as much as she'd like, but she knew he loved her, probably more than anyone else ever would. So why was she doing this?

Tom waited and then sighed. "I don't know what's happening here, Trace. I don't know whether you're freaking out about the wedding or what . . ."

She interrupted. "It's not the wedding, damn it! It's the whole being married part."

"And what about that is the problem? Isn't it you who were waiting for me to ask?" His voice rose. "Wasn't it you who dropped all the hints and told me how wonderful it would be when we were, quote unquote, a real family? Aren't you the person who told me how much she wanted to have children with me?"

She couldn't look at him. "Yes."

"So what the hell happened? How can you tell me with what, three months to go, that you don't know if you want to marry me?" He snorted. "I can tell you one thing, Tracy. You'd better be serious about this because this isn't something you can cry about and take back tomorrow because you're PMS. I am not taking this shit from you or from anyone else." He folded his arms over his chest.

"I told you, Tom, this is *not* PMS! This is my whole life! And I don't want to marry you. Not now," she tried to add, but it was too late.

"You don't. Well, you know what, babe? You get your wish. The wedding's off." He turned and grabbed his gym bag from by the front door. "*You* tell your family, and *you* tell your friends, and *you* figure out what the hell I'm supposed to tell my parents and my friends and my partners. Because I'm not selling them some load of crap about how you 'just don't think you want to marry me.' They'll think you're fucking nuts. I think you are, too."

"I'm sorry!" She was sobbing by this point. "I'm so sorry."

"You're sorry, all right." He slung his bag over his shoulder. "Oh, you'd better figure out where you're going to be living.

Because you'd better believe you're not staying here in my house anymore. Find a place to live. You don't want to marry me, fine. But you're not living here in the meantime."

"What? Tom, wait!"

He had already slammed out the door. Tracy slumped to the floor, put her head on the couch, and cried.

Chapter 23

Roomies

Kate was looking over her pathetic list of assets once again when the phone rang. "Hello?" It took a minute for her to figure out who it was on the line. "Tracy? Tracy, what's wrong?" She listened for a moment. "Of course. Do you want me to come over? Help you get some stuff together? OK, I'll be here then. Take it easy, sweetie. It will be OK."

Tracy buzzed an hour later. Kate jumped up from the couch—she'd straightened up the apartment and had cleared some space in the closet for her—and buzzed her in. She opened the door to her apartment and met her on the landing.

Tracy was dragging two suitcases, wearing a backpack, and had her gym bag and her briefcase slung across her body. Kate would have laughed at the load except for the stricken look on her face. She bit her lip to keep from crying for her friend.

"Come on, let's get this stuff inside." Tracy obediently piled her belongings in a small mountain by the couch and then collapsed on the floor, her head down. "Are you all right?"

Kate knelt by her and gently stroked her hair. She could feel Tracy's shoulders shaking.

"I don't know what I thought would happen," Tracy managed to say. "I guess I just thought we'd be able to talk about everything and work it out, you know? But he said it's over. He wants me out."

"That's what you said." Kate filled a glass of water and handed it to her friend, and then grabbed a wad of toilet paper as well.

Tracy half smiled. "Thanks." She wiped her eyes and blew her nose, and then leaned her head back on the couch. "I'm in shock, you know? I can't believe this. Three hours ago, I was three months away from getting married. Now I'm single and homeless."

"Tracy, what happened?" Kate listened as Tracy recapped their conversation, careful not to interrupt.

When she finished, Tracy lifted the glass of water and drained it. "Do you think I'm crazy?"

Kate considered. "No. I think if you had this many doubts, you did the right thing. Better now than later, right?"

"Really?" Tracy started to cry again. "You don't think it's just cold feet?"

Kate spoke carefully. "If this had happened out of the blue, I might think so. But I think it goes deeper than that." She reached out and squeezed Tracy's hand. "Hey, I'm on your side no matter what. Even if I thought you were making a mistake, I'd have your back."

"You think I'm making a mistake." Tracy's voice was flat.

"Listen to me. If this is how you feel, I think you're doing the right thing. But you're the only one who can make that decision. What does your gut say?"

Tracy didn't say anything. Then, "That I just don't want the same thing anymore. I guess that's what I've been trying to escape from." She considered telling Kate everything—about William, about how bad her eating habits had gotten—but she just couldn't face it on top of everything else. "Can I stay here until I find a place?"

"Of course. You know you don't even have to ask." Kate stood and pulled her friend to her feet. "What about the rest of your stuff, though?"

"I'll get it later. I just couldn't stand to be there anymore."

Kate pointed to the closet. "Well, I cleared a little space for you—geez, how much stuff did you bring?"

Tracy started to laugh. "I know. I was psycho, just throwing stuff in the suitcases. I'm sorry."

"No problem." Kate dragged one of the suitcases over to the closet. "It'll be fun—we'll be wild single girls again, OK?"

"Kate . . . I have to ask another favor. Will you go with me to cancel the wedding plans? And tell people?"

"Oh, shit. You haven't told your mother yet?" Kate sighed. "Yes, I'll do it. You're going to owe me, though. You are going to owe me big time."

Chapter 24

Moving Day

Tracy took a last look around the apartment. It already seemed strange to her. While most of the furniture was Tom's—after all, he had paid the lion's share of nearly all of it—a few of the prints, candles, and photos that were hers were gone, tucked away in the boxes stacked neatly by the door.

Tom had told her she could stop by and pick up her belongings today. He'd agreed to be gone that afternoon, but she was still somewhat surprised that he hadn't been there. Apparently he didn't want to see her at all.

She couldn't understand the way he felt. She still *loved* him, after all—she just didn't want to marry him. It seemed short-sighted of Tom to simply cut her completely out of his life, eradicate every trace of her as easily as if removing a rotten section of an apple. But that's what he'd done.

Her new apartment was about a couple of miles away, closer to Loyola and six blocks from the Thorndale el stop. She hadn't been able to find anything she really liked in such a short time period—her new place was a tiny one-bedroom with a minuscule kitchen and a bathroom barely bigger than a closet—but it was in her price range and had a month-to-month lease. No one except Kate even knew that she had moved out; she figured she'd have to drop the bomb at work sometime.

Her mother had taken it better than she'd hoped. Well, she hadn't screamed or thrown a tantrum, anyway, and that was probably the best she could hope for. After expressing her extreme disappointment—not only that Tracy wouldn't be marrying Tom, but in Tracy herself as a person (at least that's how it seemed to her)—her mom had been somewhat reasonable. She'd decided to keep the hall and throw an early twentieth wedding anniversary party for her and Max, Tracy's stepfather. The guest list would be smaller, and there might not be any exchanging of lifetime vows, but the party would go on.

Tracy had only E-mailed William once during the last week, sending him a brief note. "Hi, William. Things are pretty crazy here. Tom and I have called off the wedding, and I'm moving out. It's a long, long story, and I'll be busy dealing with everything for a while, but I'll be back in touch soon."

Not five minutes later, the phone on her desk had rung. "Tracy. I just got your E-mail. Are you all right?"

"Yeah." She took a sip of water. "Still in shock, I guess. But I'm OK."

"What happened?"

"I can't go into the details right now." She lowered her voice. "I just couldn't do it, and I told him so. But I didn't realize it was all or nothing."

"What do you mean?"

She sighed, toying with the bowl of paper clips on her desk. "Well, Tom told me it's over, and that I have to move out. So I guess I got a little more than I bargained for."

"That's rough." He was silent for a moment. "That's really rough. Are you sure you're doing OK?"

"I'm all right." She picked out a handful of paper clips and began stringing them together. "At least I don't have to feel guilty about talking to you anymore." She tried to make her voice sound light. "That'd be the consolation prize, I suppose."

"Don't worry about that right now. I just wanted to make sure you were all right."

He sounded concerned, warm. She swallowed hard. "I am. But thank you."

"I should get back to work—it's crazy here. I just wanted to tell you I'm here if you need to talk to me or anything."

"I know that. Thanks, William. Give me a little bit to find an apartment and move and everything, OK?"

"You got it. But in the meantime, if you need me, I'm here."

She hung up the phone. She was touched that he'd called, but it worried her somehow. Hadn't she been using Tom as an excuse not to sleep with him? Now her excuse was gone—presumably forever—and she would have to make any other decisions based only on her own desires. It was a frightening thought.

Chapter 25

Still Googling

OK, thought Kate. *At what point* do *you cross the line and become a stalker?* She'd become addicted to Googling people. She'd Googled all six exes, a couple of guys she'd had crushes on, friends she'd lost touch with. She'd googled Ned, and at Tracy's suggestion, William. Ned had a few hits—quoted in a couple of *Trib* articles and he was profiled on the gym's Web site—but William came up empty. She reported the news to Tracy, who seemed disappointed.

"Oh. I hoped you'd find something out about him." The two of them were sitting at Kate's kitchen table, drinking Diet Coke. Tracy was wearing baggy gray shorts and a striped gray and black tank top, and she sat with her legs tucked neatly up under her. She had circles under her eyes, and her hair looked dirty.

"Well, William Brown—how generic can you get? There're like, a million hits, Tracy. It's too hard to wade through them and try to figure out if it's even the same person. You gotta date guys like Victor Musnisic—names that are unique. They're much easier to track."

"Well, I'll keep that in mind when I start dating, then. 'Oh, you're fabulous but your name is John Smith? So sorry—it won't happen!' 'You're a moron but your name is Thomasino Kregglestein? Let's get it on, baby!' "

Kate laughed. "OK, shut up." She punched in a new Web site. "Here's another thing you can do," said Kate. "See? Put his name in classmates.com and you can search for him that way. How old is he? When would he have graduated from high school?"

"He's thirty-five, I think."

"OK." Kate typed in his name and wound up with seventy-seven hits in the classmates database, including a handful in the 1982, 1983, and 1984 range. "See? He could be any of these guys. Do you know where he went to high school? What state, even?"

"I'm not sure. I just know he lives in Minneapolis now."

"Well, he hasn't given any additional data, so that's only going to give you his E-mail, which you've got." Kate closed the window and turned to her friend. "Oh, well. Guess you won't be able to stalk him."

"That's OK. I kind of like not knowing that much about him, anyway," said Tracy. "I think it ruins it to think of him as having annoying family members or pimples on his shoulder or credit card debt. He's still perfect to me, you know?"

"Except you said he has a girlfriend."

"Yeah, but he says they're only together for convenience now. They have a place together, the same friends, it's easier for them to stay together. They hardly even have sex anymore—they're just really close."

"They hardly even have sex anymore." Kate nodded her head. "And you believe that?"

"Why wouldn't I?"

"I don't know, Tracy. It just seems like that's one of those lines that every married guy uses."

"He's not married."

"They've been living together for how many years? Same difference. The only thing worse than that is, 'she just doesn't understand me' or 'we've grown apart' or 'I'd leave but we have kids together.' "

Tracy colored slightly and stood up. "It's not like that. This is different." She turned back toward Kate. "I told you what it's like. And maybe I don't care if he's married or has a girlfriend, OK? Why does that have to be my problem?"

"God, Tracy, I'm sorry. Relax. I'm not trying to upset you."

"I know." Tracy sat down again. "I'm sorry. I'm PMS and I feel like a total bitch." She bit her lip. "But Kate, you don't know how it is between us. We've talked about everything. We E-mail all the time. It's like I can tell him things I can't tell anyone else."

"Even me?"

"No. Yes. I don't know. I just know that I feel this bond with him, you know? And it's just gotten deeper and deeper." She took a sip of her Diet Coke. "It's almost better that he doesn't live here, actually."

"But Trace . . . what kind of a future can you have with him? It just seems weird to me."

"It seems weird, huh? When you're the one, what, Googling all these guys."

"Point taken." Kate checked her watch. "Come on, let's get out of here. Hey, I've got an idea. Why don't you come along with me and Ned tonight. We're going to see a movie or something."

"Oh, that's great. So now I can tag along on your dates?"

"It's not a date. At least I don't think so. Besides, who cares? He's nice and you'll like him."

"I don't know. I'll feel stupid."

"OK, then, don't go." Kate sighed, exasperated. "I'm just trying to give you some options aside from going home and sitting at the computer and E-mailing William all night."

"I told you, it's not like that. Besides, he's usually busy at night," she admitted.

"Really? Doing what?"

"I don't know." She knew what Kate was thinking—that he was with his girlfriend. But she didn't say anything. Tracy looked down at her hands. "Actually, he's going to be in Milwaukee next week. He wants me to come up and see him."

"Tracy, that's great! You're going, right?"

"I don't know," confessed Tracy. "You don't think it's kind of slutty to just go up there? Because you know what's going to happen."

"I don't think it's slutty. I think you're two grown-ups who've been having electronic, long-distance foreplay for what, five months? I think it's time you got together and consummated your relationship."

"What about his girlfriend?"

"Isn't that my line? And you're the one who said you had the Vibe. And maybe you just need to stop thinking and analyzing so much and just fucking do it, you know?"

"Maybe." Tracy drew circles with her finger on the tabletop as Kate checked her face and teeth in the mirror by the door. "I have been thinking I'd take a couple of days off and just go up there . . . and see what happens."

"Yes. Please. Do it, girl. That's the only way you're going to get him out of your system. Now why don't you come out with us, please."

Tracy looked down. "I can't go out like this."

"Well, let's look in my closet. Hey, now that I'm skinny, we can finally share all our clothes!"

They were just stepping out as Kate's phone rang. "Hold on—I won't get it. Just want to see who it is," said Kate, her keys in her hand.

"Katey, what's up? Andrew here. Thought maybe we'd get together later. Call my cellie."

Kate rolled her eyes at Tracy. "God, he will not leave me alone. Ever since I lost weight, he's been whipped."

"That's good, isn't it?"

"Sure, at first. But after a certain amount of someone worshiping you, you start to crave a guy who's a dick, you know?

At first, all that 'you're wonderful, you're beautiful, you're so funny, you're so smart,' it's all great. But after a while you think, hey, wait, I'm not all that. And if you really think that, maybe you need some help. It's not fun if you know you've *got* the guy, you know what I mean? Or is that just messed up thinking?"

"I think it's messed up, yeah," said Tracy, laughing. "But I must be messed up, too, because that's how I think."

They pushed open the heavy door of the apartment building to a gorgeous evening. "Kate, what if it's not as good as the build-up? What if it's totally lame?"

Kate knew what she meant without having to ask. "Then you tell me all the details and we laugh about it afterward. OK?"

Chapter 26

Taking the Plunge

Tracy stood up and checked her watch. Her palms were sweaty and she felt slightly sick to her stomach. The time was nearly here. She was going to see William. And she was going to go to bed with him. "I am going to bed with him," she said aloud. OK, she was losing her mind.

It was the only time in her life she had planned for sex so practically. Before, the men she had slept with had been the ones to set the pace. Not that there had been that many, which worried her. Sure, by a certain point, she'd accepted the inevitability of sleeping together—even looked forward to it, anticipated it, worn sexy underwear, and shaved her legs with care. But actually take steps to make it happen? Absolutely not. That wasn't her at all.

When she E-mailed William to tell him she'd like to meet him in Milwaukee, he'd replied almost immediately. "That's great. When will you arrive? How long will you be here? Where will you be staying?"

"Actually, I thought I'd just stay where you were staying—if that's OK with you," she wrote back.

The phone rang. "This is Tracy," she said.

"The Pfister. It's downtown."

She laughed. "OK, then. So . . . I'll see you on Thursday, right? What time?"

"These meetings should wrap up by late afternoon at the latest. Why don't we meet in the hotel bar at five."

"OK—I'll see you then."

"Tracy," he paused, "I cannot wait to see you. I mean it."

She took a deep breath. "I know. Me, too, William." It was unspoken but understood that this was it. She couldn't back out now.

She'd driven up that afternoon, using one of the bank's cars, and checked in a little after 3:00 P.M. She'd been unable to eat anything all day, and now she was starving. Finally she cracked open the minibar and ate a bag of pretzels. She didn't want her stomach gurgling loudly later.

At 4:55 P.M., she walked into the bar. She'd changed her outfit several times, finally settling on a short gray skirt, nude hose, black sling backs and a gray and white patterned blouse. Black panties, black satin bra. Light makeup, pale pink lipstick, simple pearl earrings. She'd called Kate and described her outfit to her.

"Geez, Tracy, you sound like an undertaker! Don't you have anything that screams 'take me now' a little more emphatically?"

"Shut up. The skirt is short, I swear. And besides, I don't want to look like a slut."

"Trace, you look about twenty years old even with makeup on. I don't even think you could look like a slut if you wanted to."

So she was sitting here, playing with her glass of wine. She'd drank the first half of it in a rush and then realized if she didn't want to be crocked by the time he arrived, she'd better slow down.

The bar had a gold-veined mirror hanging behind it, which let her watch for him without turning her head every five seconds. When he came in, she saw him scan the bar for a moment. His eyes met hers in the mirror and he smiled, a slow, sexy smile. She didn't move. *Remember this moment*, she thought. He walked over and placed his arms on her shoulders.

"Tracy Wisloski from Chicago. Fancy meeting you here in Milwaukee. Who would believe it?" William gently squeezed her shoulders and leaned toward her to kiss her cheek. She turned toward him and smiled, reaching up to squeeze his hand.

"Hi!" she squeaked and coughed slightly. She took a sip of wine, which only aggravated it. After a good ten seconds on hacking away, she recovered her composure.

"Well, that was classy," she said, setting her wineglass down. "Aren't you wondering what I'll do for an encore?"

William just smiled and sat down next to her. He was wearing a dark gray suit, cream-colored shirt, and a cream and black patterned tie. He looked tired but incredibly handsome. "I'm sure I'll enjoy whatever you decide to do next." He gestured at her nearly empty glass. "Another drink?"

"I don't know," she flirted. "Every time we have a drink together, we seem to wind up talking about sex."

"It's true. So, another drink?"

"Sure." He ordered their drinks and she took the opportunity to run a complete body check on herself. Her heart was racing, her stomach was slightly nervous, her arms and legs felt tightly wound and like they might fly off in any direction. Her face felt warm and she had that curious sensation of heat throughout her body. She pictured a deep chord being strung inside her body and the reverberations shuddering through every cell. She touched his arm.

"Actually, I don't think I want this drink." He'd already paid for them and turned to her, his eyebrows raised. She slid off her stool in what she hoped was a smooth, graceful motion and picked up her purse. "I think I'd rather, um, go upstairs. To my room."

He smiled and his lips twitched, and he gestured in front of him. "I told you I'd enjoy whatever you suggested next."

They didn't speak in the elevator or as they walked down

the hallway to her room. She could feel him watching her, but she didn't look at him. She unlocked the door and he entered behind her, shutting it and sliding the chain on. The sound made her suck in her breath.

She stood in the middle of the room, waiting for him, her arms at her sides. She suddenly felt shy and awkward. What happened next?

What happened next was that William walked slowly toward her, his eyes on hers. She gulped and blinked rapidly, looking down at the carpeting. He closed the distance between them, placed his hands on her waist, and then withdrew them.

"One question. Is this what you want?"

"Yes." She bit her lip, and spoke in a whisper.

"Then tell me."

"I want you." But she still couldn't look at him. He put his hands on either side of her face and lifted her head toward him so she had to look into his eyes. "I want you," she repeated more loudly. "Please."

"That's all I need to hear." He bent and kissed her slowly, his hands pulling her body against his. She thought for a brief moment how different he felt from Tom—how lean his body seemed compared to his. His tongue was pointier than Tom's— she'd forgotten that. He kissed her hard, and darted his tongue into her mouth. It felt different, but she liked it.

Chapter 27

Dropping the Ax

Kate popped the top of her ballpoint pen off and on, off and on. It was a bad habit of hers when she was nervous, but she was doing it under the table—no one should be able to tell. All of the firm's attorneys were gathered in the conference room for a "critical firm meeting," the memo had read. Some, like Kate, who had arrived early were sitting at the large cherry table surrounded by twenty or so chairs. The rest were standing around the perimeters of the room. No one said much, and she noticed that everyone seemed to have unconsciously formed little groups. The newest associates were clustered by the door, the oldest partners held the north end of the table, the junior partners had set up camp at the south end, and the mid-associates like her and Danny were loosely arranged in the center of the room.

Matthew Londrigan, the firm's managing partner, sat at the head of the table. His suit was wrinkled and his hair managed to be both receding and in need of a cut. He looked tired and his glasses were smeared.

He took them off and polished them as he began speaking. "I'm going to get right down to business. I'm sure all of you have heard rumors about this firm's future. Some of them are true. And some are not." He finished polishing his glasses and slipped them back onto his nose. "Unfortunately, the ones concerning the financial condition of this firm are true. If things don't change, we won't be able to continue operating for another year. So," he paused, "we've decided to make some cutbacks. These decisions haven't been easy, but they're necessary for the financial viability of our firm, both in the short- and long-term."

No one said anything. Someone coughed. Kate accidentally poked herself in the finger with her pen end and looked down at her hand, which was smeared with ink. She shoved her hand back under the table and tried to appear nonchalant.

"Based on our current billable hours and profitability, we'll be cutting back on our staff, both attorneys and support personnel. Eighteen jobs will be eliminated."

Kate felt rather than heard the collective gasp in the room. Then Matthew answered the unasked question they were all thinking—how many lawyers?

"We'll be losing twelve support staff and six lawyers. I just want to say that these decisions were among the most difficult the other partners and I have had to make." Matthew looked around the room. "Every person in this room is a fine attorney with a bright future ahead of him or her. No one should take this personally or as any sort of reflection on their professional abilities. And it's my hope that those who will remain at the firm will do their best to support those who will be leaving in terms of networking with their fellow lawyers, mentioning job openings, and the like. I wouldn't expect any less from anyone here."

Matthew turned to look at several of the other senior partners. Even Lawless was uncharacteristically quiet. "Anyone want to add anything? All right, then." He took out a piece of paper. "We'll also be changing the firm's organization and restructuring our departments. Litigation will consist of . . ." He started reading the firm's new organizational chart and Kate gave a start when her name was read. Danny had made the cut, too, but Michael and two other litigators were being let go. She wasn't one of the unlucky ones. She still had a job. So why didn't she feel happy?

Chapter 28

Less Than Perfect

The rain continued to pound outside, slashing against her apartment windows. Tracy curled up with her cup of tea and tucked her legs underneath her. She'd lit a half dozen candles and was wearing her favorite comfort clothes—the same old ratty gray sweats she'd had for years and a faded red checked flannel shirt. She'd put on an old Indigo Girls tape she hadn't listened to in years, and felt perfectly content to sit there and "veg," as Kate would say.

How long had it been since she felt this kind of peace? She couldn't remember. At home, living with Tom, it always seemed like she'd had the television on for background noise, for company of a sort. Now that she lived alone, she rarely turned her set on. Mostly she listened to music at night or read. Sometimes she just sat and toyed with the stamps Kate had given her. She had dozens of them now, and she made greeting cards, wrapping paper, and mini note cards. She'd been taking them to work and people loved them.

After dreading the idea of living alone, she was surprised to find that sometimes she liked it. She still felt lonely, especially on the weekends, but it was a different loneliness than she had felt with Tom. With him, she had sometimes felt just as alone, even when he *was* there. "There are worse things than being lonely and single," she had said to Kate. "Being lonely and part of a couple."

She was surprised that she hadn't heard from William since their two days together last week. She'd spent a lot of time playing the events with him over and over in her mind. It still seemed surreal, like a dream she was remembering.

It really had been perfect, at least at first. Walking in her hotel room was like walking into a different world. With William she didn't think about how she appeared to him or what he might like. She simply responded to his touch, to his mouth, to his fingers.

"Take these off," he'd murmured, his fingers gently tugging at the waistband of her panty hose, and she had complied. Then he had slid one hand up the length of her thigh, and very gently slipped it inside her panties. She'd sucked in her breath.

"God, you are so wet." He'd pulled away from her to look at her face. "Are you that wet for me?"

She'd nodded, unable to speak, wanting his fingers to touch her again. When he did and he slid his finger in her, she moaned and arched her back.

William bent her head and kissed her neck. "You can't wait for it, can you?" He was still touching her with one hand and tugging at his belt with the other. She helped him as best she could and he unzipped his pants. He was straining against his underwear, and when she reached to touch him, he groaned.

"I can't wait. I've got to be inside you." He took a condom out of his back pocket (*at least he was prepared*, she'd thought), slid it on, and was inside her in one smooth sweep. She'd gasped, and William had maneuvered her to the desk while she remained impaled on his cock and set her ass carefully down on the edge. Balancing on her tiptoes, she was able to support her weight on her hands enough so that she could lift her hips off the desk to meet him. He'd groaned as he'd dug his fingers into her hips, so tightly he'd left little finger bruises she'd find in the morning. She was just beginning to respond to his thrusts when William had suddenly groaned even louder and jammed into her hard enough to hurt. Her mouth had opened. Oh, no! No!

He shuddered and then very carefully pulled out of her, holding onto the condom in one hand. She dangled off the desk for a moment, feeling ridiculous, and unsure of what to say. *Umm . . . do you usually ejaculate prematurely?* didn't seem appropriate.

"Tracy, baby, you make me incredibly hot." He reached out and squeezed her left nipple. "Give me a minute and I'll take care of you." He sprawled on the bed, slapping the mattress next to him. "Come 'ere."

"OK." She gingerly sat down next to him, still half dressed, glancing at his penis, which was returning to its flaccid state. Why did they always look so ugly and weird after sex? It must be something about the shriveling.

William laid on his back, his arm across his face. Looking at him naked, she could see that his body was softer than she would have thought. He looked leaner, more athletic in his clothes, but out of them he had the beginning of a definite potbelly and even his arms were, well, pudgy. "Fat naked," Kate would call it. "Some people look better with their clothes on, some with their clothes off," claimed Kate. "You know, there's, like, thinner naked and fatter naked." William was the latter.

"What's on your mind?" His voice was lazy, unconcerned.

Tracy thought it was wise not to be totally truthful. "Um, nothing." *You're not as sexy-looking as I thought? I'm totally frustrated?* What did he expect her to say?

"You need to come, don't you, baby?" He rolled over to face her.

This baby thing was getting sort of icky. And she really wasn't a big fan of the "come" word. *Can't we just do it and not talk about it, please?* Tracy was still turned on, but all those hot and juicy sexual feelings were quickly being replaced by what-the-hell-am-I-doing-here feelings. Then she thought of what Kate would say when she reported the entire tale to her and had to stifle a snicker. But he was trailing his fingers down, reaching between her legs, and she squirmed.

"Oh, yeah, you like that, baby, don't you?"

Had he called her baby before? Had she not paid attention? He was good with his fingers, but her pleasure was distracted by his incessant, though soft, chatter. It was like watching football with Tom—everything was play-by-play analysis with a little color commentary thrown in. She shut her eyes tight, focused on his fingers, tried to drown out his voice, and finally, after at least fifteen minutes, managed to eke out a small, not very satisfactory, orgasm. It was more of a relief than anything else—like when you try and try and try to sneeze and finally trigger it by staring at the sun with your eyes as wide open as you can stand.

"Oh, baby, I'm hot again just watching you." She could feel his cock bumping against her hip. His penis was smaller than Tom's, and not as big around as Tom's was, either. *That's great,* she thought—*I'm with Tom, thinking about William, and now I'm here with William, thinking of Tom.*

At least Tom knew that Tracy didn't like to be touched right after orgasm—everything down there was too sensitive and any sensation was almost painful. He reached for another condom—at least he seemed religious about that—and slid in her. She nearly jumped out of her skin, but after a few strokes, she realized she liked it. She was just starting to enjoy herself when she felt the muscles of his back tense under her hands. Oh, no. Yup. Again.

Chapter 29

Girl Fight

It was after 8:00 P.M., and most of the lawyers had already left the office. Kate leaned back in her chair and stretched her arms behind her and then raised them up as high as she could go. She checked her watch again, debating whether she should head home or finish up the client letter she'd been working on.

Shit. She put her fingers on the keyboard and then closed Word. Her brain was fried—no sense in trying to work anymore when she was barely able to complete a sentence. She gathered her purse and briefcase and walked down the hallway, trying to recall what she had to eat at home. She hadn't been to the grocery story for at least a week, and she had a sneaking suspicion that her fridge contained nothing more than rotting fruit and a couple of yogurts.

When she got home, she was depressed to note that her instinct had been correct. She did manage to find a Lean Cuisine—chicken with rice and vegetables—that she tossed in the microwave. She changed out of her work clothes and sat down at her PC with the dinner next to her to check her E-mail. She'd been so paranoid about getting canned that she no longer checked her personal account from the office.

The usual spam and then an unfamiliar E-mail address came

up. She opened the E-mail as she took another bite of chicken and was so surprised she forgot to chew.

The message read:

"Hello, Kate. I hope this is the Kate Becker I'm looking for—a lawyer who went to U of I for undergrad and law school. If this is you, let me know—I'd love to know what you've been doing with yourself the last few years. Mike Cooper." And it listed his E-mail.

Mike Cooper. Mike Cooper was E-mailing her. While she was Googling Mike Cooper (not to mention many others!), Mike Cooper had been Googling her.

What the hell could he possibly want? she wondered. Out of all the guys she'd dated except Ben, Mike had made the biggest dent in her heart. He'd pursued her, even though her gut had warned her about him. She'd had a business writing class with him, and he'd asked her out three times before she'd finally agreed to meet him for coffee. Even then, she'd chosen to ignore all the warning signs—like the fact that he openly ogled other women in front of her and couldn't understand why it annoyed her—and believed that he'd change for her. Mike had been smart, and charming, and a near-perfect physical specimen, a career student who was nearly as fascinated with his own physiological functioning as Andrew was.

God! Mike and Andrew actually had a lot in common but she'd never stopped to think about it. Why was she falling for guys who were men with great looks, great bodies, and little else? I'm a mimbo-lover, she thought, reminded of the Seinfeld episode where Elaine dates a gorgeous guy who's also none too bright—a "mimbo," according to Seinfeld.

Maybe I'm really a man in a woman's body, and I want a good-looking guy to make myself feel better. But that theory never panned out—she didn't feel more attractive by osmosis. Instead, all of her insecurities came raging out because no matter how smart or funny or accomplished she might be, she simply couldn't match the other person's physical attractiveness. And yet she kept picking the hotties. Andrew. Gary. Even

Ned was pretty hot himself in an older-sexy-Sean-Connery kind of way.

"You know, I've been thinking about it, and I need to date an ugly guy," she said to Tracy a few days later. "I think that's the only way to get over this."

Tracy rolled her eyes. "How are you going to date an ugly guy? You won't even *talk* to an ugly guy."

"Thanks. You make me sound pretty shallow."

Tracy sat up on the bench. The two of them were working out at Kate's gym on a Saturday afternoon. Tracy had been bugging her about getting together, and Kate had insisted on the gym before they spent the rest of the day together. She'd been so busy her workout routine had suffered and she was starting to see the returns of pudge, especially around her waist. It wasn't condition critical yet, by any means, but it was definitely not a good sign.

"I'm not saying you're shallow," said Tracy, wiping her face with a towel. "I'm just saying that how are you going to date someone you're not attracted to? And I really don't think you'll be attracted to 'an ugly guy.'"

"Maybe I just haven't tried hard enough. I've been dazzled by good looks. Just like a man, see?"

Tracy rolled her eyes again. "Yeah, you're a real man. That's why every guy you date you wind up falling in love with and then get your heart broken." Her tone had an edge to it.

"Hey." Kate set the pair of dumbbells down. "That's not true."

"Sure it is. Look at all the guys you've dated. You always get over-involved, even when it's clear from the start the guy's got major relationship problems. Look at Andrew! He dumped you—broke your heart and then stomped on it I believe were your words—and you're sleeping with him again. Where's that going to lead?"

"He's a fuck buddy, all right? And what's your point?" She narrowed her eyes at her friend.

Tracy shrugged. "I just think you expect too much out of

every relationship. You'd probably be happier if you didn't get in over your head with every guy."

"Uh-huh." Kate could feel her face getting hot. "So basically, I should be able to, say, fuck a guy that I hardly know and not fall for him, right?"

Tracy turned to face her friend. "What are *you* saying?"

"Hey, what are you saying to *me?* You're the one who started this whole thing."

"I'm just trying to make a point about your relationships with men."

Kate couldn't believe the conversation they were having. She was getting angry, really angry, and was afraid she would say something she'd regret. "And how many relationships have you been in, anyway? If I remember right, you don't have a great track record, either."

"I got out of my relationship for all the right reasons," said Tracy, somewhat smugly. "And I'm not in one now by choice."

"Wow, listen to you. What, six weeks ago, you were crying your eyes out about how terrible you felt. And now you just don't give a shit?"

"I didn't say that. I've just had time to process everything, that's all."

"Well, good for you." Kate picked up her towel. "You know what? I've got to get out of here. I'll see you later."

She started to walk away, her shoulders stiff. She half thought Tracy might say something, but she didn't, so she continued to the locker room. She unlocked her locker, pulled on a sweatshirt and strode out of the gym, her face still warm. It wasn't until she was home in the shower that she let herself cry.

Chapter 30

All Alone

Spam, spam, and more spam. A note from Elizabeth, inviting her for lunch. Great. Nothing, not a peep, from William.

Tracy shifted in her seat. It had been three weeks since Milwaukee, and she'd noticed a definite decline in the frequency of their E-mails. During the weeks before she'd gone on her "vacation," he'd respond to her E-mails almost immediately. Then he took a half day, sometimes a full day to respond. It had been three days since her last E-mail to him—a light, breezy message—and he hadn't answered. She might have been out of the dating scene for years but she could do the math.

She wished she could talk to Kate about it, but they hadn't spoken since that stupid argument in the gym. She was so used to having her to talk to—they spoke nearly every day and E-mailed back and forth—that her days felt strangely lonely without her. She hadn't heard from Tom, either, though she'd seen a couple of guys from his firm at Au Bon Pain at lunch yesterday. They'd nodded but hadn't come over to say hi like they used to. She'd been slightly stung but reminded herself that this was of her own making. Tom could play the martyr all he wanted—at least she was free of that horrible, hand-wringing anxiety she'd had for so long.

In fact, now that she thought about it, her eating habits had been a little better since they split up. She was still bingeing occasionally, but not every night the way she had been for a while. Sometimes she felt like she was engaged in a battle with her body. When she tried to consciously limit what she ate during the day, it almost always backfired. Instead, she was trying to eat more like a normal person—not starve herself and not clean out the refrigerator, either. It was like learning a new language—listening to her body, trying to figure out what she really wanted to eat, eating enough to quell her physical hunger so she wouldn't binge later. She'd read some of those compulsive overeating books like *Overcoming Overeating* and *Feeding the Hungry Heart* years ago, but now, some of the message was starting to sink in.

She'd even summoned up the courage to go to an Overeaters Anonymous meeting. She'd purposefully chosen one close to Loyola, far from Lakeview, praying that she wouldn't see anyone she knew. The meeting was held in a church basement, a dingy little room with uncomfortable cracked plastic chairs. There were about fifteen other people there, not surprisingly, most of them women. Several were hugely, grotesquely fat. About half were noticeably heavy, and the rest save one were what she would consider normal-sized. One woman—girl, really—was just this side of alive. She was about Tracy's size, height anyway, but her face was all bones and sharp angles and her wrist bones protruded painfully from her sweatshirt sleeves. When she moved or ducked her head, you could see her clavicle, the skin stretched tightly across it.

Tracy had tried not to stare at her, but she was remarkably aware of her presence the entire meeting. She was a compulsive overeater? What, was she compulsively eating celery or what?

She had been distracted by stick-girl and fascinated by her, too, in the same way that she was fascinated by those who were hugely fat. Normally the two immense women who sat together, looking like two massive sumo wrestlers, would have commanded her attention.

When she looked at people who were that large, she couldn't help but wonder exactly how it had happened. Did they just wake up one morning and start eating and eating, never to stop? Were they born fat and then just grew fatter with every passing year? And how did they get so incredibly, massively, hugely big?

Still, a body like that had to be some kind of comfort, some sort of shield, of protection. Certainly the fat made you invisible in a way—invisible to a society where you're judged first and most importantly by your looks. *We're visual by nature,* thought Tracy. *Maybe that's what makes it so fascinating—because anytime someone looks at you, they're automatically judging you, rating you, classifying you without even being aware of it.* Some line of T.S. Eliot's about being stuck and wriggling on a pin came back to her suddenly, but she couldn't quite recall it.

The meeting consisted of the people there introducing themselves. Then the apparent group leader introduced the topic—about how people often turn to food to cope with loneliness—and asked everyone there to share any stories they felt comfortable with.

"My name is Angie and I'm a compulsive overeater," said a woman who was wearing a tight but expensive-looking navy suit, pink blouse, and navy heels. Her blond, permed hair spilled over her shoulders, and she wore shiny pink lipstick that was too young for her, but she had a sweet face. "What Marla said really hit home with me," she said, nodding at the leader. "When my husband and I were married, I'd make dinner for us every night—pot roast, pork chops, meat loaf, you name it. I probably could've trimmed down a little but he never complained. He said he liked how soft I felt."

She paused and fumbled for a tissue, her eyes beginning to fill. "He fell in love with another woman and told me he wanted a divorce," she continued. "I tried then to lose weight." She half laughed. "I thought I could win him back if I looked the way I used to although after three kids, that's probably impossible. I lost twenty-seven pounds, but you know what? It didn't matter."

She was crying now, and a woman sitting beside her put a comforting hand on her shoulder. "He left anyway. And then I thought, why am I trying to lose weight? Who would want me anyway?" She gestured at her body with a look of disgust. "It's so hard. I really try to diet, I do. But I get so hungry and food is the only thing that makes me feel better. It's there when I need it and it's my comfort. I know it's terrible," her voice broke, "but I feel like food is my only real friend."

Tracy just sat there. She felt both sorry for the woman and deeply, profoundly grateful that she wasn't her. Food wasn't her friend, that was for sure. How could anyone think that? It was her enemy.

Later in the meeting, another one of the women described how she had started carrying her safe food with her. "Sugar, white flour, candy, all that stuff are triggers for me," she said matter-of-factly. "So I've been making my own food and measuring it and carrying it with me in Tupperware. It's helped a lot."

The woman went on for another five minutes or so about her legal foods, trigger foods and non-trigger foods and Tracy frowned. It sounded like the woman was just as obsessed as she had been, when, by her own account, she had been bingeing and purging up to ten times a day. Ten times a day! How had she ever even managed to leave the house?

She left the meeting feeling not a sense of community or of hope but of not belonging. She should have been able to relate to these people, shouldn't she? But all she had seen in that dingy room was a group of people she didn't want to emulate in any way, shape, or form. *If this is the club, please don't make* me *a member.*

Besides, she wasn't that bad. Sure, she binged when she was really stressed out, but she could learn how to control it. Once she got down to 118 pounds, she'd start eating normally, and she wouldn't binge anymore. It was as simple as that.

Chapter 31

An Old Flame

Kate scanned the restaurant, looking for Mike. She fiddled with her earrings and shifted her weight. Maybe she should just get a table and wait for him. That would show him how at ease she was with this whole meeting.

Mike had suggested they meet at Nick & Tony's, not far from her office. She was surprised—it was nicer than the places he had preferred in college. Mike had always been one to opt for the loudest, rowdiest places—bars where a fight might break out any night of the week and girls wore miniskirts so short their asses hung out when they bent over to play pool. Not that she had a problem with places like that, especially by the time she got to law school. They had offered the perfect antidote to the mind-numbing hours of contracts, torts, and civil procedure she had dutifully crammed into her head. Maybe she had just wanted to put off becoming a lawyer for as long as possible.

She and Tracy had spent many evenings at the Do Drop Inn, a townie bar, during their second and third years of law school. The first year, both were too terrified to do anything but study—as the saying went, the first year, they scare you to death, the second, they work you to death, and the third, they bore you to death. She couldn't think about law school without thinking about Tracy, and she sighed. They'd never had an argument like that before. Sure, they'd disagreed, but not so hotly—and certainly not to the point they were at now. It had already grown to be much more significant than it was to begin with. Much longer and it might sever their friendship.

She was so deep in thought that she didn't even see him come in. "There she is," he said. "The woman I've been looking for."

If such a thing were possible, Mike looked even better. He was still tan, his face still lean, his hair still thick and wavy. Maybe there were a few more grays mixed in with the brown, maybe a few more lines around his face and around his eyes, but it only made him more appealing. And he knew it.

"Well, hello!" Her voice sounded strangled.

He strode up to her with that easy, athletic grace she had always envied. "What do I have to do to get a hug? It's been six years, hasn't it?"

She stood up and hugged him. Bad idea. Very bad. Even in that brief moment, she could feel his lean muscular back, the breadth of his shoulders, and the strength of his arms. They pulled apart and she shook her head.

"What?" Mike grinned at her and motioned for a beer.

"You're still gorgeous. Aren't you ever going to get old and ugly?"

Mike looked down at his body, as if considering. "I certainly hope not. But look at you! You're the one who looks gorgeous, Kate." He surveyed her body with the practiced eye of someone who's done it many times before. "I bet you've lost fifteen pounds." He gestured at her arms. "And you're lifting, too, aren't you?"

"What is with you guys? How can you tell this stuff?" She recrossed her legs. "Another guy told me the same thing a couple of months ago."

"An athlete?"

"Yeah. He does triathlons. He might even be faster than you," she added, aiming for his soft spot.

But Mike only grinned. "You still know just how to get me, don't you, Kate?"

Kate laughed. "I'm sorry. That was gratuitous, wasn't it?" She playfully punched him on the arm. "Only joking." Any nervousness she'd had was fading away. When Mike had suggested getting together, all she'd thought of was when she'd first discovered he'd been screwing around—with nearly every attractive female he knew—and how devastated she'd been. She'd forgotten their easy banter, how they could joke around about anything, and give each other shit like brother and sister.

She wasn't sure why she had fallen so hard for him. He wasn't even that good in bed, a straight missionary man if there was one. On rare occasions he might want her on top but he wasn't comfortable unless he was in control. And forget about oral sex. Sure, if she wanted to give him a blow job, go for it! But he "didn't really like" to go down on women, he'd confessed. Once again, it came down to his physical beauty. Like Andrew—or the Andrew of old—he was somewhat lazy when it came to sex. But it hadn't really mattered with Mike. No matter what he did, she couldn't help but forgive him. Until she found out about the other women.

Mike leaned over toward her. "You still alive in there?"

"I'm sorry. Just thinking, I guess."

"Recalling all our happy days together?"

"You're still the same cocky bastard, aren't you?"

He grinned. "Yup. Did you ever think I'd really change?"

"I guess not." She finished her glass of wine, debating whether to have another.

"Come on, go for it. My treat."

"If you insist." She sat and sipped her drink and the two of them chatted desultorily. It only took twenty minutes before she blurted out what she'd sworn she wouldn't. She should have called Tracy for a pep talk ahead of time.

"So, why did you call me, Mike?"

"It's driving you crazy, isn't it?" He leaned over and pulled her hair away from her face. "Your hair looks good this length, you know."

She took his hand and put it back on the bar. "No fair avoiding the question."

"Well, it's a question with a long answer," he said, finishing his beer. "Remember how I always said I wanted to write the great American novel?"

"Yeah . . ." *You and every other post-grad,* thought Kate.

"Well, I did. Actually, I don't know how great it is, but it's done. And I've found an agent, and it looks like he's found a publisher for it."

"You're kidding! That's great, Mike. So what's it about?"

"Sport as a metaphor for life. It's about a guy coming to grips with being in his thirties and realizing that he may not be able to do everything in his life that he thought he would. A looking back, looking forward kind of book, an early midlife crisis novel I suppose."

"I still can't believe it. I thought all that talk about wanting to be a writer was just part of your mack," Kate teased.

But Mike took her seriously. "Come on now. I didn't need that to get you, did I?"

"Don't start. This is supposed to be a friendly little drink, right?"

"I can be as friendly as you want me to be."

"Okay . . ." Kate wasn't sure what to say. Was he coming on to her or was she imagining it? She'd seen him turn on his charm with other women without having to think about it. It was probably the same now. But what he said next surprised her.

"It actually took me three years to write it," said Mike. "It was the hardest thing I've ever done—I trashed the entire manuscript and started from scratch several times. Finally I decided to revisit my own life and let that set the framework for the book."

"Are you trying to tell me that it isn't actually fiction?" Kate narrowed her eyes. "Mike, am I in this book?"

"Sort of. You come off fine, Kate, I swear. I have a character based on you but it's not you entirely."

"Well, how much is me and how much is fictional?"

"Meg looks different physically but I stole some details from you. The way you point when you talk, how you snort when you laugh, your sense of humor, those kinds of details."

"You're not writing anything else, are you? Like about sex?" She waved her finger at him. Shit, she was pointing at him just like he'd said. "Don't forget I'm a lawyer. I can sue for defamation, don't forget."

"Relax. No one will ever know it's you. Besides, that's not why I called. I've just been thinking about you ever since I started the last draft, and I wanted to know what you were doing, find out what was happening in your life."

Kate couldn't help but laugh. "You're kidding. Great minds must think alike."

"What do you mean?"

She shook her head. "Do you know what Googling is?" Mike shook his head and she explained the term.

"Oh, yeah, I get it. That's what I do, too, but I use Alta Vista. Is Google better?"

She'd found a fellow stalker! "I think so. OK, so now you know my secret. Who else have you looked for?"

Mike actually had the grace to look embarrassed. "It's a pretty long list, actually. But I've been looking for you for a while. You were just so much fun. Most girls, if the sex is good, you can't talk to or just hang out with them afterward. You were like a cool sister or a cousin or something. I always felt like we were friends . . ."

"Friends, huh?"

"Friends who fuck." He shrugged. "You know what I'm talking about."

"I know that now, Mike. I guess the problem for me is that I took it a little more seriously than that."

"How could you? You knew I wasn't the monogamous type."

"How was I supposed to know that?"

"Kate, don't play that game. You knew what you were getting into."

She pursed her lips. "Maybe," she admitted. "But I suppose I thought I'd make you different."

"I hadn't grown up yet," said Mike. "And I wasn't ready to make that kind of commitment to a woman."

"Not screwing, oh, what, half a dozen women in addition to me was a major commitment?"

"It was then." He looked at her closely. "Are you still pissed about that?"

"Not pissed. I just remember being pretty heartbroken over you. Although looking back, I'm wondering why."

He pursed his lips. "Low blow."

"Nothing personal. You're right, though. You never gave me any reason to believe or expect that I was going to be anything more than what did you say, a friendly fuck. I just wish I'd known that back then."

"So, how's your love life now? Or did that experience ruin you for anyone else?"

"Don't flatter yourself too much." But Kate smiled. "It's been, well, interesting. Do you really want to hear?"

"Yeah, I do. I told you I want to know what's going on with you." Mike looked at his watch. "Do you want to get something to eat? I'm thinking some pasta, or pizza sounds pretty good."

They sat in a booth and ordered, and she filled him in on Andrew, both before and after. "This is what I don't understand," she said. "When I wanted him more than anything, he dumped me. Now that I don't know if I even want to have a relationship with him, he won't leave me alone."

"Some guys are like that. It's the thrill of the chase. We want women who don't want us."

"Oh, *some* guys?"

"All right, most guys. Maybe all guys. But women are the same way. I know I was a dog. I was only out for what I could get from you or from any other woman. But people can change. I've changed."

"Really? What happened?"

"Believe it or not, *I* had my heart broken. Some kind of karmic revenge. I fell in love with a woman who was everything I'd always wanted—beautiful, sexy, intelligent, ambitious. Great athlete—but you'd figure that, right? She was actually a lawyer, too. Vicious in the courtroom, incredibly talented golfer. Probably could have been pro."

"So what was the problem?"

"There wasn't one at the outset. We lived together for a year, and I realized I wanted more. I proposed, she accepted, and we set the wedding date. She broke it off two weeks before. Said she wasn't ready to commit to me. That she didn't think I'd be able to keep up with her professionally, and that she needed a man who'd be her equal in every sense of the word."

"Ouch."

"Yeah." He pushed aside his plate. "I was pretty messed up. Couldn't eat. Couldn't sleep. Called her constantly. Sat outside her house until she threatened to have a restraining order put out against me. But it didn't matter. I would have done anything for her."

"So what happened?"

"Well, I was already teaching at a community college, but I got serious about my career. Decided to finish my doctorate and started writing the first version of the novel. Started coaching high school track, too, which I love. And I realized that I wanted to come back to the Midwest, and the job at DePaul opened up. I'm shooting for tenure, and I'm ready to settle down. I realized that I wanted more than someone to have great sex with. I want a partner. I want to have kids. And I have to have someone who would be a good mom and a good wife and a good friend."

Kate was starting to wonder where this conversation was

leading. "Well, sure. I think friendship is the most important part of a relationship. I suppose you can't have sex every minute of the day."

"Nope, not anymore." He smiled and looked away. "So, I thought about the women I'd been with and I kept coming back to you. How you could make me laugh and the way you'd put your hair in those little ponytails and leave funny notes in my underwear drawer. And I think that's what you should have with someone—that friendship."

"Mike, that wasn't just friendship. I was in love with you."

"I know and I was too stupid to know or to care. But you've got a lot of qualities that anyone would want in a partner. You're generous. You're nice to people. I know you like kids. You've got a good work ethic."

"A good work ethic?"

"Sure. Look at your legal career. How many people can even get through law school? And here you are, working at a Chicago firm. That takes some serious motivation." Mike ran his fingers through his hair and grinned. "And I thought before I went out looking for someone completely new, I should decide whether there was anyone in my past that I wanted to reconnect with. You were the person who kept coming up."

"What are you saying, exactly?"

"I thought we could try going out again. See what happens. And see if there could be enough to make a commitment to each other."

"You mean start dating again?"

"Start with that. And then we see," said Mike. "And then who knows? Maybe we eventually get married, have kids, the whole nine yards."

Kate just stared at him, openmouthed. She could think of nothing to say in response.

Chapter 32

Straight Talk

The weather was finally starting to cool off, and the leaves on the trees were beginning to change. It had been almost two months since Tracy had seen Tom. She'd known that he was upset, and hurt, of course. Still, though, she had thought that maybe they could be friends. It wasn't her fault that she felt—or rather didn't feel—the way she did. She'd called him once and listened to his voice mail message.

"This is Tom. I'm not in but if you leave a message, I'll get back to you shortly." And the beep. It had been strange to dial her number and not hear her own voice chirping for callers to leave a message and that she and Tom would get back to them "as soon as humanly possible!" Her message had been friendly but brief, but she hadn't heard anything from him.

So she was surprised when he called and asked her to meet him in the park, near the zoo. She'd agreed, wondering what he wanted. When she first saw him, her stomach twisted. She took a deep breath and blinked back tears. His size, the way his hair curled around his ears, the way he rocked back on both feet when he was uncomfortable. Everything was familiar and yet strange.

"Hi." He seemed hesitant.

"Hi." She wrapped her arms around her body.

"You cold?"

"No. Just nervous."

He nodded. "I know. Feels weird, doesn't it. You want to walk or you want to sit?"

"Let's sit." Walking might be easier, but Tracy wanted to be able to watch his face and focus on what he was saying. With sudden surprise, she realized she wanted to be physically close to him, too. The thought of him holding her sounded so comforting, so right, that she swallowed hard and looked away.

"It's good to see you."

"You, too." Her throat hurt and she was close to tears. "Nice jacket," she added, as a joke. She'd bought it for him several years prior.

He glanced down and smiled. "I know. I was so pissed I almost threw it out along with a lot of other stuff you gave me, but I couldn't help it." He paused. "I've always liked it, too."

"Tom—"

"No, Tracy, let me say something," he interrupted. "I don't want to screw this up. I was so angry at you and so, well, hurt, I couldn't even see straight. And to tell you the truth, I was embarrassed. It made me look bad, you know?"

She waited, not speaking. They were sitting on a park bench, and he put his arm on the back of it as he continued.

"I know I'm not the most perceptive guy in the world, but I have to admit that I thought something was wrong, even months ago. I just chalked it up to nerves or something." He shook his head. "I'd even wondered if we were doing the right thing, getting married, but I didn't want to say anything. You just seemed so freaked and I didn't want to hurt you."

She smiled a sad smile. "I didn't want to hurt you, either."

"Ah, Christ, it's unavoidable, though. I wanted to tell you, though, that it was the right thing. Things didn't feel right between us. I don't know. When you're with someone you love and you know they love you, you just take it for granted, you know? You don't even consider that maybe there's someone else out there who'd be a better match."

Tracy felt stabbed with jealousy. A couple in their early twenties strolled by and she waited for them to pass. "Really? So you're dating someone?"

"Uh, yeah. I've gone out with a couple people."

"Anyone I know?"

Her tone must have been strained because he looked at her more closely. "Yeah. Julia and I have been going out, and I've been fixed up a couple of times, you know, friends of friends, that sort of thing."

"Oh." She interwove her fingers together and looked up at him. "That's good, I guess."

"I miss you though, Trace." He reached over and took her hand, gently squeezing her fingers. "It's not the same as being with someone who's known you so long."

"I know." She blinked, hard. "I've missed you, too. I am so, so sorry, Tom. I should have talked to you about how I was feeling a long time before I did. Maybe we could have worked through it together."

He leaned back, pulling his hand away from hers. "Maybe. But I'm starting to think this was for the best. Two people can love each other and not be good for each other."

"I know." She sat there for a moment and then couldn't help herself. She scooted across the bench so that she was pressed up against him, and reached for his right arm. It's what she always did when she wanted him to cuddle her. He laughed and slid his arm around her, pulling her next to him.

"This seems familiar." They sat there in silence for a few minutes. She listened to the birds and the traffic going by, and the occasional whiz of a bicycle or roller-blader. She could feel the solidness of his body and smell the Drakkar he was wearing. She closed her eyes and tried to savor the moment, knowing it couldn't last.

Tom leaned toward her ear. "Is this what you wanted?"

She nodded without speaking, and felt him bend closer to kiss her cheek. She turned and met his lips. What was meant to be a chaste peck quickly turned into something more passionate. Tongues were flying fast and furious and Tom's embrace was almost crushing her.

They broke apart after a moment and stared at each other. Tom's pupils were brilliant and large, and his cheeks were flushed. He had that slightly stoned look he always got when he was turned on.

"Tracy, I . . ."

That's all he had to say. She stood up and they sped back to his apartment, walking fast, without speaking to each other. She didn't even have time to register the strangeness of being back there—they were barely inside the door when he grabbed her roughly.

The sex was like nothing they'd had before—direct, intense, single-minded, almost mean. Tom didn't even bother with her sweater or shirt. He tugged at her pants, unbuttoning and unzipping them with his hands while she struggled with his. His jeans and underwear at his knees, his erection stabbing upward, he pulled one leg free of her panties and jeans, grasped her ass, and entered her in one fierce motion.

"God, Tracy." His voice was hoarse and he looked at her in amazement. He started pumping into her without further comment, pressing her body against the wall and bending his knees to get better purchase. She felt him lift her whole body off the ground—she had forgotten how big he was—and had a moment where her rational mind said there was no way she'd be able to have an orgasm in this position. She was amazed to discover she was wrong.

Chapter 33

Friends Again

In the world of dating, it never rains—it pours, thought Kate. What had happened to those long dry spells when she wondered whether she'd ever meet a man who was reasonably good-looking, straight, somewhat motivated, decent in bed and at least passably funny, and, oh, yeah, nice to her, too? Now she had Andrew pestering her to do things like go to the Art Institute—Andrew, the jock, taking in the latest exhibit of pre-Columbian art; Ned suggesting that she come over for dinner (she knew the subtext of that particular invitation and had been holding him off so far—was she really ready to sleep with someone new?) and of course, the new and improved version of Mike, who wanted to "date" again to see if they could progress into lifetime partnership. The situation was bizarre, to say the least.

But at least she and Tracy were talking again. Tracy had called her last week.

"Hello?"

A short pause, then, "Hi. It's me."

Kate shut her eyes a moment. "Hi, Me." It was an old joke between the two of them. Then they both spoke at once.

"Kate, I'm sorry . . ."

"Tracy, I'm so glad you called..." And then they both laughed.

"Me first," said Tracy. "I've been an idiot and I'm sorry."

"I'm the idiot, Trace. I've thought about calling you so many times and then I was afraid that you'd still be mad."

"I know!" said Tracy, laughing. "And every time I thought that we weren't going to be friends anymore..."

"I was totally depressed," finished Kate.

"OK, let's just agree that I was a bitch and move on."

"It wasn't just you, Tracy," said Kate. "I've been really stressing about work and everything and I probably took it out on you. Oh, my God! I have so much to tell you! You won't believe who called me last week."

"Who?"

"Nope, I'm not going to tell you on the phone," teased Kate. "This is a definite in-person kind of conversation."

"Well, what are you doing now?"

"I was working on this motion but it's not due until Friday. You want to go out or stay in?"

"Why don't I come over there? I'm dying to get out of here anyway. This place is so small it makes me claustrophobic."

Tracy showed up thirty minutes later, a grocery bag containing a bottle of chardonnay, a bag of fat-free tortilla chips, and a big jar of salsa. "I figure we can be bad but not too bad. Oh, and I brought this, too," she said, producing a pint of Häagen-Dazs Chocolate Chocolate Chip, Kate's all-time fave.

"You rock!" They hugged and both started apologizing again, then started laughing again, too.

"Never again," said Kate. "I'd rather break up with ten guys than break up with you again."

"Me, too." The two ended up staying up until nearly two in the morning, and Tracy slept on Kate's fold-out couch. They had nearly three weeks to catch up on, after all.

Chapter 34

Post-Breakup Sex

Tom rolled over and groaned. His face was damp with perspiration. "Jesus, Trace. Where is this coming from? You about killed me."

She just grinned, and he sat up and got up off the bed. "Water?"

"Yeah, please." She stretched her arms above her head. She had no idea how this had started. Since that first encounter post-breakup, she and Tom had fallen into a routine of sorts. About once a week, he'd call her or she'd call him, and they'd make plans to "get together"—and wind up having sex. Earth-shattering, sweat-popping, muscle-straining, soreness-producing, moan-initiating sex. She'd never experienced anything like it—it was animalistic, ferocious, kinky, and depraved. And fantastic. Afterward, the two of them would fill each other in on what was happening in their lives.

She got up and pulled one of his T-shirts over her head, which fell to the tops of her thighs. "Hey," she said, taking the bottle of water he offered. He opened the refrigerator to check its contents, and she checked out his body. He'd lost a few pounds—his stomach was flatter, and his arms seemed more defined.

"What?" He was looking at her as he slapped together a

sandwich. "See something you like?" He grinned. This was what she had always loved about Tom—his utter lack of self-consciousness. Only a man could have that total body confidence—women had too many years of societal expectations, airbrushed models, lollipop girls, and *Cosmo* covers to be able to pull that off.

"Maybe." She reached over and wiped at his brow. "You're still sweating."

"Well, it was a workout, wasn't it?"

Tracy nodded. The other thing with Tom and their new sex life was that the two of them had gotten cruder and cruder. Tracy had always been the kind of a girl who found it hard to say "fuck" in the literal sense of the word. And forget cock or suck or pussy or even tits.

Well, at least the previous Tracy. This Tracy had no problem using various sexually oriented profanities and slang and stringing together raunchy combinations of adjectives, nouns, and verbs that would have made her blush just to read them.

Tom said something and she looked at him. "I'm sorry, what?"

"So, what happened to you in the past couple of months?" Tom took another long drink of water. "Don't get me wrong— I'm not complaining! It's just that you're different, you know?"

She wasn't sure what to say. How could she explain it herself? It had something to do with William, maybe, and something to do with the relief of not committing to Tom for the rest of her life. Something had been unleashed in her that she didn't think she'd be able to cram back into the box.

She'd tried to talk to Kate about it, but had been embarrassed when she tried to explain the dynamics. "It sounds like PBS—post-breakup sex," said Kate reasonably, sipping at her coffee. "All those feelings are still there and it makes it incredibly intense."

"No, it's more than that. It's like, ferocious!" Tracy looked around Cousins where they were having a Saturday lunch and lowered her voice. "It's like we're animals."

"Animals? Really?" Kate ate a bite of her vegetarian moussaka. "How so?"

"Oh, I don't know. We're just all over each other. I'm sore afterward but I don't even care. And we, well, talk dirty, stuff like that."

Kate brightened. "Talking dirty is good!"

"No, I mean *dirty* dirty. Filthy dirty."

"Like . . ."

She couldn't even bear to look at her friend. "Like 'oh yeah, suck my dick, you little slut . . .'"

Kate choked on her Diet Coke. "*Tom says that!*" She wiped at her mouth. "I'm sorry, Trace. I just can't believe it."

"It's true! And I'm," she lowered her voice again, "just as bad."

Kate's expression said she didn't believe her. "Like *what?*"

Tracy shook her head. "I can't even say it."

"Well, then write it down!" Kate pushed a piece of paper and a napkin toward her. Tracy thought a minute and then printed in tiny letters, "You like it when I suck your hairy balls, don't you?"

Kate squinted at the note, trying to read it and realization dawned. She looked at her friend in amazement and shook her head.

"Wow. I never knew you had it in you."

Tracy giggled. "I never knew it either, but I almost feel like I'm crossing the line, you know? If I'm like this now, what is it going to be like in the future? Am I just going to get kinkier and kinkier until it's like threesomes and bondage and, I don't know, animals and stuff?"

Kate leaned toward her friend. "Tracy, I think you're worrying for nothing. Maybe you've just been repressed all these years and your, I don't know, your inner sexual self has been unleashed, you know? And is that so horrible?"

Tracy considered. "No, I guess not. You're right."

Chapter 35

Taking the Next Step

For a Thursday night, 312 wasn't that crowded. Kate looked for Mike in the popular restaurant, but he hadn't arrived yet. She was seated at a two-top and ordered a Diet Coke from the waitress. She was exhausted and figured if she had any alcohol, she'd be asleep before dinner.

She knew Mike meant well, but this dating-to-see-if-we-can-marry thing just wasn't happening. Every time they got together it was like a job interview. Mike quizzed her on her ethical values, her feelings about working after they had children, how she felt about "quality time" (ugh!), how she would talk to their kids about sex and drugs, and what she thought the formative experiences of her own childhood had been.

Finally she'd thrown up her hands. "Enough, already! I'm sick of the constant Q and A!"

He'd seemed genuinely puzzled. "But Kate, if more people talked about all this stuff before they got married, they'd be happier together. And there would be lots fewer divorces."

"I don't care, Mike. Isn't part of the idea to just spend time together? I'm starting to feel like Eliza Doolittle here."

"Who?" He wrinkled his brow.

"Never mind." She'd exhaled in frustration and he'd slid closer to her on the couch.

"You seem tense. How about a massage?"

What was it with guys and massages, anyway? It was like they all read the same seduction handbook. "Only if it's a silent one." She knew she sounded like a bitch but she didn't care. Could he just shut up already?

Thankfully, he did. He plied her tense shoulders and neck with skillful fingers and then worked his way down both sides of her spine.

"Mmmfh," she moaned into her pillow. "That feels great. Thank you."

"No problem." He moved his hands lower, kneading her buttocks and she stiffened for a moment and then relaxed. She had a sudden thought of Andrew—this was one of his favorite seduction strategies.

"What?" His hands paused. "You want me to stop?"

"No, that's OK. It feels good." Eventually they had wound up having sex, and she had to admit that he'd become a much better lover since they had first dated. Whereas he hadn't noticed or even thought to ask if she'd had an orgasm before, he was all about giving her them now. Not that that was a problem. But lying there afterward, he spoiled it by asking what she thought about raising children on a meat-free diet.

Yet she was here, to meet him for dinner. She'd been tempted to cancel, blaming her schedule, but then he probably would've wanted to come over and make her dinner. There was such a thing as too devoted, she realized—she'd never realized such a thing was possible in a man before.

How had this happened? A relationship was like a legal negotiation—the one who had all the power was the one who was more willing to walk away. The person who needed the deal more would never be able to negotiate as fearlessly as the one who had a dozen other lucrative cases—that was the nature of the beast. It was the same with relationships. The pursued always had the upper hand over the pursuer. In every couple, there was an adorer and an adoree, one who loved more and one who was loved. The balance was never equal although it could and sometimes did change over time. That's what had happened with Andrew, and now with Mike.

Kate had liked it before. There was nothing as heady, as sexy, as much of a turn-on as a man wanting you—assuming he was desirable and not just some weirdo, that is. Who would think you could get bored with it?

By the time Mike arrived, her mood had gotten even darker. He apologized and blamed the traffic, but he didn't seem fazed at all. That was one of the things she had forgotten about him—he wasn't the kind of person to worry about what he considered minor things like being late. As a self-admitted type A, Kate couldn't stand to be even five minutes tardy anywhere and always showed up in court a good ten or fifteen minutes before a motion was called.

During dinner, she was aware that she was snapping at him. He ignored it at first, then finally commented. "I apologized for being late. Enough of the attitude."

Aha! *This* was the Mike she had known before—not this simpering, let's-talk-about-how-we-want-to-raise-our-children sensitive guy he had become. She was so excited by his turnaround she pushed it even further.

"What does that mean? Attitude?" She said with attitude to the extreme. She crossed her arms and gave him the look that every women knows how to give—the one that can start an argument without saying a word.

"Two can play this game, Kate." He finished his salmon and pushed the plate aside. "I told you I was sorry for being late. You want to spoil a pleasant meal, that's your problem." He pulled out his PalmPilot and started checking his E-mail—another annoying habit he had adopted. He had yet to make it through a meal without referring to his Palm at least once, or even—gag—taking a phone call. Was anyone really that important?

To be fair, they hadn't had PalmPilots when they were going out before. And where Mike had been concerned with nothing more serious than the size of his biceps, he had morphed into a full-blown academic. He constantly regaled her with tales of departmental politics, and who was in favor with whom, and who was publishing and where, and who would definitely make tenure and who wouldn't. She'd conveniently forgotten his ego. No matter how many stories he told, Mike always seemed to be the one getting the last word, coming out on top, looking good while the supporting characters got the shaft. She suspected that some of these stories had been embellished if not outright manufactured.

Worst of all, she was expected to follow all these stories, remember them, and ask probing questions about them later. "Don't you remember?" Mike had whined the other day. "Erik is the one who just published the paper on the relationship between intrinsic motivation and athletic performance. I've mentioned his work several times."

God, my whole life will be listening to these stories and worse yet, having to act like I care. And that idea—despite his gorgeousness and his newfound attentiveness—suddenly seemed much less appealing. It was one of those moments where something shifts in your head and settles into a new groove, and you're never quite able to recapture the feelings you had before. "You're right, I'm being a bitch."

He nodded in agreement. She spoke carefully. "I think I know why," said Kate. "I feel like you're trying to turn me into this little fem-bot wife, mother, and career woman all rolled into one, and you're not even interested in what *I* really want. You just want to make sure that you can shoe-box me into the fantasy you've already created."

"What? You're crazy. I told you, if more people had these kinds of conversations and worked all the details out before they got married, there would be fewer divorces . . ."

"And more frustrated, unhappy wives," Kate finished. "I'm not the right woman for you, Mike. I've been trying to be the woman you want, give the right answers to all of your exceptionally annoying questions, and fit this idea you have, but I haven't even thought about what I want. I want to have a partner and have kids someday, too. But it can't be forced like this."

"I disagree."

"What happened to you? We used to have a good time together! You were so much fun! Even when you screwed around, I knew you didn't mean it in a malicious way."

Mike misinterpreted her and reached for her hand. "I'm not like that anymore, Kate. I've changed."

"I know. And I don't think I like it."

He scowled and she lowered her voice. "Mike, be real. Do you think you can manufacture a relationship out of nothing? We're different people now. I don't think I can feel the way about you I did before. I'm just not going to love you the same way I did, don't you see that?"

"Who's talking about love? Love doesn't last. Love is an outgrowth of lust. I'm talking about partnership, respect, companionship, shared goals, a family, decent sex . . ."

"And that's not enough for me." Kate stood up. "I'd skip a lot of that for love."

Mike snorted. "I would've thought you'd grown up by now. But I can see you're still the same immature, unrealistic girl you were when we were together."

Her mouth opened. So the gloves were off. "And yet you want me to bear your children! What does that say about you?"

"That decision hasn't been made yet."

"Wanna bet?" Kate stood up. "I'll be seeing you, Mike. Thanks for the google." She waved as she left the restaurant, feeling lighter than she had in months.

Friday night she skipped the usual drinks-after-work scene with Danny and the guys from work, and headed straight for the gym. She needed to sweat. At first exercising had been all about losing weight. Then her motivation had been to maintain the admittedly not-bad body she'd somehow discovered under that extra twenty pounds. But unexpected things had happened. If she didn't work out, she felt antsy all day. She didn't sleep as well. She just didn't feel very good.

She'd told Ned about it and he'd laughed. "You're hooked now."

"What? What are you talking about?"

"You're an endorphin junkie. You can't help wanting to work out because you need the buzz, man." He leaned his head back in what she assumed was his hippie imitation. Of course with his ponytail and his age, he probably fit the bill better than most. "Like, every day, man."

"You are very strange." But maybe he was right. So here she was, after a quick Balance bar at her desk, cramming in a workout just for the stress release and that sensation that nothing really mattered all that much.

The gym wasn't as crowded as usual, and after a quick mile jog, she moved over to the weight machines to circuit train. She was just finishing up her leg presses when she noticed a woman at the triceps pull-down station. She was grabbing the bar of the machine and letting it travel all the way back up instead of keeping the bar between her waist and her thighs. Kate watched her for a moment, and then walked over.

"Can I suggest something?"

"Sure." The woman looked up and grinned. "Is is that obvious that I'm clueless?"

"Hey, I was the same way when I started, too." Kate showed her where she should be holding the weight. "Then straighten your arms, and bend your elbows like this, see?"

"Ooof," the woman grunted. "Wow. I can feel it."

Kate checked the stack. "You know, that may be too much weight for you. Why don't you try this one." She adjusted the pin and the woman pushed the weight down.

"That's better."

"That's good," said Kate. "Keep your elbows in at your sides. Got it?"

"Thanks for the help. I guess it's obvious I'm not here very often, huh?" the woman said with an embarrassed smile.

"Hey, we all start somewhere. Have a good workout."

Kate started walking toward the leg curl machine—she hated this one but it was great for your butt—and saw Ned grinning at her. "So, you want a job here, or what?"

"Shut up." She laid facedown on the bench. "I was just trying to be helpful."

"No, seriously, Kate. You should think about it. You're good with people and you've already got a pretty good background. You could get certified. We've got more clients than we can even train here, and it's getting busier all the time."

She was sweating now, breathing deeply as she finished the set. "Oh, that's a great idea. Quit my job and become a personal trainer." He didn't say anything. "Oh, shit, Ned, I'm sorry. I didn't mean that the way it sounded."

"Sorry to suggest something beneath you."

She slid off the bench and reached for his arm. "Wait, Ned. I wasn't thinking, and I'm really sorry. It's not like being a lawyer is so great. Most of the ones I know are jerks anyway."

"Don't worry about it." He shrugged. "My job is just something I do—it's not everything I am. But I did think that you saw past that label."

God. She'd hurt his feelings, and there was nothing worse. "I did, and I do. Look, how can I make it up to you?"

He considered. "Dinner? How about a homemade meal?" He'd suggested that before, and she hadn't been ready. Dinner at someone's house? That meant S-E-X, pure and simple. And was she ready to go to bed with a guy who could be, by a little bit of a stretch, her dad?

"OK, OK. You've got me. Actually, you want to do it tomorrow? I don't have any plans." Way to sound desirable, Kate.

"I've got a client to train until eight—is after that OK?"

"Sure. I promise to make something good and fattening."

The next evening found Kate doing something she rarely did. This went beyond throwing a frozen pizza in the microwave or making microwave popcorn or even a batch of chili. She opted for a simple recipe regardless—pasta with peanuts, broccoli, chicken breasts, a green salad, and bread. She bought a bottle of burgundy, a bottle of sauvignon blanc, and a six-pack of Amstel Light. He was bound to like something.

Ned's hair was pulled back in his usual ponytail. He'd brought a bottle of wine—*how sweet*, she thought—and wore faded black Levi's, a mint green shirt, and what looked like Doc Martens. He might be in his forties, but he dressed much younger. She liked it.

"Something smells good in here," said Ned, kissing her cheek.

"Well, I've been slaving over a hot stove all day, you know." She was chopping cucumbers and tomatoes to put in the salad.

"Can I do anything?"

"Nope. It's all under control. How about a drink?"

"A beer sounds good." She handed it to him and he sat down at the little table just off the kitchen. He looked around. "This is a nice place. I love the crown moldings and the floors."

"That's right, I forgot you haven't been here before." She gestured. "That's the living room," she said, pointing at the corner, "dining room," motioning at the table, "kitchen, of course. Oh, and that's my office," she added, gesturing at her desk. "My bedroom's in the back."

"Wow. I'd have never thought this was such a big place."

"It's all in the attitude, isn't it? I don't know. It's small, but I like it. If I got a bigger place, I'd just have get more furniture, more stuff, more possessions . . ."

"Keeping you rooted to the earth?" he finished.

"Something like that. I've never been into clutter or anything. That's probably why I hate having piles of work on my desk. It offends my natural sensibilities, I suppose."

Ned was looking at her bookshelf. "I'm surprised you don't have any law books here." He read aloud. "Margaret Atwood,

Sue Grafton, Galloway's *Book on Running*. Hey, what's this? *My Secret Garden? Forbidden Flowers?*" He pulled one off the shelf. "Women's sexual fantasies. Kate, I had no idea."

"Oh, God! Don't look at those."

Ned turned the pages. "These look pretty dog-eared, you know? You spend a lot of time reading this stuff?"

She laughed. "OK, call it safe sex. What do you want?"

He grinned at her and put the book back. "This one's good, though." He held up *What Color Is Your Parachute?*

"Yeah, I've been looking at that lately, actually," she admitted. "Hey, Ned, again, I'm so sorry about yesterday. I felt like an idiot."

"Fuggedabout," he said in a bad imitation of Tony Soprano, waving his beer bottle. He picked up Andrew's sunglasses, which were sitting on her bookshelf. "Nice shades."

"Oh. Yeah." Crap. Should she say something? But Ned had pulled out *Parachute*. "So, tell me more about your career crisis."

"I don't know. Most days, I hate my job but I don't know what else I'd do. I've been looking for positions where I could use my legal background—contracts administration, employee relations, maybe even working for a legal publisher. Or doing HR, like my friend Tracy. But all I do is read the classifieds and stew. I guess I'm too afraid to make the leap."

Ned finished his beer and got up to get another, refilling her wineglass. "Why?"

She added the vegetables to the salad and mixed the peanuts into the pasta. "Lots of reasons. I'm starting to make decent money now; I do like some of the people I work with; and it's a known quantity, you know?" She took a sip of her wine. "Plus I just hate to admit I made a mistake in going to law school."

"Life's about making mistakes, Kate. That's how we learn."

"Who are you, Yoda?"

Ned laughed. "OK, that was pretty Zen. Give yourself a few years. You'll be a lot easier on yourself, I promise."

"Can you guarantee that?"

He stood up. "Almost certainly. Now, can we eat? I'm starving."

"Yeah, it should be ready." They sat down and she dished up their plates.

"Kate, this looks great!" Ned took a bite. "Tastes great, too."

"What can I say? I told you I'm a multifaceted individual."

"A woman of many talents." Ned took another bite, chewed, and then looked at her. "This is excellent, really. The food and the company." He leaned over and kissed her very gently on the mouth.

Kate was so surprised she didn't respond. He drew away and looked at her for a long moment. Neither said anything. She pressed her lips together slightly and leaned toward him, her hand on the table. His lips felt warm and soft against her own.

They kissed that way for a moment, and then Ned opened his mouth slightly and teased her lips with his tongue. She closed her eyes and opened her mouth to him, feeling his tongue gently probe her own.

What had started as a sweet, soft, romantic kiss was rapidly turning into something much more dangerous. Kate felt her insides start to get that familiar twisting feeling, that tightening she couldn't quite explain, and she leaned forward in her chair to continue the kiss. Without pulling away from her, Ned moved his chair so that he was closer to her, and put his hands in her hair.

They were both breathing harder now, and the kissing had become more intense, more urgent. Ned had his fingers in her hair and pulled gently at the nape of her neck, bringing her head up as he kissed along her jaw and the side of her neck. He stood, pulling her to her feet, and wrapped her arms around his neck, accidentally snagging his ponytail. His hair was silky against her fingers.

"Oh, I'm sorry." She giggled. "Gosh, your hair is so soft."

Ned looked at her with a curious expression and they both started laughing. "Did I really just say that?" Kate laughed harder. "God, next, I'll be asking you what kind of conditioner you use."

Ned thought a moment. "Pantene. It gives me shiny hair and smells great, too!" he said brightly.

Kate guffawed, bending slightly. "God, Ned, I'm sorry. I didn't mean to ruin the moment. That was really . . . nice."

"No problem." He smiled at her, and reached over to stroke a piece of hair out of her eyes. "I like laughing with you. It's one of the things I like about you."

"Me, too." She smiled back, and a sense of relaxation flooded over her. This was what she wanted, she thought—to be able to laugh with someone the way she could laugh with Tracy. How come that was so hard to find with a guy?

Chapter 36

The Recycled Groom

"**Y**ell-oh."

Tracy smiled despite herself. Tom was in a good mood. She'd been thinking maybe they'd get together this weekend, but maybe she could talk him into coming over tonight. She was bored and a little, well, horny.

"Hey, Tom. It's me."

"Tracy." He lowered his voice. "What's up?"

"Nothing. Wanted to see what was new with you."

"Well, I'm sort of in the middle of something, Trace," said Tom. "I was just sitting down to eat."

"Can I call you back in a little while?"

"Uh, could I call you tomorrow instead? I've got company over."

"Oh." She got it. "Oh, that's OK. Don't worry about it, I'll just talk to you later."

"Trace, look . . ."

But she'd hung up. If he was having someone to dinner, it had to be serious—he'd only done that for her after they'd gone out, what, six times? Must have a new girlfriend, but he hadn't mentioned that before.

And what did she have? Other than William, she hadn't even considered dating someone since Tom. The thought of having to put herself out there again made her depressed. She curled up on the couch and stared at the ceiling. What if she never met someone to love? Worse yet, what if she met someone but the person didn't love her back? Life seemed incredibly bleak all of a sudden. She turned on the TV and channel surfed for the rest of the night, looking for something to distract herself. It didn't work.

Tom called her before nine the next morning. "I'm sorry about last night, Tracy."

"That's OK." She kept her voice light. "So, did you have a hot date?"

He cleared his throat. "I've been meaning to talk to you about this, but I hate to do it this way. I have been seeing someone—do you remember Julia? From the firm?"

Oh, sure, Tracy remembered. Julia was petite, dark-haired, pretty, and funny. She and Tom had joked around at their parties, but Tracy had never been jealous—after all, she knew he loved *her.* "Oh, yeah. She's really nice," she said, wondering if she was laying it on too thick. "So, you're dating her now?" She hated how her voice sounded, tinny and false to her ears.

"We've always been good friends, you know that. And once you and I were over, she told me that she was interested in me." Tracy didn't say anything and he continued. "Crap, Tracy, there's no easy way to tell you this. We're getting married."

She nearly dropped the phone. "Married?" she squeaked. "I mean, congratulations. That's great. That's really great."

But he heard what she was really saying. "This probably seems sudden to you, but I think it's the right thing. She knows what she wants and"—he half laughed—"that's me."

She knows what she wants, thought Tracy. *And I don't.* She managed to make all the right congratulatory noises and then the thought struck her. "Tom, how long have you guys been going out?"

There was a long pause. "Since we broke up, actually."

"Wow, you move fast, huh?" She blinked back tears and then

had a sudden thought. "So, I'm assuming she doesn't know about our little—what did you call them—fuck fests?"

"Uh, no. But that's the other thing, Tracy. We can't do that anymore, either. I kept meaning to tell you that but it's been so hot between us I didn't want it to stop."

"But it's stopping now."

"Yeah, it is."

"Well, that's good to know." She turned too fast and knocked over her open water bottle on her desk. "Damn it! I just spilled my water. I've got to go. I'll talk to you later."

She hung up and hurried to the kitchen for paper towels to mop up the mess. At least she didn't have any files open and she'd only gotten a little on her keyboard.

You didn't want to marry him, she reminded herself. *You should be happy for him that he's found someone who wants to, someone who will love him. I am happy for him,* she thought, rubbing at the desk until the paper towels were shredding in her hands. *I am simply thrilled.*

Chapter 37

Is He the One?

Lawless was on the rampage once again. He'd called a meeting of the litigation department yesterday morning. Sitting there with a stack of computer printouts in front of him, he systematically decimated the entire department. No one escaped his notice. Gregory Koi, a young partner, hadn't been billing enough hours. Christine should have won a motion for summary judgment that would have resolved an auto accident case, but had "blown a no-brainer." Mitch Younger needed to devote less time to pro bono and get his ass in gear. It didn't matter that Mitch's billable hours were among the highest in the firm—he was a billing machine with a conscience who donated time to representing low-income residents in landlord disputes. "Look at the numbers, Younger," snapped Lawless. "We don't have the time for your fuzzy-headed liberal charity work."

Kate had seen Mitch, who rarely rose to the bait in any situation, flush a deep shade of pink. He'd licked his lips as though to say something, and then thought better of it.

"And Kate." Lawless fixed his glance on her. "What has happened to that productive young lawyer who joined the firm several years ago? She seems to have more important things on her mind lately, like her workout schedule."

"That's not true," said Kate hotly. Lawless and several others around the table looked at her in surprise. No one else had even bothered to mount a defense to Lawless's onslaught.

"Then would you care to explain why your billables have dropped by seven percent in the last quarter? At a time when this firm needs every billable dollar we can generate?"

Kate looked down at her legal pad. She wasn't going to give him any ammo to hang her with, and getting into a pissing contest with Lawless was a bad idea. No matter who won, she'd be the one coming out with wet shoes.

"Your response?" Lawless was waiting, and the other lawyers were avoiding looking directly at her.

"I guess the numbers speak for themselves, don't they."

"They do, indeed."

Not for the first time, Kate thought of how much she hated Lawless. Detested, really. Abhorred. And someday—within two or three years, actually—she could be his partner. The thought made her cringe. Maybe he'd leave the firm before then, she thought. Or maybe he'd be killed by a disgruntled client. Or any maniac wielding a handgun. Or a drunk driver. The method didn't matter.

But consoling herself with fantasies of Lawless's bloody, painful departure from this world wasn't helping her mindset. Sure, it gave her a momentary burst of guilty pleasure, but the end result was that it made her question once again if she really wanted to do this for the rest of her life.

She'd been reading the want ads and looking on monster.com, but so far she hadn't seen any jobs that even remotely appealed to her. And she was twenty-nine, for God's sake! Thirty was practically around the corner. Shouldn't she have her life together by then? She'd spent her twenties in a career she didn't enjoy, so how much longer was she going to keep treading water furiously, trying to maintain her sanity? The thrill of billing two hundred hours a month was gone. The pride she used to feel when she told people, modestly of course, that she was an *attorney* had evaporated. And the sense of accomplishment when she wrote a compelling motion or argued and won a motion in court was fleeting at best.

Later that night, she fantasized about what she should have said to Lawless. Something about how working out might do something for his disgusting fat gut but nothing for his balding pate. Why hadn't she stood up to him? Why hadn't she just told him to fuck himself with his billable hours and stormed out? Or quit on the spot. That would have given her some satisfaction, wouldn't it?

She'd talked about it a little with Ned. Ned. She hadn't seen him coming at all. She hadn't been sure about the Vibe when she met him, but it was definitely there now. In some ways, he was the first man, the first grown-up, she had dated. Ned was easy. He didn't bitch about her working late or complain that she was distracted when they did see each other. He didn't pepper her with questions about whether she planned to serve her children free-range chicken as opposed to farm-raised or what her opinions were on having a family bed. And unlike most of the guys she'd met, he seemed to have no interest in the amount of money she'd pull down as a partner.

Ned's attitude toward life was different than most of the people she knew. He liked his job, but he wasn't motivated by money. "Time is more important than money," he'd said. "What difference does it make if you make six figures but can't do what you enjoy?" She teased him sometimes, calling him Yoda or Mr. Miagi. But she liked the way he thought and respected him because he wasn't hung up on the almighty dollar like most of the men she knew.

And then there was the sex. She wasn't sure what she had expected. Maybe she'd thought because of his age, he'd have lost some interest in the act. She really hadn't thought about it before they'd gone to bed together. But now that they had, she'd discovered a new level of lovemaking.

It was hard to explain. She'd certainly had no shortage of good sex before—or bad sex, for that matter, as well. She'd had sex that was fucking, sex that was lovemaking (albeit rarely), and sex that was sex for sex's sake, scratching an itch that needed to be scratched and nothing more. She'd had sex where she'd had to replay every fantasy she'd ever had—from mildly raunchy to extremely perverted—in order to reach orgasm. But all Ned had to do was touch her, even just stroke her hair or place his hands very gently on her breasts, and her heartbeat accelerated and every thought of work and money and working out and what-the-hell-was-she-going-to-do-with-her-life fell right out of her head.

He was tender in a way she'd never experienced before. With other men, even ones she loved, sex was all about power and who was in control. After an orgasm, she had sometimes felt a curious sense of emptiness and detachment, a nameless hunger or thirst she couldn't quench. With Ned, she felt secure, special, loved.

They spent as much time laughing and talking in bed as they did having sex. Talking with Ned was like talking with a girlfriend. He liked to theorize about people and why they acted the way they did. "It's the social worker in me," he explained. "You try to figure out why someone does what they do so you can reach and connect with them." She was sometimes surprised by his insights. She found herself telling him things she would normally only tell Tracy, and she loved it.

Was he Mr. Right? Who knew. Who cared. For right now, he was who she wanted. And that was enough.

Chapter 38

A Wake-Up Call

Tracy was walking down the hallway toward her office when the walls started to spin. She stopped and grabbed onto the wall, trying to regain her balance. She felt nauseated and dizzy.

"Tracy? Are you OK?" She recognized the woman's face but couldn't recall her name.

"Yeah." She licked her lips and tried to smile. "I'm fine."

"You look terrible. Maybe you should stop by the nurse's office."

"No, I'm sure I'll be fine. I just didn't eat breakfast," Tracy lied. In fact, she had eaten breakfast earlier—a dozen doughnuts that she had promptly thrown up. Then a nearly full carton of ice cream, and that had come up, too. Then she'd showered, dressed, and come to work, her head pounding.

Before, she'd thought it was trying to deal with the wedding stress, and her job, and all the stuff with William on top of it all. So she used food as a crutch. It wasn't like she was a drug addict or alcoholic or anything like that.

But instead of getting better, she seemed to be getting worse. She kept thinking about Tom with Julia, wondering if he made the same jokes with her, if he kissed her the same way, wrapped his arms around Julia the way he used to do with her. *I gave all that up! And for what?* The only time she could completely forget about it was when she was on a binge. Her mind shut off. Screw Tom. Screw William. Screw everyone. For a few minutes, she didn't hurt at all. Even if she felt miserable afterward, that brief respite was a blessing.

She waved off the woman's concern and made it to the bathroom. She did look terrible. And she was starving. The last two weeks had been an endless cycle of binges, punctuated by vomiting sessions. The fingers on her right hand were bruised and cut, and she'd carefully wrapped bandages around her fingers to hide the damage.

She was sitting at her desk when Winnie, the bank's full-time nurse, stuck her head in her office. "I hear someone isn't feeling well," said Winnie, her teeth white against her ebony skin.

"No, I'm fine. Probably just low blood sugar. I didn't have time for breakfast."

"Uh-huh." Winnie looked at her carefully. "You look pale, honey. And what did you do to your hand?" She reached toward Tracy's hand and Tracy snatched it away.

"Nothing. I fell and scraped my fingers, that's all."

"Uh-huh." Winnie stood there impassively. "How are you feeling otherwise?"

A tone of annoyance crept into her voice. "I told you, Winnie, I'm fine." She forced a smile. Winnie tended to be maternal—probably normal for a nurse—but sometimes she carried her imaginary authority a little too far.

Winnie paused and then turned and shut the door behind her. "Why don't you come and see me later today when you have a minute, then. Just let me check your blood pressure."

"Winnie, I'm sure you have better things to do."

"No, honey, I don't. This is my job, remember?"

"All right, all right. Will it get you off my back?"

"It's the only thing that will."

Tracy knew Winnie would hound her until she stopped by, but she still put it off until late afternoon, figuring that maybe she would have left for the day. No such luck.

"So, how are you feeling now?" Winnie motioned for her to sit down and took out her blood pressure cuff and stethoscope.

"I'm fine. I told you, I skipped breakfast. I know, it was stupid."

Winnie was quiet while she pumped up the cuff and positioned the stethoscope on her arm. Tracy sat perfectly still, hating the sensation of the tight cuff on her arm. As the air drained out, Winnie frowned and pumped more into it, then let it out again.

"Have you had your blood pressure tested lately?" Tracy shook her head. "Honey, it's only ninety over fifty-five."

"Well, I work out a lot."

"Low blood pressure is one thing. Too low is another." Winnie gave a little push and rolled her chair away from Tracy. "You should see a doctor about that, you know."

"OK, OK, I will." Tracy started to get up, relieved that the interview was over. "Can I go now?" she teased.

"Not yet. Let me look at that hand of yours."

Tracy tensed and instinctively shoved her hand down by her side. "It's fine. Just a little scraped up."

Winnie held her hand out and waited. Tracy took a breath and slowly reached her arm out. Winnie rolled a little closer and gently peeled back some of the Band-Aids. She didn't say anything for a moment, and Tracy kept her head down.

"Tracy." Winnie's voice was soft, and she was holding her hand very gently. "This doesn't look like you fell." She turned Tracy's hand back and forth, and spoke quietly. "These look like teeth marks. Is that what they are?"

Tracy could feel tears start to spill over and run down her cheeks. She ducked her head again and managed to nod.

"Oh, honey." Winnie reached over and hugged Tracy, squeezing her against her large chest. "You poor thing."

The physical contact was too much for her and Tracy began to sob, harsh, unfamiliar sounds.

"Shhh, shhh," Winnie said. "You're OK." She waited until Tracy had calmed down. "How long have you been bulimic?"

Tracy took the tissue Winnie offered her and blew her nose. "I don't know. College, I guess. It was bad for a while, but I thought I'd gotten better. Now it's out of control again."

Winnie took the tissue and threw it in the trash. "How many times a week?"

"Sometimes every day. Sometimes only once or twice a week. It depends."

"Is this the first time you've been dizzy like this?"

"No," admitted Tracy. "It's happened a couple of other times."

"That's probably because your electrolytes are low. And the purging is probably affecting your blood pressure, too." Winnie took the crumpled tissues from her and threw them away. "Have you gotten help for this?"

"Not really. I went to an Overeaters Anonymous meeting but I felt out of place there. I just keep trying to quit, but I can't." Tracy started to cry again. "I try so hard not to do it, really! I try to stop, I try to be good, but I always fail."

"Tracy, I want you to listen to me. I'm not trying to scare you, but bulimia is a serious disease. Besides the damage you're doing to your teeth and your mouth and even your poor hand, if your electrolytes get too low, it affects your heart. You can even have a heart attack."

"I'm twenty-nine years old!"

"That doesn't matter. Bulimics die if it's not treated, Tracy. They die."

Tracy crossed her arms. "It's not that bad, Winnie, really. I've just had a bad couple of weeks, that's all."

Winnie crossed her arms as well. "Do you hear yourself, Tracy? That's called denial." Tracy looked away from her and checked her watch. Surely she'd be able to leave in another minute or two.

Winnie was still talking. "Tracy, the bank has an employee assistance program that is completely confidential. I want you to talk to this counselor. I think she'll be able to help you."

"Is this something I have to do?" Another thought occurred to her. "Will this be in my employment file?"

"Of course not. And I can't force you to go, Tracy. That's up to you. But you should realize that your body is sending you a message. Your body is telling you that you can't keep doing this to yourself. Are you going to listen, or are you going to ignore it and let it get worse?"

Tracy walked back to her office in a daze. The funny thing was, she wasn't sure if she cared if she had a heart attack. That might be preferable to going through this same horrible cycle day after day. Was that pathetic or what. What was wrong with her?

Tracy sat at her desk and picked up a photo of Kate and her, taken at a law school party their first year. Both were grinning, holding plastic cups of beer in their hands. *I look normal*, Tracy thought. *So why am I so messed up inside?* She swallowed, and set the picture down. She felt exhausted, drained to the core. *I'm tired of feeling like this*, thought Tracy. *I'm tired of hating myself all the time. I'm tired of being me.*

Chapter 39

Career Crisis

Things were getting out of hand. This was the third morning this week she'd had that awful creeping awareness as soon as she woke up in the morning. That nameless dread, the sick feeling in the pit of her stomach. She tried to avoid it by sleeping as late as possible, but that just made her mornings insane, and she wound up sprinting out the door with still-damp hair, stress about making it to work on time overcoming the dread she'd woken up with. It had been a while since she'd felt like this. Her first few motions in court, she'd had the same feeling. Her first deposition. Her first trial, second chair, of course. But eventually the feeling had gone away. Now it was a regular thing.

Was she depressed? Maybe. Certainly the thought of waking up and feeling like this every day was enough to make her depressed. Her workouts helped—she felt better afterward, at least until the next morning rolled around.

She'd talked to Tracy about it, who listened and tried to help. But when Kate complained about her work load or the frustration of trying to bill fifty hours a week, every week, Tracy didn't get it. "Kate, that's awful! Can't you just talk to Lawless and tell him you're overwhelmed?" Of course Tracy had the luxury of a nine-to-five job. She might stay late occasionally—six or seven on very rare occasions—but she had no clue how a private firm functioned or the constant pressure she was under.

Of course she'd mentioned it to Ned, too. Unlike Tracy, he didn't suggest that she try to cut back her hours—he'd had other lawyers as clients and knew the drill. "How long have you felt like this?"

They were lying in bed, feeling pleased with each other. Kate had been tracing her fingers down Ned's side, noting the demarcation where his torso joined his hips. It was one of the sexiest parts on any guy, provided the man was lean enough to have it. Ned was.

"Oh, I don't know. Probably since about the sixth week of work, I guess. Which would make it coming up on five years."

Ned rolled on his side, facing her. His penis flopped over, in that state between erect and flaccid, and Kate had to will herself not to touch him. She knew from experience that he wouldn't be ready again for a while, and she didn't want to give him a complex. Not that he'd have one, but it was bad enough when a twenty-something couldn't get it up. She didn't want to deal with a boomer who had the same problem.

"That long? And you've stuck it out?"

"At first I thought it was just nerves, you know, inexperience, insecurity, whatever," she confessed. "Now I'm starting to think it's just me." She sighed and pulled the sheet up over her body. "I look at the women lawyers I know in their forties and I don't see anyone whose life I want! I can't even find a role model. All of them are unhappy or drink too much or their kids are screwed up or they're divorced or they weigh three hundred pounds. None of those things are appealing."

"So quit. Make a change. What's the worst that can happen?"

"Oh, let's see. I quit my job and find a new one only to discover that I don't like that one, either! Or I don't make enough money and I lose the apartment and can't pay my bills and basically become homeless."

"Is that your worst-case scenario?"

"No. Add in gaining a hundred pounds and never finding the meaning of life, though, and you've pretty much got it." She frowned, considering. "Oh, and I have to move home and work at McDonald's or something. So I'm fat, unhappy, poor and lonely. That'd be my worst-case scenario."

"Sounds like you've spent some time thinking about this." Ned ran his forefinger down her arm, leaving behind a trail of goose pimples. She shivered. "You know things wouldn't be that bad, Kate. You're too hard on yourself." He lifted the sheet to peek at her body. "Maybe I should be hard on you, instead." He pulled her against him and she felt his erection nudging her.

"You haven't told me what I should do," she murmured as he unrolled a condom and gently lifted her on top of him. He'd told her he liked to have her ride him—"so you can do all the work," he'd teased. She'd never really liked being on top before, but that was because she'd felt so exposed. Now that she was thinner—she never thought of herself as actually thin, of course, merely thinner—she liked it.

She liked the feeling of power she got as she controlled the pace, controlled how deep he penetrated her. She found to her surprise that she could orgasm simply by moving on him very slowly—she'd never been able to come through intercourse alone and had assumed she wasn't that sensitive where it mattered. But with Ned, she loved the feeling of moving her body slowly, feeling that indescribable building sensation, and then pressing just hard enough to feel that wonderful pressure and then letting herself go. It had just taken more patience, that's all. Feeling the orgasm approach was like the approach of a train—you could hear it rumbling in the distance, seemingly far off at first, and then as it got closer it gathered momentum, finally roaring by in an earth-shaking din of engines and wheels and raw power. Once it got going, it was unstoppable, and she knew it.

Afterward, she was lying on Ned's chest, panting and sweating and feeling like she'd run five miles. He ran his hand down her back. "You're wet," he said in her ear and she smiled and half sat up. "You know, I can tell when you get really turned on. You pop out in sweat along your lower back."

She rolled off him carefully, and reached for a bottle of water on the nightstand. "Really? I do?"

"Yeah." She handed him the bottle and he drank from it and then passed it back to her. "It's incredibly sexy."

Kate rolled over so she was lying on her stomach, her head in her hands. "What makes it so sexy?"

Ned had pulled the condom off and tied it in a neat knot, setting it on the nightstand. He considered for a moment. "It can't be faked. It's purely physiological. I suppose that's what makes it such a turn-on."

"Hmmm." Her vagina felt vaguely sore, but it was worth it. It was always worth it. For a few long minutes, too, she completely forgot about how miserable she was as a lawyer. But as the sweat dried, that nagging unhappiness returned. Even the best afterglow eventually fades.

Chapter 40

Taking the First Step

Once again, the room was half-filled with people. Chairs sat in a semicircle and small knots of people stood around in groups, talking. Tracy sat down in a chair by herself, but smiled at the woman sitting next to her. She was about her age, petite with short, spiky brown hair. She looked like Elizabeth, thought Tracy with surprise, but without the shiny veneer the latter always seemed to present.

Elizabeth had called her two days ago to invite her to yet another "I-am-so-great" dinner to commemorate her latest achievement. "I'm moving to London at the end of the month!" she'd crowed. They were sitting at the circular bar at Nine, waiting for their table. Tracy had gestured to Elizabeth's cosmopolitan.

"Should you be drinking that?"

"What? Why not? Or, they're kind of out now, aren't they. You're right."

"No! I mean, what about the baby? I thought you were trying to get pregnant."

Elizabeth had laughed and tossed away the idea of her future progeny with an airy wave. "Oh, that. Tracy, where have you been? I decided against that for now. I can always have my eggs frozen and have a surrogate in the future." She took a delicate sip of her drink. "With the move to the UK, I simply don't have the time. And quite frankly, that whole pregnancy thing just does not appeal. Swollen ankles, bloated breasts, stretch marks . . ." She closed her eyes and mock-shuddered. "No thank you! I'll find a woman who can do that for me."

"I said, is this your first meeting?" On closer inspection, the woman didn't look all that much like Elizabeth. She looked too warm, too genuine.

""Uh, no." Tracy paused. "My second," she admitted.

The woman leaned closer. "I know how you're feeling. Most of these people," she gestured with a nod at the room, "are practically lifers. I've been coming for six months and I'm still a newbie to them."

"Really?"

"Really. You'll see—it's a religion to most of us. But you don't have to be religious or even spiritual to get something out of it." She offered her hand to Tracy. "My name's Monica, by the way. Recovering anorexic/bulimic."

"Tracy." She cleared her throat. "And, uh, I'm bulimic." The words stuck in her throat. It was the first time she'd admitted it to anyone except Winnie.

"Fingers, pills, or exercise?"

"What?"

Monica rubbed a hand over her short hair. "Do you puke, take laxatives, or work out like a maniac?"

"Oh." Tracy tried to laugh. "I make myself throw up. Does that make me a puker?"

"You're here. That means you're a puker that wants to get better."

The meeting started, led by a sad-looking, thin-faced guy in his thirties. Tracy was surprised once again to see men at the meeting—didn't all guys just naturally have good body images? He talked a little bit about triggers and then invited the group to share their own.

"My job," said one woman in her mid-twenties, wearing a

lime green sweater and low-slung jeans. "I get so stressed and I come home and just have to eat."

"It's my parents," said a girl who couldn't have been older than fifteen. "They're on my case constantly. Always bugging me about who I'm hanging out with, where I'm going, when I'll be home. I can't stand it!"

"Annie, your parents love you and are concerned about you," said an older woman.

"I don't care! Can't they get off my back for a while? And since they found out about this, I've got to come here." She kicked at her chair. "I hate this. I don't have a problem. I just need to lose ten more pounds and I'll be perfect."

Tracy stared at the girl in shock. She had to be 5'6" and maybe weigh 110. Where would those ten pounds come from?

Later during the meeting, people were asked if they wanted to share any concerns. A couple of people spoke and then Tracy hesitantly raised her hand.

"Um, my name is Tracy, and I'm bulimic."

"Hi, Tracy," said the members of the group.

She looked down and twisted the edge of her sweater with her hand. "I'm here because I'm afraid. I know what I'm doing to myself is hurting my body. I feel awful afterward, but I can't stop." She stopped and bit her lip. "Every single time, I tell myself, 'this is the last time.' And it never ever is." To her shock, she realized she was starting to cry. She looked up at the other members of the group and saw expressions of not disgust or rejection but of understanding. Compassion. Kindness. Sympathy.

"We've all been there," said a woman sitting across the room.

Monica reached over and handed her a tissue. "Thanks," murmured Tracy.

The group leader nodded at her. "Tracy, you already know that food can be a powerful distraction from pain or other emotions you don't want to deal with. But it's also only a temporary one. In OA, you can learn how to accept yourself and your body and become free of the need to binge or purge or starve or whatever it is you do." He smiled at her. "I know it's scary right now. But keep coming. You'll see."

"Thanks," Tracy said in a small voice. She kept her head down. At the end of the meeting, she slipped out of her chair to head for the door.

"Tracy!" called Monica.

She stopped and turned. "Yeah?"

"I just wanted to give you my phone number. You know we're supposed to be anonymous, but if you need someone to talk to, you can call me. I've been there."

Tracy looked at the number in her hand and then back at Monica. "Thanks. But I don't think I need it."

Monica closed her fingers over Tracy's hand. "Just keep it. You never know."

Chapter 41

Full of Flaws

The light was on in Patricia Baker's office, but the door was shut. Kate knocked and waited for her response before she went in.

Patricia's short, wispy blond hair was slightly messy, and Kate could see her scalp through some of the thinning patches. She was wearing an expensive-looking salmon-colored blouse, but there was a faint stain—coffee, probably—over her left breast.

"Hello, Kate. You're working late, too?" Her voice, deep, matched her size. Patricia probably weighed in at about two hundred, but she carried her weight well. She looked big rather than fat.

"Oh, I'm about to leave. Just wanted to drop this memo off for you. It's in support of our summary judgment motion and I thought you'd like to look it over before I file it tomorrow."

"Thanks." The client was one of Patricia's long-term ones, Kate knew. Even though technically she wasn't in litigation, Kate kept the older lawyer up to date on the file. She didn't tell Lawless about it—it would only annoy him. He liked to operate under the illusion that he was the only partner responsible for making rain, or bringing business into the firm. But from what Kate knew, Patricia brought in a hefty amount of business herself.

Patricia skimmed the motion briefly while Kate waited, unsure of whether she should go or stay. "From my cursory review, it looks good," said the older lawyer with a smile. "But that's par for the course for you."

"Thank you," said Kate, meaning it. Praise was so rare at her job, she took it whenever she could get it. "Let me know if you have any changes or suggestions, and I'll get it filed first thing."

"I will, and thank you." Patricia leaned back in her chair and steepled her fingers, a move that reminded Kate of Lawless. "You know, Kate, you have a real future here. I shouldn't say anything but I know the other partners feel the same way I do. Unless something unforeseen occurs, we plan to offer you partnership in two years."

"Really?" Kate was surprised. To think that just two months ago, she'd been afraid of losing her job in the downsizing. Now she was being groomed for partnership. It was a lot to digest. "Well, uh, thanks for telling me that."

"Just thought it would be motivation for these late nights we put in."

"Yeah, uh-huh." Kate nodded and said good night, and walked down the hall to her office. She wanted to get to the gym before she went home. She wouldn't have guessed that within an hour, she'd be barking orders to a group of strangers.

Her voice blared over the loudspeaker. "All right, people! Let's step it up! Four, three, two, one, switch!" Twenty fit but exhausted-looking men and women did as she commanded, moving on to the next station whether it was push-ups, squats, jumping rope, or biceps curls.

The regular instructor for the Kick-Your-Ass Cross-Training class had been unable to teach it, and Ned had talked her into it. "Come on. You've taken the class before, and everyone in it knows what to do. All you have to do is direct the action, keep them motivated, keep them moving."

Ned grinned at her, that cute smile that showed his dimples. How could dimples look so damn good on a guy in his forties? "I know you lawyers love to talk. This will just be an hour of talking."

"No way. I won't know what to do. I'll look like an idiot. What if I screw it up?"

"You won't. Come on, I'll introduce you."

And so Ned had led her into the mirrored classroom where knots of lean, toned Lakeview twenty- and thirty-somethings were stretching, talking, and slipping out of sweatshirts. Almost all the students appeared to be in fantastic shape, and several women could have passed for models. Kate had that horrible sensation of not belonging. How had she thought she could do this, anyway? She wasn't a gym fanatic like these people—they were probably all exercise addicts.

But once she got started, she found that she liked it. The loud, downbeat-bass-pumping music, the energy of the class, the sense of effort that surrounded her. At first, she felt self-conscious in front of the class, but after a few minutes, she warmed up. She called out encouragement, and walked through the stations, giving pointers on form as the students dipped and jumped and squatted and curled. After a cool down and stretching session, she was surprised by how good she felt.

"That was great," said a blond wearing a gray sports bra and baggy red workout shorts. "Are you new?"

"Me? Oh, I don't really teach here. I got volunteered for the job."

The blond wiped her sweaty face on her towel. "This is my favorite class, but it's great when you have an instructor who's into it. Maybe you should do it again!" She waved as she went out the door.

Afterward, she looked for Ned to say good-bye before she left. He was standing at the desk, talking to one of the women who had been in her class. She had smooth, chocolate-colored skin, huge dark eyes, and shoulder length hair that hung in tight curls around her face. She was standing close to Ned, and touched his arm when he said something that made her laugh.

Kate watched, feeling a twinge of jealousy. She knew he was surrounded by gorgeous women every day, and usually it didn't bother her. No, that wasn't true. It did bother her. She just tried not to think about it too much. When it was in her face like right this instant, it was another matter.

She waited, debating, and then slung her bag over her shoulder. "Hey," she nodded at both of them. Screw him.

"Kate! Keisha was telling me you did a great job with the class."

Keisha smiled and Kate smiled back, immediately feeling like a huge sweaty oaf compared to Keisha's petite, perfectly sculpted body. "Oh, yeah," said Keisha, her eyes widening. "The class rocked. I loved the way you yelled at us!"

"I didn't really yell, did I?" She'd been into what she was doing—maybe things had gotten a little out of control.

"Not yell in a bad way. Yell in like a get-your-asses-moving way! That's what I like."

Tracy fiddled with the strap on her gym bag. "Well, thanks. Thanks a lot."

Keisha looked at Tracy and then at Ned. "Well, I guess I'll be going. I'll see you both later." She waved at both of them.

"So, what'd you think of teaching?" Ned crossed his arms and looked at her. "You loved it, didn't you."

"Oh. Yeah, it was all right." Kate looked at her watch. "I've got to get going though. Got an early day ahead of me, tomorrow."

Ned looked at his own watch. "It's barely ten. If you can wait a couple minutes, I'll head out with you."

"No, no, that's OK. I really want to get going."

He leaned toward her and kissed her. It was the first time he had done that there at the gym. "Do you want to come over tomorrow for dinner? I'll surprise you."

Of course he cooked, too. No wonder all the women wanted him. "Maybe. Can I call you from work and let you know?"

"Sure."

Kate just stood there for a moment, silent, and Ned touched

her arm. "Is something bothering you? You don't seem like yourself."

"Nope. I'm just tired!" she said brightly. "I'll talk to you tomorrow."

It was after four before she had a chance to pick up the phone. She'd had to attend a motion call that took up her whole morning, and then spent the afternoon trying to finish a brief Lawless had insisted she rewrite. She'd only had an apple and a Balance bar all day, and her lower back was killing her.

"Hey, Ned, it's me. Look, I don't think I can make it tonight. It's been crazy here today and I'm just in a terrible mood."

"Why? What's going on?"

"Just the usual nightmare. I don't even know when I'll get out of here."

"Hmmm." She could hear that weird New Age music he liked drifting through the receiver, and she felt a sudden surge of annoyance. Of course he could hang out all day and do yoga and listen to birds chirping over waterfalls and get in touch with his inner self. *Some of us don't have time for that shit.*

"What if we make it later? I've got some errands I want to run anyway. You want to say eight?"

"I don't know," she hedged. "I don't think I'll be good company."

"Come on, Kate. Come over and let me be nice to you. You sound like you need it." He said it matter-of-factly and she felt guilty for thinking such evil thoughts.

"All right. I'll just come straight from work."

When she arrived a little after eight, he had a glass of water and a glass of wine waiting for her. "Hydrate first, and then the wine," said Ned, taking her briefcase. "But why don't you take a quick shower."

She protested that she didn't have anything to wear, but he smiled. "I laid out some sweats for you. And thick fluffy socks, because I know how you love them."

She had to admit she felt five hundred times better when

she got out of the shower. And when she'd finished half her wine, she felt almost human. Ned had already set the table, and offered her French bread with olive oil.

"Oh, I forgot," she said, her hand over her mouth. "Can I do something?"

"Yes. Sit, drink your wine, and relax."

She started complaining about the day she'd had and then stopped. "God, I sound like such a bitch. I can't even stand myself." She ate another piece of bread. "How do you stand me?"

Ned simply continued to stir his sauce, which smelled of tomatoes, basil, oregano, and a spice she couldn't quite name. "I can listen to you without getting caught up in what you're experiencing," he said. "Most of the time, people just need to vent to be heard. And I think I'm a good listener."

"Does Keisha think you're a good listener?" She'd blurted it out rather nastily, but he set their plates in front of them.

"I suppose, sure. Why?"

Kate put her head in her hands. "I'm sorry. Maybe I'm wrong. But it seemed like there was something between the two of you. And I was jealous."

Ned set his fork down. "There was something between us. But it didn't last long and it's over now."

"When?"

"When did I see her or when did I end it?"

The room felt very still. "Both, I guess." She realized she was holding her breath, and her appetite had disappeared.

"Several months ago. And a couple of weeks after you and I went out the first time."

She swallowed. "Why?"

"Kate." He leaned forward and took her hand. "Because I liked you. Keisha is a beautiful girl, but she's a girl. She's wrapped up in herself and doesn't have much time for anything else. You're different. You're funny and warm and sexy and open. You work too much, but so do most of the women I meet. I'm attracted to that drive and energy, I suppose."

"So why am I feeling so awful?" She said it quietly.

"I don't know. You probably think she's better-looking than you are, or younger, or skinnier, or some such BS. Or you've been cheated on before, and you think that's what's happening now. Or that's what's going to happen." He took a sip of water. "It's your natural defenses kicking in."

"Maybe." The day, the week, shit, the month caught up with her, and Kate realized her eyes were filling with tears. She hung her head so he wouldn't notice. "I'm sorry. I feel so stupid. I should've just said something to you last night."

"Uh-huh." He got up and came over to stand behind her chair. "You've got to let me in a little. Sometimes I feel like we only really connect in bed. I love making love with you, but I want more than that."

"Ned, look at you. You could have anyone at the gym. You could have anyone anywhere! I still don't know why you want me." She closed her eyes. "I'm crabby, I'm stressed, I'm getting gray hair, I have cellulite, I have no idea what I want to do with my life. I'm full of flaws."

"Kate, I'd rather have a great relationship with one flawed person than go from bed to bed looking for some idealized version of perfection, which doesn't exist anyway. I did enough of that in my twenties and thirties. I want more than that now."

"Really?" She looked at him for a long moment. She wanted to believe him.

"Really." He leaned over and kissed her lightly. "Can we eat now? We can talk later, but I'm starving."

She picked up her fork, and twirled her pasta on it. The sauce was delicious, and she had two huge servings. "God, I'm a pig."

"Your body's hungry." Ned reached over with his finger and wiped a smudge of sauce off of her chin. "Sometimes you just need to stop and listen to what it's saying."

Chapter 42

Girls' Night Out

Tracy wasn't sure why she'd agreed to this. "It'll be fun, Trace," Kate had urged. "You already know Teresa, and Connie is so much fun. It'll be a riot."

Privately, Tracy had doubted that. Teresa was one of Kate's oldest friends—the two had known each other since first grade or something. She'd met her several times before; Teresa was a teacher in Elmhurst and didn't come into the city very often. Connie was a college roommate of Kate's who lived in Dallas but was in town for the weekend. Tracy didn't want to go— Connie got on her nerves—but Kate had insisted.

"You never do anything anymore, Trace," she'd said. "You need to get out. Besides, maybe you'll meet someone."

She thought the chances of that happening were slim to none, but a night out wouldn't kill her. So here she was, sitting around a tiny round table at a bar she couldn't even remember the name of, drinking beer from a pitcher and feeling bored. Connie had wanted to check out the scene on Rush Street, and Tracy's suggestion of someplace classier like the Sky Bar had been voted down.

Connie was all hair and posturing and large, dramatic gestures and look-at-me squeals of delight. Tracy had never particularly liked her before, but as the evening went on, her obnoxiousness quotient seemed to be increasing. When Kate was around her, Teresa wasn't so bad, but she could be a downer. She was heavy—probably a size sixteen or so—and always seemed to be coming off a bad breakup.

When Tracy came back from the bathroom, Kate was deep in some intense conversation with Teresa, probably about her most recent boyfriend, Tracy assumed. From what Kate said, the guy was a real asshole. He'd cheated on her at least twice that she knew of, but she insisted she loved him.

And Connie—well, Connie was busy making eyes at some Ricky Martin wanna-be at the end of the bar. He oozed over to their table and Tracy groaned. Clearly she was the only one at the table without a buzz. She hated feeling like the one person who would be responsible and make sure that nothing terrible happened to anyone.

"How's it going?" The Ricky Martin wanna-be nodded his head at Connie.

"Oh, I'm fine. Just fine," said Connie, laying on her Texas accent extra thick. You'd think she had a mouthful of honey. *Gag*, thought Tracy.

Ricky smiled a cursory smile at Tracy and she forced a quick grin. Would this night ever end?

By this time, Teresa was in tears, and Kate was handing her bar napkins to wipe her eyes with. Kate caught Tracy's eye and shook her head. Tracy hoped the subject of their conversation didn't wander into the bar tonight—Kate would probably smack him one.

Ricky had bought Connie a drink, and the two had their heads together, giggling. He didn't seem to notice the carat and a half diamond on her finger, but that was all right, thought Tracy—Connie didn't seem to notice it either.

But who cared? So Connie was engaged. What was wrong with a little innocent flirtation? Her thoughts turned to William, and she took another swallow of beer. What had that been about? Maybe it had been about sex, but she'd thought that maybe it was something more. All those E-mail conversations had made her think there was something more between them, something special. Was that wrong? Was she that naïve?

Connie and Ricky's conversation seemed to be getting more intimate when suddenly Connie said something sharp. It wasn't so much what she said as the tone. He'd apparently stepped over the line, and after a few feeble attempts to smooth things over, he strode off.

"Fuck you, bitch!" was his parting comment. *Charming*, thought Tracy.

Connie tossed her hair. "What an asshole. He thought buying me a drink meant he could get in my pants." Tracy tried to arrange her features in a sympathetic expression but said nothing. "Hey, I've got an idea!" said Connie, signaling the waitress for another pitcher of beer. "Let's play 'I never!' "

"Come on, Connie," said Tracy, pushing her glass away. "We already tried quarters. Isn't that enough?"

"Oh, come on," whined Connie. "It'll be fun. Come on. Kate? Teresa? You want to play, don't you?"

The two conceded and the game started. The object was twofold—to simultaneously get your friends drunk and humiliate them at the same time. You sat in a circle with your closest cronies, each with a drink in hand, and racked your brain for all the dirt on them you could come up with. Then you raised your glass and nailed them with their past transgressions and your faultless memory.

"I never . . ." Connie said, grinning at Kate. "Had sex in my parents' bed."

"Oh, come on," laughed Kate. "Who hasn't?" She took a big swig of beer. "Come on, Tracy, I think it applies to you, too."

It did, and Tracy drank the required swig of beer. Teresa was next. Her eyes were red, but she thought for a moment. "I never . . . hit on a guy who turned out to be gay."

"Hey, that one's not fair. That could've happened to all of you, too—you just don't know it!" But Kate lifted her glass and drank it.

Kate's turn. "I never . . ." she shot a look at Connie. "Had sex with a guy in the bathroom at a party!"

"Oh, you bitch! You suck!" squealed Connie, throwing back her head and shaking her trailer park hair all about. Her affected embarrassment was designed to attract male attention and it did. Tracy saw several guys look over, and Connie made sure to arch her back so her overly large breasts—*really, unattractively large*, thought Tracy, *way too big for her frame*—would also be spotlighted. Tracy drank more beer.

"Oooh, Tracy's drinking! Tracy, do you have something you want to share?" Connie turned to her delightedly, all smiles and sugary-sweet menace.

"No, Connie. I was just thirsty." *I so much do not like you, you little twat*, thought Tracy.

"Your turn, Trace." Kate grinned at her. Tracy felt guilty. Kate just wanted her to come out and have a good time. It wasn't her fault that Connie was the most annoying person on the planet. And there were a few decent-looking guys scattered among the Neanderthals at the bar.

"OK . . . I've never dated three guys, all of whom have the same name," said Tracy. It was lame but it would have to do.

Teresa and Connie immediately started laughing. "That's right! The Mikes!" And Kate shook her head and finished her beer.

"Hey, what happened with Mike Cooper?" asked Connie. "Didn't you say he'd tracked you down?"

"Oh, my God, I didn't tell you!" Kate started Connie in on the latest, and Teresa turned to Tracy.

"Are you having a good time?"

"Um, sure." Tracy nodded at Connie. "She's just kind of . . ."

"I know," Teresa finished for her. "She's grating on my last nerve." She paid the waitress for their new pitcher of beer and smiled at one of the guys at the next table. "Thank God she lives in Texas." She changed expression. "Oh, Tracy, Kate told me about you and Tom. I'm really sorry. How are you doing?"

From someone else, the question might have rankled. From

Teresa—who was one of the genuinely nicest people she knew, even if also the most gullible—she knew it was a gesture of concern. "I'm doing OK." Tracy refilled her glass. She didn't usually drink beer, but tonight it was tasting good. "Get this— he's dating someone else now, actually."

"Really? Already?"

"Oh, not just dating. He's marrying her, too."

"Get out!" Teresa was indignant. "But you guys were together so long! It just seems so weird."

"I know, it does seem weird sometimes." Tracy drank more beer. "To spend that much time with someone and then just have them out of your life is hard to get used to."

"Do you mind if I ask . . . what happened?"

Tracy exhaled, thinking. "Well, I guess you'd call it the classic case of cold feet. I met this guy and I was really attracted to him, and it got me thinking that if married Tom, that would be it, you know? I guess I wasn't ready."

"Wow." Teresa set her glass down. "Don't take this the wrong way, Tracy, but I'm surprised. You seemed so content with Tom, you know what I mean?" She laughed. "And he was just so nice. I was always kind of jealous of you, actually. All the guys I meet have major hang-ups of one sort or another." She half laughed. "Like cheating on me. I wonder if I'll ever find the right guy."

"Teresa, come on. What's the big hurry?"

"I know I shouldn't say this, but I want to get married! I want to have kids. It's totally politically incorrect, but it's true."

"Come on. You're smart, you're pretty, you're nice, you've got a job you love," Tracy said. "You've got plenty of time to get married and have kids, all that."

"But I'm fat." Teresa poked her thigh. "You don't know how it is, Tracy, you're so pretty and thin. When you're fat, you just don't have as many options."

"Teresa, please. A real man, a good man isn't going to care whether you're fat. He'll fall in love with you for *you*." Jeez, now she sounded like a romance novel. A bad one.

"Do you really think so?" Teresa perked up, sounding hopeful. Tracy suddenly felt very old. She wasn't sure if she did believe that, but she wanted to.

"I hope so. If I don't, I guess there isn't much point in looking for love, is there?" She finished her beer. "I'll tell you one thing. Forget physical attraction. I tried that and it doesn't work. All it did was totally mess with my head. Next time I want to fall in love with someone from the inside out." She considered. "It would almost be better if you could fall in love with someone over the Internet, you know? That way hormones and all that physical stuff doesn't get in the way."

"I don't know." Teresa giggled, and Tracy realized that she really was exceptionally pretty. But Teresa was right, too—most guys would only look at the size of her ass and pass her over. "I really like all that physical stuff."

"Yeah, I do too," admitted Tracy. She lowered her voice. "Well, if they know what they're doing, anyway."

"Agreed." Teresa refilled both of their glasses.

Tracy motioned to Kate. "You know, she's got this thing with the Vibe. Do you believe in that?"

Teresa, smiling, shook her head. "I don't know. She's such a goof about that. But yeah, I think I sort of get what she's talking about. I've had that feeling with a couple of guys." She sighed. "Who both turned out to be jerks, actually."

"Well, I didn't believe in it, you know? Then I met someone who I was sure I had it with. That's the guy I was talking about."

"You mean this was recent?"

"Earlier this year."

Teresa stared at her. "Did you cheat on Tom?"

"No, no. I would never do that. But it started me thinking about everything. I was afraid if we didn't get together, I'd never have it again, you know? Feel that attracted?" She felt very depressed all of a sudden. Tracy could hear herself speaking, her voice droning on. *You'd better shut up*, warned that little voice in her head, but she continued. "And I don't even

know if it was a real Vibe! It was all about sex, but I was thinking it was a lot more than that. And the sex itself wasn't even
that great."

Teresa sat there, openmouthed. "Wow. You're just full of
surprises, Tracy! We should hang out sometime. You always
seemed nice, but I thought you were a little stuck up." She
made a quick apologetic grimace. "No offense, I mean."

"Don't worry about it. Maybe I was. I don't know."

Teresa glanced at Connie and Kate, who were laughing
hysterically at something. "So, what happened?"

Tracy glanced over at Connie—she didn't want her to hear
any of this. "Well, we finally hooked up and it turned out to be
not what I expected," she admitted. "And after we got together, he sort of blew me off."

"I can't believe that! What a prick!"

"I don't know. I think I came on a little too strong for him.
I'd just broken up with Tom and I think I was looking for a re-
placement for him . . . maybe I scared him off." Tracy
shrugged. "I kept thinking that we had some special connection and all he really wanted was to, well," she lowered her
voice, "you know, screw me." She shook her head. "Whatever.
And it was weird. We had this amazing sexual chemistry, but
when we slept together, it wasn't what I expected. At all."

"Why not?"

"Ummm . . . let's just say you could call him the one-
minute man."

"Oooooh, no." Teresa shook her head sadly. "I hate it when
that happens."

"Yeah, I kept thinking, oh, this is what I've been fantasizing
about?" Tracy fluffed her hair. Her face felt warm but she didn't
mind. It felt good to talk about William instead of keeping it
all inside. "But it still hurts a little, you know? I just feel stupid
about the whole thing."

Teresa touched her arm. "Hey, I know. Remember, we've
got to kiss a lot of frogs, don't we?"

"You've got to do more than just kiss them!" They both

laughed and Tracy leaned forward. "OK, to be honest, it wasn't all that bad. He did do some things with his tongue that no one has ever done before."

"OK." Teresa scooted her chair closer to Tracy. "Spill. Now."

"I can't describe it exactly." Tracy was starting to feel an exceptionally nice sense of relaxation. "But you know how with some guys when they give you oral sex, it's like they're doing you a favor? This was different. This was like he loved it and he was going to keep doing it until I begged him to stop. And finally, I had to!" She didn't mention that even during oral sex, William had kept up his play-by-play monologue, which had made it a little creepy.

"Ooooo!" Teresa pretended to fan herself with a bar napkin. "I love that. Why can't guys understand that if they did that more often, we'd happily give more blow jobs?"

"Well, maybe not happily. But at least not as begrudgingly!" Teresa and Tracy both laughed again, and Kate looked over.

"Hey, what are we missing out on?"

"We're talking about sex." Tracy refilled her glass. "And I'm just getting warmed up."

Kate looked at her, eyebrows raised. "I guess I wasn't wrong about you needing a night out, Trace."

"Sex, huh?" Connie interrupted. "My fave subject!" Connie grabbed a handful of pretzels from the bowl Kate had commandeered from the bar. "Even if it seems like ancient history lately with Bill traveling all the time. Maybe Kate should tell us her secret. What's it like getting it on with an old man, anyway?"

"Ned is not old. And let's just say that his years of experience have not been wasted." Kate grinned at the three of them. "He does this thing where he gets inside me just a little, just a little, just a little . . . and then when you just can't take it, he slides all the way in." She shut her eyes and squeezed her shoulders together. "It's amazing. And he can go forever."

"And this is a very good thing," said Teresa.

"Oh, yes. A very good thing."

"The tease is the best part about sex," said Connie. "But guys just think the key is banging the hell out of you. If you can't walk afterward, they must be great in the sack."

"Hey, sometimes not being able to walk isn't so bad," said Teresa.

"So, what do you guys think? Does size really matter?" asked Tracy.

"Listen to you!" Kate said to Tracy. "Don't you know by now? Yes!"

"Definitely. It's got to be big and meaty." Connie raised her hands shoulder-width apart to show them just how big and meaty.

"It doesn't have to be huge, but it has be enough that you know it's like, in there." This was Teresa.

"Well, how big is that?" Connie again.

"I don't know." Teresa rolled her eyes. "Bigger than this, all right?" She held up her pinkie finger and the four of them laughed.

The next morning, Tracy woke up with an unfamiliar hangover. Her mouth was parched, and her head seemed to be throbbing in time with her pulse. She couldn't even remember what time she'd gotten home—or how? She drank a gigantic glass of water and then slipped outside to grab the Sunday paper. She had worked her way through to the classifieds when the phone rang.

"Tracy! How are you feeling this morning?" Kate's voice sounded exceptionally loud.

"Crappy, thanks for asking. Why?"

"Why do you think? You were a wild woman last night! Did you give that guy your number or not?"

"Guy? What guy? What are you talking about?" Tracy looked at her fingers as she spoke. Gross—her fingernails were filthy.

"Tracy. The total hottie who was hitting on you at Sauce! Tall, cute, gray sweater, black pants, kind of a scroungy Brad Pitt thing going on . . . hello! Don't you remember this?"

Tracy frowned. She didn't even remember being at Sauce, let alone any Brad Pitt look-alike. "Uh, yeah. Sure." She sighed. "Did I make a fool of myself or something? Kate, I can't even remember how I got home."

"No, you were fine. You were funny and kept talking about the 'one-minute man.' Then you were telling everyone that the key to good sex is to break up with the person first. Don't you remember? You were saying 'breakup sex is the best!' like it was a cheer or something. You were pretty wound up."

Tracy cringed. "Oh, no. Was anyone I know there?"

"Nah, not really. It was a pretty young crowd—college kids, early twenties, that group. Don't worry about it."

"I was blabbing about my sex life to total strangers and you're telling me not to worry about it?"

"Tracy. This is me, remember? Sometimes you just need to have a wild night. It doesn't mean anything. Lighten up." Kate said something she didn't catch. "Hey, Connie and I are going to grab a late lunch. You up for it?"

The thought of food even now made her stomach twist. "No way. I'm just going to stay here and try to recover by tomorrow."

"Okey-doke. I'll talk to you later, sweetie. Oh, Connie says last night was a blast."

True to her word, Tracy spent the rest of the day lounging about her apartment. Her one big achievement was taking a shower, and even that seemed to require an enormous amount of effort. She made some soup and crackers for dinner, and was asleep by eight that night.

Chapter 43

Retaliation

Kate groaned and glanced at the alarm clock. 3:27 A.M. Eleven minutes after she had checked it last time. OK, forget sleep. Maybe she could at least get up and get some work accomplished. She got a glass of water and sat down at the computer, pulling up her personal and work E-mails. Several spams, a short note from Tracy, who was traveling for work, a reminder from Lawless about the upcoming firm social. The so-called social was an excuse to invite major clients—and those minor clients who might become major clients—for an evening of drinks and kissing up. Kate hated them, but attendance was mandatory. It was easy for the guys, who would talk about the Cubs or the White Sox or the Bears or the sadly lamentable Bulls. Most of the clients, even now, were men, after all.

Kate wished she could care about sports, but she rarely paid attention to what was happening. She knew Sammy Sosa was a good ballplayer, but couldn't have told someone his position or his number if she'd had to. This event was supposed to be business casual, which for men meant khakis and a golf shirt. Who knew what it meant for women. She felt underdressed in chinos, overdressed in a suit. Everything she had was either too casual, too formal, or too inappropriate. At least when it was over, she'd have the weekend to herself. Ned was taking a couple days off, and had asked her if she wanted to visit some friends in Valpo with him just before the holidays started up.

Kate settled on flat front black pants, flats, and a short-sleeved pink sweater. She'd made all the requisite mouth noises to all the clients she'd worked with, and was wondering when she could slip away. If she left before nine, Ned said they'd be there by 11:00 P.M.

No such luck. Lawless spotted her as she was edging toward the door. "Kate, you know Bradley Worth, don't you? Key Insurance?"

"I don't think we've met, no," she said, offering her hand. "Kate Becker."

"Kate's one of our senior associates in the litigation department," said Lawless. With clients, he came off as an affable uncle to the younger attorneys. It was only those at the firm—and the attorneys who had the misfortune to be on the other side—who saw his true nature.

"How long have you been at the firm?" asked Bradley, who clearly couldn't care less. He was in his early forties with a slight paunch, receding hairline, and sweaty marks around the neck and armpits of his maroon shirt.

"Four years now," answered Kate. "All in litigation."

"Oh. So what made you go to law school?"

God, I am so sick of these inane conversations. She whipped out her standard answer. "I wanted to do something that would be intellectually challenging, something that I'd never get bored with," said Kate. "And the law seemed so complex and multi-faceted that I thought that would do it."

She didn't add that she'd been wrong—that although law was certainly complex, she'd lost all interest in trying to understand it. She could still give this answer with a straight face, though, which made her wonder about her own duplicity. Maybe she was as bad as Lawless.

Lawless left to freshen his drink, and Kate struggled for something else to talk about. Her mind suddenly felt empty. Bradley glanced at his watch.

"I'm going to have to get out of here to make the next train," he said apologetically.

"Oh, where do you live?"

"Geneva. Way out west."

"Oh, I've heard that's a nice town." After a few more moments, Bradley excused himself and left. Lawless strode over to her, his normally pink cheeks red. It was the only sign that he'd been drinking.

"What happened to Bradley?"

Kate took a sip of her Diet Coke. "He had to catch his train."

Lawless sighed. "You know, Kate, these events are important to the firm. I hope you don't feel that you're sacrificing your social life to help develop stronger relationships with some of our most important clients."

"What?" She stood and looked at him. "What are you talking about?"

"I'm talking about your attitude. You're making it perfectly clear that you don't want to be here, and people can tell." Lawless leaned toward and grabbed her elbow. "I can tell. This is a team sport, Kate, remember that. You have to be a team player."

Men and their sports metaphors. Kate fought the urge to wrench her arm away from his grasp. Instead she remained motionless and looked directly at him. "I am a team player. I think my work and my attitude reflects that. Now take your hand off me. Now." Her voice was low, too soft for anyone to hear.

Lawless stared at her and then abruptly let go of her arm. He seemed nonplussed for a moment, but quickly recovered. "By the way, I'm going to need that discovery in the Nationwide case on my desk by Monday. I want to review it before we produce it."

Oh, so it was to be a pissing contest. "It's not due until Friday," Kate said, trying to keep her voice neutral. "The client has the draft interrogatories and I'm just now pulling together the docs for the production request."

"That's not my problem. On my desk, Monday morning." He glanced at his watch. "You shouldn't have any trouble if you work on it tomorrow."

She stared at him. What, did he know of her plans? She'd worked every Saturday for the past, what, eight, nine, ten weeks in a row? "That's not fair," she said. "I've got plenty of time to do it next week, and I have plans this weekend."

"Not my problem. I'll see you on Monday." He strode away on his fat little legs and Kate shut her eyes. Goddamn him. It wasn't fair. She hurried to the bathroom and stood in there for a full five minutes, torn between tears and screaming.

She knew Ned wouldn't understand. "How many weekends do you think I can get off? You promised, Kate," he said on the phone. "I thought you were looking forward to this."

"I know," she said miserably. "Shit, I am so sorry. He's just doing this to punish me because I stood up to him. But I can't go, knowing it's hanging over my head. I'd just have to come back and do it Sunday night."

"So do that. Come with me, we'll have a great time, and you can come back and do your work."

"I can't, Ned. It will take me hours to go through everything. I'm sorry. Please. I'll make it up to you, OK?"

"Uh-huh." He didn't say anything for a minute. "Look, I'm going to get going then. I'll talk to you when I get back."

Kate hung up the phone in her office, close to tears for the second time that night. She was angry at Lawless for being such an unreasonable jackass, and angry at Ned for not understanding the position she was in. But most of all, she was angry at herself.

She spent most of the day at the office on Saturday, fine-tuning the interrogatory answers for the client's OK and reviewing the documents they'd be producing. By 4:00, she was almost finished—she could proof the stuff tomorrow—and packed up her briefcase. The air was chilly outside, and she was relieved once she was home. She took a shower and stuck her head in the fridge. Not much to eat—maybe she'd splurge and get a pizza.

She was still debating when the phone rang. She grabbed it, hoping it was Ned. "Katydid, what's going on?" It was Andrew. "I'm out on my bike and thought I'd cruise by in a few. Sound good?"

"You're biking tonight? It's in the thirties!"

"Yeah, but I'm trying to get some long rides in before we get snow. What do you say?"

Kate debated. She should have talked to him before—at least she could get it out of the way. At first it had been kind of exciting juggling Mike and Andrew and finally Ned. Now even with Mike gone, it felt wrong. She hadn't slept with Andrew in weeks, but only because the opportunity hadn't presented itself. "Um, yeah, sure."

"All right, doll. See you."

She buzzed him up ten minutes later. He was wearing his cycling gear, his muscular thighs bulging against the tight, damp lycra of his tights. As usual, he headed for the sink and downed two large glasses of water. "You mind if I take a shower?"

She sighed. "You know, this isn't your crash pad. What are you going to wear?"

He grinned. "Towel's fine with me. Or I can just stroll around butt-naked if you prefer."

She started to say something and then caught herself. "All right." He emerged from the shower a few minutes later, wearing her striped robe. It was as if they'd never broken up. He easily slid right back into his former routine of taking her for granted.

"Andrew, we need to talk."

"About what?" He was lifting the hair off the back of her neck, and reaching around for her breasts. God, he knew just how to touch her.

She grabbed his hands. "Look, I should have said something before. We've got to end this fuck buddy thing."

"Why? What's the problem?"

"Look, I'm seeing someone. I really like him and this just isn't cool."

"Oh, it's that Mike dude, right? You told me he wanted to hook up."

Had she told him that? She couldn't recall. "No, not him. We're done. Someone else."

Andrew reached behind her to pull a Diet Coke out of the refrigerator. "Yeah. So? What does that have to do with us?"

"What do you mean?"

He shrugged. "I don't mind if you're kicking it with someone else." He grinned. "That doesn't mean you've got to give up some fun on the side."

He had a point, but then she thought of Ned with Keisha. The thought of him with her had made her stomach twist. Sure, with Andrew it was just sex, and she knew it was just sex, but she doubted Ned would feel that way. She wished it were him standing in her kitchen in her robe, not Andrew. "Maybe, but I just don't want to do that. I think," she said slowly, "I think I love him."

Andrew looked at her for a moment. "I thought you said you were giving up on love in favor of lust."

"Yeah, I know what I said. I was wrong."

Andrew stood there for a minute, but he was too proud to try to convince her further. "So, I should blow out of here, huh?"

She shrugged. "It's up to you." *Yes, please leave*, she thought. But she didn't want to be mean. He couldn't help it if he was only her boy toy. "We can still be friends, can't we?" She managed to say it without laughing.

"Yeah, sure, whatever." Andrew disappeared into her bedroom, emerging in his biking gear. "I should head out." He started to kiss her, then thought better of it, and wheeled his bike out the door.

Kate let out a long breath. That wasn't so bad. At least it was out of the way. The only question was whether she should tell Ned about the whole thing. She thought he could handle it, but then again, maybe he didn't have to know everything about her. She'd maintain a little mystery.

She hadn't known until she said the words to Andrew, but she did love Ned. At least she thought she did. It wasn't just the way he looked, although that didn't hurt. It was the way he was so completely present with her. He made her feel fascinating, funny, sexy, even beautiful. If a guy did that, it *had* to be love.

Chapter 44

Making Strides

Tracy looked at the calendar and was shocked. One month. An entire month of not bingeing and puking. There had been so many times that she had been tempted to give in, but she hadn't.

She had eaten more than she meant to, especially at night. As soon as she felt too full, those feelings came galloping back—why not just eat more and then puke? She could get rid of the calories that way. She had been so close to giving in that she'd had to leave the house. She walked over to Borders and had a decaf latte and read, or popped in a yoga tape and tried to focus on her breathing. It sometimes took some time, but eventually the urge dissipated.

The meetings had helped a little, too. She had hoped that as soon as she started going, she'd tap into a hidden reservoir of strength she hadn't known she had, but it wasn't like that. She had the same urges and the same feelings, but what did help was simply listening to the other men and women—mostly women—talk about their obsession with food, with their bodies, with control.

"It sounds awful, but I feel better when I hear someone who's worse than I am, you know?" admitted Tracy to Monica.

The two were out for coffee after an early Sunday evening meeting.

"That's not terrible. We compare ourselves against other women, so when you hear of someone who pukes five times a day and you only puke two, you think, well, I'm not *that* bad." Monica half laughed. "Which is pretty sad, when you think about it."

"Yeah, you're right. It's that whole 'it could be worse' thing." Tracy tore off part of her bagel—plain, no butter or cream cheese. She was working on breaking the diet mentality, but it was harder than she'd thought it would be. She couldn't help mentally counting every calorie and fat gram she put in her mouth.

"How long did it take you to get so comfortable?"

"What do you mean?"

"You just seem comfortable in your own skin. Like you don't worry about how you look or appear to people."

"That's a strange-sounding compliment, isn't it?"

"That came out wrong. I mean, you seem so unself-conscious."

"I'm not, though, Tracy. There are plenty of times I can't help thinking about how I look. Forget about going on a date, much less getting naked with a guy." Monica took a sip of coffee. "But on a day-to-day basis, I guess it has gotten easier. I think I finally figured out that I was spending the vast majority of my waking hours worrying about my body, worrying about how fat I was, obsessing over what I was going to eat next, freaking out if I had to go to a party or a dinner when I was dieting, hating to even look at myself in the mirror."

"So, what happened?"

"I was dating this guy who was a real dick. We broke up about this time last year, actually. He was supposed to come home with me for Thanksgiving, meet my family, the whole thing. He calls me the day before and says he can't—he's going to stay in town and work."

"Well, maybe it was unavoidable."

"No, he was seeing someone else. He dumped me the next week." She sipped her coffee and continued. "And he did it over the phone! So I get off the phone, and I'm crushed, and I realize why he broke up with me. It wasn't that he was a jerk or selfish or couldn't commit. It was that I was too fat!" She lowered her voice. "That was the reason! All I could think was how completely disgusting and horrible and ugly I was. Of course he wouldn't want to take me home with him. How could he even touch me?"

Tracy felt her expression change. She knew just what Monica meant. "Yeah," she nodded. "I've been there."

"But what happened next was amazing. I'd read all those eating disorder and love-your-body books and nothing had ever sunk in or helped. Then all of a sudden I remembered something I'd read—that a bad body thought is never about your body. And I realized that what was really going on was that I was angry and frustrated and hurt. But blaming the way I looked was easier than admitting I was in love with an asshole." She sat back. "Does that make sense?"

"Yeah, I think so."

"Well, that was the turning point for me. It's a lot easier to express your disgust at your body than admit you're unhappy or lonely or frustrated or bored, I think. Look at our society! We're all conditioned to think that if we can simply look the right way, everything else will come our way. Forget whether you're happy or feel good about yourself—are you a size four? Do you have washboard abs? Are your breasts simultaneously full and perky?" She shook her head. "I'm sorry, I think I'm getting off on a rant here."

"Oh, I love Dennis Miller! The only problem is I never get half his references."

"I don't think even *he* knows them all," laughed her friend. "But I know what you mean."

Tracy drained her cup. "Hey, do you want more?" she asked. "Let me get it."

Monica reached for her purse but Tracy shook her head.

"No, this is my treat. Every time I talk to you, I feel like I learn something valuable." Tracy set a ten on the check. "You're my personal OA idol."

"Shhh. Don't tell anyone—remember, we're supposed to be anonymous!" Monica grinned.

"Seriously. I'm glad we met."

"Me, too, Tracy. It'll get easier, I promise. It will be hard, too, no lie. But over time, you'll look back and think, 'how did I ever come this far?' "

"I'm glad you said that. Because sometimes it sucks."

Chapter 45

Girl Talk

Kate wrote out the check with her usual scowl. Three hundred ninety-seven dollars and thirty-eight cents, payable to the Student Loan Servicing Center. God, why hadn't she really thought about what she was doing before she went to law school? She'd be paying for her education for years regardless of whether she used it.

Ned had called her Sunday night when he got home.

"How was your weekend?"

"It was good. They're great people. I would've liked for you to have met them."

"I can't feel any guiltier than I do already, Ned."

"You'll be able to meet them another time."

"I know, but I'm tired of waiting for another time. Do you know how many Saturdays I've worked? Do you know how many evenings I've stayed late or brought work home or worked through lunch?" Her voice cracked. "I'm sorry. I don't mean to bitch at you."

"You're not bitching. It's only bitching if you keep doing it without making any changes. You know—insanity is doing the same thing over and over but expecting different results."

"What? Where'd you hear that?"

"I've got it wrong, maybe, but the idea is the same. Your whole life isn't your job, Kate. It's only a part of your life."

"It's not a job, Ned . . ."

He interrupted her. "I know, I know, it's a career. Same difference, Kate. Life is short. If you're so miserable, I don't understand why you don't quit."

"And do what?"

"Anything else. You don't have to make that much money to pay your bills. So it will be tight for a while. So what?"

She didn't admit to him that she'd been fantasizing about getting fired. That way, the decision would be made for her. She wouldn't agonize over being a quitter or seemingly irresponsible or being shortsighted or unable to keep up with the guys. It would simply happen, and then she'd have to deal with it. That probably wasn't the best attitude to have toward your career.

"At the very least, couldn't you talk to that female partner you like at your firm? Maybe she can give you some insight."

It was a good idea, and one she'd considered before. On Tuesday, she stopped by Patricia Baker's office.

"Hi, Patricia. Um, you know how you said I could always talk to you if I had a question?"

"Uh-huh. What is it, Kate?" She glanced at her watch. "I'm sorry, I've got a client meeting in ten minutes, so we'll have to keep it short."

"Actually it will probably take longer than that," Kate said. "Do you have time for lunch?"

"You know, this week is just crazy. I don't think . . ." She looked at Kate and then back at her calendar. "How about if we have a drink on Friday? Everyone likes to clear out of here early then anyway, right?"

"That sounds good. But it will be just you and me, right?"

"Of course. We don't have to join the usual gang. You do still all go out to Harry Carray's, don't you?"

Kate grinned. "Yeah."

"So we'll go anywhere but there."

Friday night, Kate waited for Patricia and they rode the elevator down together. Ben Dolan, one of the younger partners, was already on it when they got in.

"The lady lawyers are heading out?"

"Yes, we're going to talk about hair mousse and bikini waxing," Patricia said with a perfectly straight face. Kate stared and then laughed. So did Ben, nervously.

"Ha, ha! You girls and your sense of humor."

" 'Girls,' " said Patricia, after Ben had walked off. "I'm older than he is." They wound up in the atrium bar of the Renaissance Hotel. It was just a block from the office, and airy and well-lighted inside. "Guaranteed not to see anyone from work."

The bartender nodded at Patricia and brought her a martini without being asked. "Chardonnay, please," said Kate. A couple in their forties came in and the waiter walked over to serve them.

"Do you come here a lot?" Kate regretted the question as soon as it left her lips. Why didn't she just ask Patricia how it felt to be a problem drinker?

"Occasionally." Patricia had already drained half her martini. "My apartment's another six blocks east of here, down on the lake, so this is a nice halfway point." She motioned at the bartender. "So, Kate, what's on your mind?"

What was on her mind? Her job. Ned. Money. Becoming a crazy cat lady or worse, a bag lady. Disappointing her parents. Being a failure. Whether she'd ever get rid of that last patch of cellulite on her thighs. The fact that she'd found three new gray hairs above her right temple. Realizing that even if she had a kid nine months from today, she was going to be in her fifties when the kid was in college.

"I guess I don't know where to begin," said Kate. "Can I assume that this conversation is just between us?"

"You mean you don't want anything you say to be recalled when you come up for partnership, for example?"

"Exactly."

Patricia had finished her drink and the bartender had replaced it, neatly sweeping away the empty glass. "Strictly between us girls."

"Do you still like your job? Practicing I mean? Being a partner and everything? Would you do it again if you could?"

Patricia considered, picking out the toothpick and sliding it into her mouth to eat the olive. "No. No. No. And I hope to hell not."

She hadn't expected her candor. "Really? So why are you still doing it?"

"I don't ask myself that question very often anymore, Kate. Look, I made choices. I know I'm a token at the firm, but I've grown to like the benefits my salary affords me. You stick it out long enough, you'll see them as well. You can get a nice condo, a Lexus or a Beemer and you'll stash plenty for retirement." She gestured to herself. "You may wind up gaining a lot of weight and not have a date for years, but you'll be financially secure. Or as secure as you can be these days."

Kate didn't know what to say. *You're not that fat*, didn't sound like the right response. Instead, she took a sip of her wine, and said nothing.

"I'm not complaining. Sounds like I am, doesn't it? But life is choices. I made my choices and I'm not always thrilled with them, but that's where I'm at. I'm a middle-aged, overweight, single, somewhat successful Chicago attorney. I'm good at my job, I'm reliable, and clients love what I can do for them. I don't have time for much outside of work, but I don't know what I'd do with the time anyway. So I work my ass off and save for retirement and figure that eventually I'll get to do what I want. I'll have enough to move someplace hot and raise dogs and trade in martinis for tequila. And that's it."

"That's what you want? What kind of dogs?"

"Jack Russells. Smartest dogs you'll ever see, but they're ornery. Can't have one with the hours I work, but I'll have a houseful of them twelve years from now. I've got it all planned."

"Oh. That sounds good," said Kate, hoping for an encouraging tone. Dogs? Hot weather? Tequila? *God, if this is what I have to look forward to, please shoot me now.*

Chapter 46

An Unexpected Offer

Tracy glanced at her watch. Tom was late, as usual. At least she'd prepared for it and brought something to read—the latest *Fitness*. She realized as she flipped through it, though, how much of it was about losing weight. An article on eating less to lose weight, a workout to tone your trouble spots, ways to incinerate calories and blast away body fat. Ugh. Forget *Fitness*. Why not just call the magazine *Hey, You're too Fat*? Tom came striding up, his overcoat flapping.

"Hey, Trace." He bent and kissed her cheek. She forgot for a moment and turned toward him and he accidentally brushed her lips, and then quickly sat down. "You look great."

She smiled. "Thanks. So do you. I like your tie." He was wearing a black suit with a gray stripe, a French blue shirt, and a blue and yellow speckled tie.

He fondled it and smiled. "Yeah, Julia picked it out. She's got great taste." He dropped the tie. "Not that you don't have great taste. You know what I mean."

"I do. That's fine. So how are you guys getting along?"

"Great. Great. Really great." He was probably as nervous as she was. At least she knew that they weren't going to wind up screwing their brains out this time. Tom abruptly changed the subject. "What about you? Are you dating anyone?"

"No, not really. Just working, going to the gym, the usual. You know I like the quiet life."

"Um-hm. What about Kate? What's she up to?" Tom took a sip of his latte, carefully wiping his lip.

"Well, she's still going out with that personal trainer, Ned—did I tell you about him?"

"How's her job? I hear things are really tight at her firm. Bad time to be looking for a job, too."

"Yeah, I know. It makes me glad I never did the practice thing. Banking seems so much safer."

"Probably. You know, that's what I wanted to tell you. My firm is transferring me to D.C. They offered me a pretty sweet deal, a moving package, the whole thing. So we're moving there next month."

"We?"

"Yeah, me and Julia. I don't think I told you. This has been in the works for a while, and she's already taken a position at another firm there. That way there'll be no issues when we get married."

"Oh, that sounds good. Well, congratulations! That's great!" Now she sounded like him.

"It is, but I'll miss Chicago. It'll be strange to leave, you know? I hate to give up the apartment, too."

"Oh, I didn't think about that."

Tom ran his hand over his hair. "Look, Tracy, I've thought about this and I don't want the hassle of selling the place—the market's terrible and I'd probably barely get my money out anyway. I thought if you wanted, you could lease it from me—stay there indefinitely or at least for now. Isn't that place you're in a month-to-month?"

"Yeah, but I don't know, Tom . . ."

He continued. "Look, the mortgage is practically what you're paying now, and you said that place is a rathole. Talk to Kate. Get a roommate. I don't care. I just want someone who will take care of the place." He looked at his plate. "You're the one who did everything to fix it up anyway, you know, and I feel crappy about kicking you out. It seems right that you live there."

She felt a rush of love for him. Her eyes prickled. This was the same sweet person she'd fallen in love with years ago. "Are you sure? You don't think it would be too, you know, weird?"

"Tracy. How long have we known each other? I've thought about it and it makes sense. Julia thinks so, too. If you don't want it, that's fine. But if you want it, it's yours."

She'd told Tom she would let him know about the place in a few days. She hated the idea of moving again, but she really didn't have that much stuff, and she missed Lakeview. Still, Kate had been talking about cutting her expenses—and it'd be cheaper for both of them if they moved in together. It could work. It could even be fun.

Kate probably wondered about it, but she hadn't asked her about William in a while. Sometimes, when she couldn't sleep, she replayed some of their conversations in her head, remembering things he'd said to her, looking for clues to what had happened. She knew they'd had a connection of some kind, but she realized now that she'd expected, or hoped for, more. She'd let him get in too close, believing that they had this special bond that no one else could possibly experience. She'd even thought that maybe, possibly, they could wind up together. She'd let herself fantasize about that, think about a future with him. It hurt discovering that he'd presumably wanted nothing more than to have sex with her. And he hadn't even done a great job at that.

Still, she couldn't help wondering what had happened to him. Maybe he'd turned out to be the king of premature ejaculation, but there had been a few moments there, not during sex and certainly not after, but in the moments of foreplay, that she'd felt something between them. She remembered the first time he'd kissed her, the conflicting swirl of desire and guilt. How they'd grown closer, first sharing the mundane events of their days and then opening up to each other in an intimacy she'd only had with Kate and later Tom. Had he felt that too?

Or was it just a game for him? She was past the point of being angry and eventually she'd get over being hurt. Now she just wanted to know if everything he'd said to her had been one big manipulation, a means to get her into bed.

Kate said if she wanted to talk to him so badly, to call. "Forget your pride. You want to talk to the guy, call him up," she'd said. "Ask him what the deal was. Tell him to fuck off. Tell him he's an asshole. Tell him *you* were using *him*. Just get it off your chest, Trace."

"Uh-uh." Tracy had shook her head. "If I call, it gives him the upper hand. I'm not doing that. I'm not making myself look stupider than I already have."

"I think it's 'more stupid,' " said Kate practically.

Tracy reached over and shoved her friend. "Shut up."

"OK. But aren't you curious, at the bare minimum? Don't you wonder what the deal was? Was it just a big mind fuck or what?"

Even a month ago, Tracy would have rushed to his defense. Kate hadn't been there. She hadn't felt that electricity, that spark, that Vibe, for God's sake. But now it seemed cloudier. She remembered how she'd reacted, how conflicted she'd felt, but the actual attraction seemed distant. Had she really wanted him so badly? Or had she created something in her mind that hadn't even been there? She felt fragile, though. If she talked to him again, she was afraid she might lose the ground she'd gained, might start wanting him again.

"I am curious," she told Kate. "But you know what? I can't talk to him until I don't want him anymore. And right now there's still a part of me that does."

She didn't have to say anything else. Kate understood perfectly.

Chapter 47

Moving On

Kate took a deep breath. Her stomach had been rumbling all day, but she'd been unable to eat anything. She'd bought a turkey sandwich for lunch, but had thrown it away after three bites.

Finally, five o'clock approached. She'd purposely chosen Friday afternoon for this meeting. All she had to do was have this meeting, talk to Lawless, and then she and Ned and Tracy would celebrate.

Lawless's door was slightly ajar and Kate rapped on it. "Come!" he called. God forbid he spare a word, thought Kate.

"Hi, Dick. Do you have a minute?"

"Just one." He finished scribbling his name on several letters, and looked up at her.

"I just wanted to give you this." She set the letter on his desk and he looked at it and then at her.

"What's this?"

"My letter of resignation. I've decided to leave the firm. I'm happy to stay on for four weeks to wrap up any loose ends, make sure that all my files are current, you know." She licked her lips and then hated herself. Why did he always make her so nervous?

"You going to another firm? Someone make you a better offer?"

"No, actually not. I'm leaving law, at least for now. I've got a job at a gym and I'm going to focus on that for a while and figure out what I really want to do."

"You're joking." He shook his head. "You could make partner here. You're going to throw it all away to wipe sweat off exercise equipment? Your parents must be so proud."

"This isn't about my parents. This is about me. And that's really none of your concern anymore."

"How true. And this firm is really none of your concern anymore. You can clean out your desk and leave immediately."

"What?" She stood there openmouthed for a moment. "What do you mean? I told you, I'm only giving my four-weeks' notice."

"And I'm telling you, you can pack up your stuff and leave. We'll manage without you. You'll get your final check next week, on payday."

"I . . . I don't . . ." She couldn't even finish her thought. He had already turned his chair away from her, dismissing her. She bit her lip, trying not to cry.

She walked into her office, stunned. This wasn't what she had planned at all. She'd thought there would be congratulations, maybe some heartfelt good-byes, a few lunches and drinks out with the guys. At the least, a chance to review her files and to mentally say farewell to the office she'd spent the majority of her waking—hell, both waking and sleeping—hours.

She walked down the hall to the copy room and took an empty paper box back to her office. She took her diplomas down off the wall, and picked up the photo of her and Tracy and a shot of her with her parents that usually sat on her desk. A few knickknacks—her stress ball, her crystal clock, her business card holder—and her stash of pretzels, Balance bars, extra panty hose, her tennis shoes and socks, bottle of Aleve, a few tampons. She'd thought it was a lot, but it all fit in one small cardboard box.

By the time she left, most of the office had cleared out for Friday night drinks or to head home to their families. She should leave a note for Tiffany or Danny, but she was overwhelmed by the urge to leave. She took a long look at her office before she stepped out. She took three steps away, and then returned to shut off the light.

She was supposed to meet Tracy at Rock Bottom to celebrate finally giving her notice. Ned had said he'd stop by later for a private celebration. The bar was crowded, but she found an empty stool and ordered a glass of chardonnay, raising her voice to be heard. Then she changed her mind. "You know what? Forget that! Give me a bottle of champagne." She'd worry about her budget tomorrow.

"All by yourself?" the bartender grinned at her. He couldn't be older than twenty-three, but he was cute, his hair worn long-ish.

"No, I'm waiting on a friend."

"Ah-ha." He nodded and walked down to the corner of the bar. He squatted on his heels and then stood back up, leaning close to her to speak. "Just how much celebrating are you doing? Do you want a twenty-dollar bottle, a sixty-dollar bottle or a one-fifty-dollar bottle?"

"Just your basic twenty-dollar celebration, please."

"You're the boss." He wrapped the cork in a towel and slid it out with a muffled pop in a practiced move. "Here you are." He handed her a delicate flute. "What shall we drink to?"

"To me. To escaping from the law. And to the next step, whatever that is." She pulled out a twenty and a five and slid it over to him. "Keep it."

He was surprised. "Thanks very much!" He glanced around to make sure no one was clamoring for a drink. "So, what, you're on the run from the authorities? Could I be aiding and abetting you here?"

"No, I just gave my four-weeks' notice at work. But it became my ten-minute notice when my boss found out."

"Ouch."

Kate took another sip of champagne and checked her watch. Tracy should be here any minute. She picked her purse up.

"Hey, um, what's your name?"

"Vincent."

"Vincent, I'm going to run to the bathroom. Will you watch this box for me?"

He grinned. "For a good tipper, anything."

She peed, and washed her hands in the sink, dutifully checking her reflection. She noticed one of those annoying magic eye posters framed in glass on the bathroom wall—some kind of pattern of purple, pink, and blue lines and swirls. She glanced at it for a moment, then away, then suddenly back. It looked like one of the ones Tiffany kept on her desk, but who could tell?

Maybe it was the light in the bathroom, or the angle, or her distance from the print. But for the first time she could clearly see the hidden image. It was a rhino standing in the grass, its head lowered, about to charge. She squinted to make out the words beneath the picture. "Solution: Rhino" was printed upside down. She grinned, and walked around the print, looking at it from all angles, amazed. Once you saw what was hidden in the picture, it was impossible to miss.

Chapter 48

Voluntary Celibacy

Tracy looked around her minuscule apartment. Most of her stuff was already packed; it wouldn't take long to move. Tom had even offered to stop by in his Explorer to help, and she'd agreed. By unspoken agreement, they hadn't talked about what Kate called their "fuck fests." She was sure Julia didn't know, though, and the thought gave her some satisfaction. She just wished that they would've been able to connect like that when they'd been together. Maybe it would've saved their relationship. Or maybe not.

She still loved Tom, but she could see now that on some fundamental level, they'd never really connected. He made her feel safe and secure, and she'd thought that was enough. Meeting William had shown it wasn't, and she was grateful for that. What if they had been married and had kids and then she'd met William—or someone else like him? It could've been much worse.

Kate was after her to jump back into the dating scene. It was funny—now that she was with Ned, their positions were reversed. The three of them had gotten together a couple of times, and she could tell by the way he looked at her friend that he loved her. She remembered Tom looking at her the same way. Maybe they'd get married. "I can't even think about that yet!" Kate had said. "I've got to get this job/career/whatever thing straightened out first. Then I'll worry about the next step."

But while Kate was helpfully pointing out good-looking guys their age when they went out, Tracy was favoring a more gradual entry back into the single world. Her strategy was to start by reading the personals. Every week, she picked up *The Reader* to check out what new ads were listed. Some were funny, some had to be exaggerations, some were pathetic. And some were downright scary.

She should stop doing this—it was too depressing. Kate had warned her about it before. "You're not going to find anyone in those personals, babe," she'd said. "Only weirdos and losers write those things."

She checked her watch. Tom should be here any minute, but she might as well kill some time. She called Kate from her cell. "OK, listen to this." She read from the paper. " 'Polyester girl wanted, fifty to sixty-five, whose slacks and blouse fit her to a T, who can nurture and arouse me wearing rubber gloves. Anal action and diapering a must.' "

"Oh, my *God*. You're lying."

"I'm not! It's one of those 'None of the Above' ads."

"How many times do I have to tell you to stop reading those things? They're going to warp your fragile little mind," said Kate, imitating Cartman from *South Park*. Kate had begged her to see the movie during one of their video rental nights, and Kate had laughed hysterically throughout. Tracy had thought it was gross and completely idiotic. Of course, look who was reading *The Reader* for entertainment.

"I can't help myself. I'm bored. Listen to this: 'Oral Pleasures! Ladies, do you have a fantasy whereby an attractive home repair serviceman comes to your house, gives you some fantastic oral pleasure, and leaves—no strings attached? Let this home repairman cool your hot spots and warm your cool spots'." The phone slipped and Tracy repositioned it. "Oh, and then it says 'treat yourself to a talented tongue.' "

"OK. That one actually sounds interesting."

"Kate! Give me a break."

"I'm just saying in theory. In reality, what? You're going to call this guy and say, 'sure come on over, here's my address'? Then he comes over and rapes you or robs you or beats the crap out of you and what do you say to the police? 'Uh, actually I invited this total freak stranger to my house for no-strings oral sex'? That's a conversation I don't want to have."

"How about, 'I'm sorry, officer, but I was really, really, really, really horny'?"

"I'm sure that would make you a much more sympathetic victim." Tracy could hear Kate crunching on something.

"Apple?"

"Yeah. Sorry to chew in your ear. Tracy, seriously. Why are you reading these things? Should I be concerned?" Her tone was teasing, but Tracy heard the undertone.

"No. I told you, I'm waiting for Tom. Besides, I would never actually call any of these guys—not even the normal-sounding ones. I bet ninety-nine percent of the people who read these things never pick up the phone and actually call someone."

Kate relented. "Well, maybe there are a few nice guys in the bunch, but the whole thing just seems too weird to me. You know, if you want to get fixed up, there's this really nice guy at the gym that Ned knows . . ."

"No. I'm not ready for that."

"Tracy, it's been, what, three months since William, and that weird sex thing with Tom doesn't count. Just go out on a date with someone. You're not thinking of getting a cat, are you?"

"I'm not turning into a crazy cat lady. I'm just not ready to put myself out there yet."

Kate continued talking, but she wasn't listening. "I'm sorry. What?"

"I said, the longer you wait, the bigger a deal it becomes. Come on, go out with this guy one time and I'll get off your back. Tracy, it's not normal to spend all your time alone. You hardly even come out with me anymore."

"I know." It wasn't the first time she felt bad about lying to her best friend. Now that they were going to be roommates again, she'd have to come clean about OA and her bulimia. Many nights Kate thought she was home, she was attending OA meetings or getting together with Monica. She'd even spent a Saturday at a body image workshop. Some parts of it were stupid—like drawing an outline around their bodies to see how big they really were—but it had helped to see that she wasn't alone.

It seemed like every woman she knew had some kind of eating problem or body image issue or just plain didn't like the way she looked. When you considered that, the idea that so many books suggested of loving and embracing and accepting her body wholeheartedly seemed like it might be too much to shoot for. Given the odds, maybe loving her body was too much to shoot for. But making some kind of peace with it now seemed possible.

And then . . . she could look for love, search for the Vibe. Right now, finding Mr. Right—if there was such a person—wasn't high on her list. It wasn't just that she wasn't ready to risk the possibility of rejection. She didn't want to experience that rush of interest, have the hope that a guy would call her only to be disappointed when he didn't. Her eating habits were much better, and she was learning to be kinder to herself, but she felt a little fragile. She wanted to feel more confident—more normal, more comfortable with herself—before she threw herself back into the dating arena and had to worry about how men would react to her.

In a way, deciding not to date, and not even to look, was a relief. It reminded her of a card she'd seen in a bookstore years ago. On the outside, it read "As my friend, I just wanted to let you know that I've decided to embark on a campaign of voluntary celibacy." The inside of the card read "all that involuntary celibacy was getting boring." That was the difference—when it was by choice, not by happenstance, it didn't seem such a bad thing. For now, at least, the Vibe could wait.

Chapter 49

A Little Tiny Vibe

Kate hummed under her breath as she walked down the hall to their apartment. The place was empty; Tracy wasn't home yet. It was Tuesday—she was probably at an OA meeting.

Looking back, Kate couldn't believe she'd been so ignorant. All the signs had been there—Tracy's fixation on her body, the way she constantly bad-mouthed the way she looked, the pinched, unhappy look she had when she ate. Kate had had no idea Tracy had been so sick, but she seemed to be doing better. She certainly laughed more, and she seemed more comfortable with the way she looked. She'd given up her killer exercise routine in favor of some low-key hatha yoga classes at Kate's gym.

"I'm swearing off intense exercise until I feel better about my body," Tracy had explained. "I have to be at the point where I *want* to work out, not feel like I *have* to work out."

Of course the irony was that Kate now spent six to eight hours at the gym every day. But she wasn't exercising—she was training clients or teaching classes, or less often, simply working the desk. She'd gotten her personal training certification last month and now was working with clients one-on-one. She loved it. Finally she felt like she was in the right job.

"Hey!" Tracy came in, closing the door behind her. She was

wearing a light blue scoop-neck T-shirt, khaki shorts with a belt, and Doc Martens. She'd let her hair grow since she broke up with Tom, and it now hung below her shoulders.

"Is that a new shirt?"

"Yeah, I picked it up at Filene's at lunch. Like it?"

"I do. It looks great on you."

Tracy looked down at the shirt. "Yeah, it does, doesn't it?" She grinned. "I got you one just like it, but in lime green."

"Oh, my God. We've got to wear them at the same time. Be Twinkies."

Tracy opened the refrigerator, looked inside and shut it. Kate looked at her without saying anything.

"I'm not quite hungry," Tracy explained. "Just habit."

Kate nodded. One of Tracy's new habits was to "check in with her hunger" before she ate anything. She did the same thing during a meal. It was a little annoying at times, but Kate wasn't about to tell her that. Friendship wasn't any different than a love relationship—you learned to put up with your partner's less-than-charming quirks.

Tracy suddenly spun around. "I totally forgot to tell you. Guess who called me today?"

"I don't know. Tom?"

"Nope."

"Oh, that guy from work? In the loan department? Adam?"

"No, no, not him. I saw him at lunch today, though. We're going out on Saturday." Tracy bounced down on the couch next to Kate. "Guess again!"

"I have no idea." She stared at Tracy. "Oh, my God. Not William."

"The very one."

"After all this time?"

"Oh, yes. See, he's had a difficult time of it, you understand. He's been struggling with a lot of issues, and hasn't had any emotional space to even *begin* to deal with me."

Kate wrinkled her nose. "Does he really talk like that?"

"Yeah." Tracy continued. "But—get this—he hasn't been

able to forget about me. 'I've tried, Tracy, God knows I've tried. But I can't get you out of my mind.' "

"What did you say?"

"I said, well, what does your girlfriend say about that?"

Kate started to laugh. "You didn't."

"I did." Tracy's eyes got round. "I was so sweet. Sickeningly sweet. And there was a pause, and he said he didn't know what *that* had to do with anything. And I didn't say anything."

Tracy got up, walked into the kitchen, and poured herself a glass of water. Leaning against the kitchen bar, she continued. "So then, he says, 'well, how *are* you, Tracy?' Like he's so concerned. And I said, I was great, work was great, I was living with you, and it was great."

"Did you say anything about your eating thing?"

"No way! That's none of his business. So we're talking and I'm thinking, you know what? This guy is trying way too hard. He's saying all the same kinds of things as before, but I'm not interested, you know? Which makes me feel good, right? But I can't help wondering, so why is he calling me? Why now?"

"Because he's going to be here in Chicago."

Tracy stared at her. "How'd you know?"

"Because he's a guy, Trace. It's a long-distance booty call."

"You are so right. That's exactly what it was. So he just sort of mentions that he's going to be in town, and I didn't say anything, and then he says he'd love to get together with me. For dinner, of course."

"And a fuck. A rather quick fuck, as I recall."

Tracy pointed at Kate. "Bingo! So, I said, thanks, William, but I don't think I have the time. I'm super busy, all that."

"And?"

"And then he goes all out. He starts whispering that he'd love to be able to touch my skin, and see my—and I quote—incredibly beautiful body—and you know what I said?"

"No . . ."

"I said, 'you know what, William? Tell it to someone who cares.' "

"You did not."

"I did." Tracy laughed. "I don't know where that came from. I just thought, ewwwww. Why would I even want to see him again? He'd just spend the whole night trying to get me into bed. And then not do a very good job when we got there."

"Meow!" Kate made a scratching motion.

"Hey, the truth hurts." Tracy lifted her hands. "And he's all about being open and honest about his feelings." Tracy drained the rest of her water glass. "And you know what this means? *I* got to be the one to say no. I got to turn *him* down. Woo hoo!" She jumped up from where she'd been sitting, and did a pathetic imitation of the Cabbage Patch dance. "Go, Tracy! It's your birthday! Go, Tracy! It's your birthday!"

"Oh, my God. You're very strange." Kate got up and joined her in the kitchen.

"You know what? I feel better now," Tracy admitted. "I still don't know what happened with him, but I don't care. For all I know, he plays this game with ten other women as well. But I'm not playing anymore."

Kate considered. "Yeah, that's possible. Especially if he travels a lot. What a weasel."

"Total."

They sat there for a moment. "How was your meeting?" Kate asked.

"It was good, thanks." Tracy smiled. "OK, I *am* hungry. Did you eat already?"

"No, I thought I'd wait for you. I was thinking of making stir fry. Hey, do you mind if I call Ned? I told him I was planning on cooking."

"Of course not. I like him a lot."

"I do, too."

"You *love* him," Tracy teased.

"Yes, I'm aware."

"And you were wrong, you know," said Tracy.

"Wrong how?"

"Wrong about the Vibe. You said you didn't get it with him at first. You thought he was gay."

"I did not."

"You did! I remember. And now look at you guys. You'll probably get married."

Kate reached into the refrigerator and pulled out several peppers. "I am in no hurry to get married. I like the way things are now. And I did get the Vibe! It was just a little tiny Vibe, so I didn't feel it right away."

"Uh-huh."

Kate started chopping the peppers into neat little strips. "Okay, maybe it was a baby Vibe. A little infant Vibe. An embryo Vibe. But it was there, I swear it." She pointed her knife at Tracy.

"Whatever you say."

"Don't disrespect the Vibe, my dear," said Kate. "You never know when you might get it."